TURNING FORWARD

TURNING FORWARD

Liz Aab

WENLOCK
PRESS

Paperback ISBN: 978-1-7397004-0-9
eBook ISBN: 978-1-7397004-1-6

Wenlock Press
705 Wenlock Building, 56 Wharf Road
London N1 7EW
United Kingdom
www.wenlockpress.com

To those who have taught me so much

Table of Contents

"I want to be in your book," she told me abruptly.

Because I tend to think of my own life in dramatic terms, I now remember reacting strongly to the moment, grasping in an instant how pivotal it would be: the muscles on the back of my neck tightening and my forehead shoving over my brow into an intense penetrating look.

But that's not really what happened, and I owe you the truth, which tends to be better than fiction anyway. The question didn't jar me, just confused me. I'm sure you know the feeling – that panicked embarrassment like when someone asks you about your cat Fluffy and you don't remember meeting the person before. A confusion that is absolutely paramount to mask.

You see at that time I didn't have a book and wasn't even a writer until three minutes ago. When this woman walked into my office at the Central Order headquarters, I was sipping coffee and reading a few newspapers at my desk. My job at that time involved moving money around the world. While we still wore our traditional tight black leather gloves (historically to make our hands invisible), in this new era of multiple flat screens and high-speed internet, it became important not just to sound omnipotent, but to appear professional as well. So my boss renamed my position "Structurer." I wore a suit to work.

This lady was driven – you could tell that immediately – and comfortable with silence the way watercolors are comfortable with white spots on their paper. She waited.

This gave me some opportunity to do a Google search and see if I did actually have a book I didn't know about yet. I typed in my name and found the link on Amazon. The blurb began: "Anne Kesheen walks into the office of the somewhat omniscient narrator and demands to be in a book …"

In a college improvisation course, I learned that you establish status by holding your head motionless and leaning back in your chair.

I held my head motionless and leaned back in my chair. "That's an interesting suggestion," I said with impressive authority. "But I don't know what to write about."

"My name is Anne Kesheen," she began, "and you will write my story. I am determined to live a good life; I just don't know what that means. I've heard you are one of the Central Order's top professionals at structured analysis, so I'm sure you'll figure it out by the end."

There was something odd about the way she put that which caught me off guard: she had "heard" about me. No one was supposed to have heard anything about me. First, I have a very behind-the-scenes job. And second, the Central Order is both a very public and deeply confidential organization, as you will come to understand in this book. Which I realize I have already started writing.

I looked at Anne frowning, pursing out my lips; probably the same look I have when my boss comes in and asks me at 4 p.m. to do something urgent for tomorrow. I'm not disinterested. But I have a lot on my plate, you know, managing financial valuations, drafting proposals about our key metrics, handling day-to-day operations of global financial flows – why would I take the hours and months I'd need to write a book about this random person who walked into my office?

"I understand you have access to the File," she drove on, ignoring what I thought to be my best discouraging frown and my widening eyes, which were quickly becoming panicked. How much did this Anne know about what we did at the Central Order anyway? "And I will authorize your access to all my Memories," she added.

Now she had me.

You see, I said earlier – no wait, Amazon's blurb said – I am "somewhat omniscient." It's not really true. I can tell you anything that happened anywhere anytime. But I can't read minds.

The reason I can know everything that ever happened is that I have clearance to access the File. The File (as I was surprised to learn Anne knew) is a secret, unlimited, immersive video record of everything that has happened, that can be viewed from any vantage point, at any moment in time. It's accessible only to those of us in the Central Order with sufficient security clearance. It's a huge perk – and the number one source of Central Order's staff's HR and legal violations, from stalking to porn to insider trading.

The first few years at the Central Order, I did what many new recruits with access do: I checked out the inside of the Oval Office during Cabinet meetings, watched baseball games from the vantage point of the pitcher's mound in Yankee stadium, visited a certain silent night in the little town of Bethlehem, watched cute cats squeezing into boxes – I'm sure you can think of a thousand things you'd do too.

Because of the File, I can tell you exactly what any moment looked like, who said what, with what intonation, what the air smelled like. But my omniscience is limited to what is objective fact. I don't have any more sense than you do about what people are thinking, how people feel or how to interpret an event. No matter how immersive the technology gets, how high fidelity the image, how responsive the VR headset, how evocative the smells and textures, something is always missing.

That missing element was best described to me on a training course during my summer internship at Central Order. One of the first questions was the idiomatic, "If a tree is falling in the woods, does it make a sound?" The answer is yes, of course it does.

Where it gets tricky is if I asked instead, "What sound does it make?"

Here, the instructors explained, it depends on my vantage point. Am I under the falling tree, or a thousand feet away? Do I feel happy that the tree is falling as part of the natural lifecycle of a forest, or angry that soil erosion from human activities has caused it to fall just then? Depending on where I am and how I feel, it can sound like a crackle, a hiss, a distant thud, a beacon of renewal, or a guillotine.

So, while I can take a snapshot of any moment in history, from any perspective, I can't tell you what the moment means. I can't tell you what it sounds like.

Or take another example from my early rotation in "Central Counselling," a department which often deals with relationship challenges (health issues are usually referred to "Central Healing"). A woman came into my cubicle (I've since been promoted to a window office) and explained a particular argument she'd had with her roommate about leaving dirty dishes in the sink. We pulled up the images and audio from that day in the File. She watched the images, and I watched her. She was clearly shocked. "Wow, I was really angry," she said coolly. "I can't believe I made such a big deal of it."

It was that experience, and a dozen others, that convinced me of the futility of forming opinions about things. Here was a woman, sane and reasonable, who even disagreed with herself about to interpret a situation: when she was tired and exhausted, the dirty dishes were a personal affront; when she was calm and comfortable, they were merely an ugly inconvenience.

So I gave up my search for absolute truth, which ironically had been one of the reasons I wanted to work for the Central Order in the first place.

But now, someone was willing to give me authorization to access to her Memories. I could experience her life firsthand, as if inside her own head. I could literally hear the tree fall from inside her own ears and would be able to say exactly what noise Anne heard it make. Unlike real human memories, the ones in the File don't degrade or get rewritten over time. This would be the closest I could get to the truth. Or a truth anyway. This might be the only time I had this chance.

Rumor has it this authorization has been offered a few times in the past, usually to Central Counselling. But even there, most often people only allow access to Memories as they are facing their own mortality, in the final days of their lives. They find something reassuring, my Counselling colleagues tell me, about knowing someone else will remember their life, as they themselves experienced it. I have no idea what happens to those authorized Memories after the person died – does anyone ever replay them, in their entirety, or even in moments? Why? Who would spend their life reliving someone else's? My only thought it that they perhaps they use them for research, to find eyewitness testimonies, or understand trauma, and study child development. But like I said, the Central Order is typically very confidential, so I have never been told what happens to those Memories – your guess is as good as mine.

I let my frown dissolve and my eyes soften, then leaned back in my chair. This could be my one chance to witness the objective truth. And if Anne was determined to live a good life, could I even find out what that means by the end of it?

I had also learned in improvisation class that you can show high status by taking up space, so I stood up.

"Well Anne," I began, unpeeling my tight leather glove and reaching across the desk to shake her hand, "it looks like we've got a book to write."

PART 1 : FREEFALL

The right side of her neck and her triceps were in agony. She was not expecting that. Her butt was bruised as you'd expect, but her neck and arms were a complete mystery.

She got out of bed and put on her slippers. The log cabin they rented next to the slopes at Lake Tahoe had no central heat; they were no longer students, but not yet a year into their first jobs, so still budgeting like they were. Plus Anne and her friends, Mary and Julie, thought the idea of a traditional log ski cabin for President's Day weekend was quaint. The fire last night was wonderful, especially after a dip in the private hot tub and a few mugs of hot cocoa with peppermint schnapps.

But it was bloody cold this morning. She grabbed the rough wool red quilted blanket off the bed and clutched it around her on her way to the kitchen nook. The equally authentic metal kettle on the stove was so heavy this morning. While she was filling it up with enough water for the three of them, she debated whether to let go of the blanket so she could grab the kettle with the other hand too.

Man, her arms were tired.

Tired from snowboarding? she marveled. Her legs were remarkably tired, but not sore. She sparked the pilot light and set the kettle to boil.

She went to sit on the massive couch in front of the fireplace but discovered that Mary had already taken it over. Mary had woken up with the dawn and was reading *100 Years of Solitude* buried in several of the ubiquitous red quilted woolen blankets.

Anne hummed a cheerful good morning and jumped on the blanket mountain. Mary scrunched up her legs to make room for Anne to sit properly on the couch, and then reached back to push herself up into a sitting position.

"Oh man," Mary said. "I can't believe how sore my arms are!"

"Yeah," Anne remarked pleased to have company in misery, "I don't get it."

"Think about it. I don't know about you, but I spent most of yesterday doing inverted pushups to get my butt out of snow piles."

So that's what it was. Nobody had told her that the hardest part of snowboarding would be getting yourself back up again.

Her otherwise excellent instructor had started their class with the most important lesson for budding snowboarders: how to fall.

"You will fall. Often. A lot. At the beginning, every turn," he had said from behind reflective goggles. The sun gleamed off his shiny black helmet, which was the only shout-out to the renegade side of the snowboard culture. The rest of him looked like any old ski instructor.

"So first, understand that falling sometimes hurts. If you catch a toe edge, your feet get locked in place while the rest of your body continues down the mountain. You pivot over your board more than 90 degrees and land flat on your face. You might get the wind knocked out of you, since it happens so suddenly that you'll probably be surprised.

"But no worries, because everyone gets their breath back.

"The key thing is to fall gracefully and not to break your wrists. Never stretch your arms out in front of you," he said demonstrating the position. "Instead," he pulled just his forearms back towards him and clenched his hands into fists, "put your arms in front of you like you are about to block a punch. This way, your whole body absorbs the fall not just your wrist. Same goes for falling backwards."

He paused, and then grinned. "And for falling in or out of love," he added. He uses this line every morning, Anne thought.

With mittens on, arms blissfully free of ski poles, snowboard strapped on one foot, Anne, Mary, Julie and ten strangers hobbled over to the T-lift. Julie fell over first, but Anne would have her moment of glory halfway up the T. Ever since then, she would think that the T-lift is the hardest part of snowboarding, and never understand why they couldn't use chairlifts for the bunny slope. Oh well.

The group got to the top of the mountain and the instructor sat down to strap on his snowboard. For a reason still mired in mystery and legend, most rental places carry strap-on boards, not clip-on ones. Clip-on boards take about two seconds to put on, and don't detain the skiers that you are with. But the strappy ones humiliate snowboarders, who have to sit down to effectively tie their own shoelaces without sliding down the mountain. One more push-up to do.

Awkwardly, they got their boards on, and the instructor continued preaching.

"Okay, some people may tell you that there are two turns in snowboarding and spend a lot of time teaching you how to shuffle down the mountain in the so-called 'falling leaf' method. They build up mystique about toe edge turns until you end up learning to snowboard like you had a wooden leg.

"Some instructors tell you great details about where to put your weight and how to shift it. Sorry kids, you're not getting that here." Anne and Mary looked at each other. Julie's gaze was fixed on the increasingly attractive instructor.

"The most important thing is falling. But the second most important thing is to relax. When you relax and just let the mountain help you find your way down, it becomes effortless and truly enjoyable."

He asked the class to stand up. Once they had stopped slipping, he advised them to lower their center of gravity. To sink into the mountain and hang out.

"Pretend for a moment that you are cool," he said, grinning again. How many pick-up lines does he have in his repertoires? Anne asked herself.

He taught them to relax their shoulders and let their arms fall where they would. He did head circles with them to stretch out their necks. "You'll thank me later," he said.

He then hopped around and demonstrated how to go a short distance facing downhill and how to put pressure to bring the board to a halt. The class followed one at a time. No problems.

He then had them slide back the other way. Anne started to accelerate and panicked. She did what any sensible person does when things get out of control: she sat down.

"Graceful," he mocked her, swiftly crossing the mountain so he was downhill of her looking up. He kneeled still facing her while the rest of the class finished coming back across the mountain.

He asked for her name and Anne told him. He then announced, "Sitting down is a perfectly acceptable way to stop if you're really out of control. It's like taking a weekend night off from partying to read a good book."

He popped back into a comfortable standing position. "But unless you let things get out of a control just a little bit, you'll never get past the bunny hill.

"There's a moment when you will be facing downhill

about to turn in. All you have to do is turn your body to look up the mountain. If you try to force the turn with your feet, you will catch your downhill edge – your toe edge – and have to practice the brilliant falling method I taught you before.

"It's one of the nice things about snowboarding. If you relax and just look at where you want to go, the mountain will try to help you get there."

The water was whistling on the stove. Anne untangled herself from the red wool quilt blankets and painfully pushed herself off the couch. She took out three mugs and spooned out a heaping tablespoon of instant coffee in each, to which she added a splash of milk and a healthy dump of sugar. She stirred the milk in the bottom of the cup until it was brown and frothy, and then turned to pick up the heavy kettle. She filled the first two cups with a groan and then emptied the pot into the last cup.

The floorboards creaked in the room next door and Julie shuffled out of her room.

"Yeah coffee!" Julie cheered, and took her coffee mug in both hands, huddling against it for warmth.

"So what does today have in store for us?" Anne asked while handing a mug to Mary.

Mary looked up from her book and took the mug. "I'd like to have another go at snowboard lessons," she said.

"Especially with the same instructor," Julie piped in. She held her coffee mug like a lollipop.

Anne checked her watch. They had an hour to get to the lesson. She rallied the team, pounded her coffee, and retreated to her room to change.

She tossed the blanket back on the bed and took off her nightclothes. After she had put on her sports bra, she went to the mirror. Yesterday she thought her arms were strong. As a setter on her volleyball team, she had developed well defined arm muscles. But they felt so weak now that she noticed the flab under her arms. She would do more pushups when she got home.

Her thermal underpants were still damp and cold, but she had no choice. Over them, she pulled on her snow pants, which were as thick and waterproof as an inverted diaper. She achingly pulled a thermal undershirt on, and over it, a bright yellow "Virgin Cola" t-shirt she had gotten for free a few years back. The white quilted arms of her thermal undershirt were exposed from her sleeves to her wrists. A roommate of hers once dressed like that even during the summer; she thought it was pretty cool, actually.

She gathered Mary and Julie, yanked on their snowboard boots (man, they looked so much better and were so much more comfortable than ski boots, she thought), pulled on jackets and hats and mittens, grabbed their boards with mittened hands, and headed to the base lodge just a few hundred feet away. (Another win for the internet.)

"Do you remember his name?" Mary asked Julie.

"Flint, I think."

So Anne took the lead and asked to sign up for Flint's beginner class, explaining that they took his class the previous day. He was only taking private lessons today, the cashier told her. When they did the math, it was only a few dollars more per person per hour, so they booked him for the whole morning.

Twenty minutes later, Flint pigeon-walked down from the lodge. His helmet and goggles were off, but they recognized him by his gait: clunky and professional, but completely confident and relaxed.

"Hello again, Anne," he said from ten feet away, and closing in. He turned to Julie and Mary in turn and lifted his hand in a half wave. "Glad to hear you guys want to go at it again today." And then facing Anne: "How's your neck? Sore?"

"How'd you guess?" she lit up, astonished. How could this guy know what she was feeling?

"It tends to hurt to look one way for a long time," he answered. He then grabbed the top of his head and pulled it into a stretch. He closed his eyes with content pleasure. She wondered if he liked having his back scratched.

She followed suit, and indeed it felt good. She then started to massage the sore right side of her neck, and let her eyelids fall. Many people, family, friends and lovers, would tell her that she had amazing hands. She knew this, and no one enjoyed the use of her hands as much as herself. She would sit in class and give herself shoulder rubs. All of Anne's tension bubbled up toward her brain, but she refused to let it in. So it collected at the base of neck, twisting into a tighter and tighter hairball of tension. But a few moments of the right pressure with her thumbs, and it would start to dissolve…

She had forgotten to put on sunblock. While she scampered through her pockets looking for the bottle, Julie was peppering Flint with questions about his experience snowboarding, his hometown, how long he'd been teaching, whether he did this year-round, what he did during the rest of the year, where people working on the mountain lived, whether he had roommates in his dorm, what the social life was like…

That conversation continued up the chairlift (thank goodness not another T-lift) where Julie and Flint paired off, and Anne and Mary followed in the next chair behind. They ascended into the sun, blinded by the light off the snow.

The bar went up. They tumbled off the lift. The top of the mountain was silent. No kids on the bunny slope, no music blaring from the lodge. Just the thin air and the rhythmic drone of the chair lift. Skiers and snowboarders swished by. The group shuffled out of the way, away from the lift.

While they were strapping on their snowboards, Flint recapped the main points from yesterday's class. Relax. Trust. Look. Let the mountain tell you where to go.

Mary was growing impatient. She was frustrated by his surfer boy style. She regretted coming to California and regretted trying snowboarding. She was okay at skiing, not graceful, but she could get down the mountain. And it wasn't that she didn't like new challenges.

It was just his teaching style. He talked in mumbo jumbo. She wanted mechanics: how to shift her weight and where to angle her board. She found that her board kept sliding out from under her when she tried to stop. She was scuttling down the mountain on her butt mostly. And she still couldn't execute that infamous toe turn that he belittled in the first lesson.

For the first hour of the class, the three of them were equally struggling. Then unexpectedly, Anne completely her first two linked turns. Julie, Mary and Flint watched in slow motion as Anne, still facing downhill and moving across the mountain below them, shot both fists up in the air in victory and tried to turn around to see them. Her toe edge caught, and without warning, she fell flat on her face, her arms still raised above her head.

She let out a gust of air that came out halfway between

an "ugh" of disgust and a laughing "huh," and slid a few inches headfirst down the slope.

"Graceful!" Flint shouted down approvingly. "Okay, Mary, give it a try. Make sure to crash at the end too." Julie laughed.

Mary pushed herself up and started down the hill, facing downhill. When she was gearing up to turn forward, she tightened up and caught her toe edge. She flopped onto her knees. Flint went over to her.

Mary was becoming exasperated. "I just don't get what my feet are supposed to be doing," she said.

"You froze up and try to push the turn with your feet, instead of letting your body weight make it turn for you," he observed.

"But what are my feet supposed to be doing?" she asked insistently.

Flint kneeled into the mountain. "I usually don't think of it in terms of mechanics, so I'm sorry I may not be able to answer that very well. Wait," he said suddenly, "let me try myself and I'll tell you."

In one fluid motion, Flint flipped over so he was facing downhill, and started slowly across the mountain. He turned perfectly and then came to a gradual stop.

He then shouted up at Mary the mechanics of the motion: the order in which to rotate his torso, transfer weight from one foot to the other, heel to toe, how to angle the board, when to bend one's knees, where one's center of weight should be. It was a turn checklist.

Mary got up and with careful study, followed his instructions to the t. There was one slight wobble, but she finished the turn completely. She had known what was coming, what to do. Anne noticed how much more relaxed she looked coming into the turn. Was that what made the difference?

Back in high school, Anne and Mary were the same organization freaks. Anne would at times take the bus home instead of walking just so she could have an extra 15 minutes to plan her homework schedule for that evening. She wrote in a journal on unlined paper in all block letters in perfectly straight, evenly spaced rows. She would still have this hallmark of compulsion later on, no matter how many times she tried to get away from it.

But snowboarding, this was liberating. She loved Flint's teaching method: board by feel. It irked her that Mary was unwilling to learn this way. Maybe she didn't trust the mountain, or herself, enough? Maybe she couldn't let one moment lead her to the next, that she had to know ahead of time what was to come?

Anne was already becoming a snob of the sport. She thought she was learning the right way, and Mary was learning the wrong way. Or maybe Mary just needed to learn this way first, and would ultimately be able to snowboard by feel?

Julie started down and managed the turn as well. Anne was still one turn ahead of them, twenty feet down the mountain sitting down. Her cramped neck was tired of looking back at them, so she lifted her goggles and turned back to face the view.

She was on top of the clouds. The virgin snowy trail spread out from under her feet, cascading into the invisible white haze of cloud tops. The sun pressed its light into the white clouds, the white snow, evenly. It hurt to look but she couldn't close her eyes, not just yet. Looking at the clouds hurt like staring at the sun, but the raw truth of the light drew her. When her eyes eventually closed, she still saw light, first white then yellow then orange then red. Random patterns of light danced like a kaleidoscope on the inside of her eyelids. Trains of random circles snaked around the palette of her retina. Then it was all dark. Silent.

Her mind filled the void with sounds, quiet white noise. A high-pitched humming in her ears that turned on, tried to find a station, and then gave up and clicked off. Then the sounds of waves moving in the middle of the ocean far from the shore. Waves crashing now, grabbing and churning gritty sand in wicked white turbulence. Spray, foam, grating against the hard saltiness of the sea. A bead of sweat climbed down over the cusp of her lip. Her relaxed mouth parted slightly, letting the sweat find its way past the Blistex-coated outer side and cautiously enter the wet underside of her top lip. Her tongue came to meet it, tasting the sweet saltiness with its tender tip. The sea sound was getting louder, sounded almost real. No wait, sounded too real, too sharp –

The icy spray of slush hit her naked neck and jolted her fierce eyes open. Flint laughed, now just inches behind her.

In her Memory, she first had to swim back to shore, reenter the world of reality. Identify her time and place – okay I'm on a mountain with my friends learning to snowboard. She then had to revisit her recent memory, determine that the imagined sound of waves was actually the impending arrival of her instructor, and determine that was a pretty obnoxious thing to do. Also a little funny.

At this point she then asks why would an otherwise nice ski instructor, sorry snowboard instructor, splash her with snow? For some people they would instantly assume it was a flirtatious move, but Anne wasn't a flirter yet. Her idea of getting to know someone was to go for the jugular – ask extremely personal questions about one's view of the meaning of life, ambitions, and weaknesses. Splashing snow on an unsuspecting victim hadn't yet been added to her arsenal of homo sapiens mating rituals.

But she's not dumb. She reasoned he was too good to have lost control. She had seen such behavior when middle schoolers flirted. And considering him to be just plain obnoxious seemed like too a harsh a judgment for a stranger, never mind someone she was growing to like.

So then emerges the key question: was she growing to like him? If so, she should reciprocate with some equally flirtatious device, perhaps tossing her voice in a higher, more childish pitch or tossing some snow at him in return? She realizes in a moment that figuring out how to hold her head and voice is no different from Mary asking how to hold her torso and toes on a turn: Anne is trying to learn flirting by checklist. And does she even want to flirt at all, she wonders?

Oh how difficult human relationships are! Half the battle is communicating what you feel; the other half is figuring out what it is that you feel in the first place.

In the File, you can see Anne turning to face Flint with a carefully constructed, peeved-yet-shocked look on her face, which she timed long enough to indicate he shouldn't make a habit of such juvenile behavior, but not long enough to truly scold him. Script complete, she then drops her eyes behind her raised goggles, and looks up at him. She says with mock inquisitiveness, "Thank you?" and then makes a show of dusting snow off her body.

Flint retains his relaxed smile and moves his gaze down the mountain. His eyes fix on the seam between the trail and the clouds.

"Do you think you can make it to the top of the clouds without falling down?" he asks, challenging her.

She licks a second aggressive bead of sweat from her lip. It wasn't salty. Must have been snow then, not sweat. She wonders briefly where it had come from, and whether it was dirty.

She turns back to watch the cloud seam. So he had noticed it too. And he knew that she had seen it. For a moment, they share the beauty of the cloud tops.

Abruptly she stands up, dusts off the last of the snow, and says "Let's go."

* * *

If I were telling this story, I would have Anne and Flint swoop down the mountain in fluent arcs, sinking into the clouds like a mythical ascension back into Eden. They would at times share the same curves, with Flint elegantly breaking apart the virgin snow and Anne effortlessly taking his lead, following in his tracks. They would be exactly a pair of turns behind each other, so they would spring off the left side of the mountain in unison, like a twin pendulum, slide to the right side, decelerate and fall back across the mountain face. They would be alone on the trail; the trail would be a perfect wide breath of soft whiteness. The clouds would consume them and then release them into a vista of brown dotted mountains and villages where grey threads of smoke start their long trek back to the stars. The vibrant green pine trees along the side would be loaded with fluffy armfuls of white powder, and maybe a bird would chirp to remind the couple of the silence in the mountains.

Their snowboards would in unison glide silently across the mountain, and then with a whisper that grew into a roar, swish into the turns. They would make it to the bottom without falling, breathless and understanding that no words could compare with that shared experience. So they would talk without caring what topic it was, whether the merits of Power Bars over Snickers (a quarter the fat, two-thirds the sugar, and twice the protein) or the best practices of drying long underwear (on a rack in front of the fireplace).

But I can't tell you that story. First because that's not what happened. And even if I stretched the truth, we would have left Anne's two good friends stranded and without instructor. Plus it's just unrealistic – mountains are never empty of fellow skiers. Runs are never without ice patches or bumps or imperfections. And Anne is a good learner, but not *that* good a learner.

So instead Anne tries her darndest and indeed makes it down five full turns (three toe edge, two leaf style) before catching her toe edge and face-planting into a patch of harder snow. The clouds were still ahead of her, though it was hard to tell exactly where they started. She was close enough to see through them. Above her, Julie was shouting down an approving whoop. Mary gave some measured words of encouragement. Anne got herself up.

I think most people would have stopped at this point and waited for the gang to catch up with her. But Anne's not like that, at least not at this point. For her, independence and ambition were king. Friends and potential lovers were great, if they could keep up. But they weren't worth waiting for.

But the clouds were so close, and she had a job to finish. So with her face still red and stinging from scraping along the icy slope moments before, Anne rolled back onto her butt, pushed with her sore arms back onto her feet, and set back off toward the clouds.

Anne described this moment to me over a cup of hot water as one of her best. She for the first time fluidly winds down the mountain an uncounted number of times before coming to a voluntary stop. The clouds unfurl around her. She feels a sense of freedom and exhilaration, pride and power, and lust for life that she would revisit many times later in her life.

Years before this moment, Anne had seen a David Ives play called *The Universal Language* which describes a made-up language called Unamunda. The words are imagined, but they echo words you know; "hello" translates as "Velco®" for instance. The whole play has struck with her, but above all is the sign hanging on the wall that counts from one to ten:

1. Wen
2. Yu
3. Fre
4. Fal
5. Fynd
6. Iff
7. Heven
8. Waitz

Here, on the mountain, falling through the clouds, Anne felt a sense of free falling that would never be repeated, not even when she went sky diving, not when falling apart, or falling down, or falling in love. She was free. A rope that had been holding her to some warped sense of reality had dissolved. She was dancing in the clouds, snowboarding naturally, fully relaxed. She was happy. She had found heaven.

Just after she told me about this moment in my fluorescent lit office, where the overzealous air conditioner was turning our fingernails blue, she remarked, "In many ways, Flint cut me free."

Then her eyes sink to the brown carpet, then through the carpet to the past where this memory lies in sepia-toned soft-focus. I let her go back to that moment and pretend I have email to check.

* * *

According to the File, the four of them managed to find their way down the mountain. By the end, Mary's technique was flawless, and she managed to make it down an entire run without falling once. Mary was satisfied. She had learned a new sport, and felt that tomorrow, they could do without lessons.

Julie on the other hand truly enjoyed playing in the snow, and it never bothered her to end up fully encased in a thick pile of it. Once she caught a toe edge, smacked face first (fisted arms in front of her in a well-practice fashion), and had the wind completely knocked out of her. Her momentum carried her entire body and snowboard into a headstand, like a break-dancer, before she tipped over and grated another hundred feet down the side of the mountain. But with one of the first breaths that she got back, she let out an enormous laugh. She remained sprawled like a snow angel until Flint was able to come down to her side, and on his knees beside her, ask if she was okay. Julie couldn't have been better.

At the end of the mountain and the lesson, the girls were

unstrapping their boards and removing their mittens. Their shirts were soaked with sweat under their jackets, which they now opened gratefully. Steam visibly rose from their t-shirts. Mary took off her helmet and her matted, damp wavy hair sprouted in all directions. Anne kept her helmet on but put her goggles up on her helmet. She clipped her mittens to her snowboard pants, on the same hook as her five-day pass. They only had one more day of skiing.

Flint leaned against the snowboard he had deftly dismounted two minutes ago. He asked the group, consciously making equal contact with all three girls, "Did you guys get a chance to check out the watering holes around here last night?"

Julie vivaciously replied, "Are you kidding? After you beat us up yesterday, we headed straight for our condo's hot tub!" But then she added, invitingly, "But is there any place you usually like to go?"

Anne flushed visibly. When we watch the File together, Anne insists that the flush was just from the exertion, the cold weather, the sudden stopping. But it's clear what was going on. I love watching these early day images of Anne. So bashful. It's endearing.

Flint would find it endearing over the course of the evening as well. The four of them decided to stow their boards at the lodge and grab some après ski beers (except for Anne who only drinks faux beer drinks like Smirnoff Ice) at some lamely named ski bunny joint, like "Ice Breaker" or "Home Base" (whose slogan was "make sure you get to home base tonight") or most lamely of all "The Ski Lodge." I forget which one they went to. It's not important, don't worry.

Wherever they went, there were a lot of snowboarders

and instructors. You could tell the instructors by their playful maturity, or if not, by their uniforms. Plus the fact that several an instructor came by their table to say hi to Flint and bestow not-so-subtle approval for his three-to-one girl-guy ratio.

The girls were really enjoying themselves. Sitting down after a hard day on the slopes, drinking some beers (or Smirnoff Ices) and admiring the "view."

Nothing exciting happened at the bar. Anne would later include this part of the night in her database of reasons why she never hangs out in small groups. She evolved this theory that when you have more than two people, the conversation always slips to the lowest common denominator. Now she has managed to arrange her life to orient around one-on-one brunches, large parties where she can create one-on-one situations, or on some occasions, small groups of people with very high lowest common denominators (e.g. single women of similar age who went to college together).

As their beers ran dry, Julie invited Flint to rejoin them for dinner at eight, so they could have a chance to hit the hot tubs and wash up first. He said he had plans with some friends, but would it be okay for them to join? Mary, warmed by two beers, interjected, "Are they single?" Flint laughed and told them to meet right at this spot five minutes before eight as the place was hard to find.

The outdoor hot tub was surrounded by a ring of snowdrifts. Mary stalked out in a towel from their condo through the dark icy air and slipped in next to Anne, who was already admiring the early stars. Julie came barreling in after. The steam floated just above the white bubbling surface.

Julie cackled mischievously, "So what do we have

brewing tonight?"

"Well," Mary replied with a grin, "looks like we might have some instruction yet ahead of us."

Anne was distant, entranced by the chaos of the mist hovering above the pool. By the motionless stars that she can never see through the bright lights of New York. By the random rhythm of the jet against her still sore triceps. She had sunk into the water down to her neck, trying to get the jet to soothe her aching shoulders. If her liver filtered the pollution from her blood, her shoulders filtered the pollution from her mind. Her closed mouth was already level with the undulating bubbles of the water, and she debated going deeper so that the water jet could hit her neck.

She pushed herself up to a full sitting position. "You seem to be getting along well with at least one of them, Julie," she goaded with a grin.

Anne wasn't just being playful. This was tactical. If Julie did have a thing for their snowboard instructor, then she had to keep her eyes and hands off. She had always adhered to a strict policy when it came to men; she never pursued men that others had crushes on and had become good at convincing herself that she was not interested in them either.

When I asked Anne about this habit, she mused that it might have come more from insecurity than benevolence. She felt that she couldn't compete with the other girls in her class.

I think there may be some truth to that, but I also think Anne has a particular keenness for the undiscovered, and a loathing for following the herd. Her need to be different extended to those she liked as well. Her need to discover extended to choosing friends.

She reflected on the situation. Clearly it worked out in

the end – she had awesome friends. But she wondered if she had passed up the chance to get to know other amazing people just because others also realized they were amazing.

Fortunately she didn't have to worry about her policy that night. Julie replied, "Flint's alright, but did you see the Scandinavian guy at the bar? I hope he comes."

Julie was being honest. She did think the Scandinavian man was more attractive than their somewhat staid snowboard instructor. But I think she also figured out two things: that Anne has this "hands off" policy, and that there had been some palatable chemistry between Anne and Flint.

Regardless of intent, one thing was certain: Anne was now free.

* * *

The three of them showed up a few minutes after eight, due to a few extra changes of clothes, some reapplication of makeup, and meek hot water pressure. Flint had been punctual but was calmly waiting for them. He had cleaned up well. He had gelled up the front of his hair like the crest of wave. But the rest remained soft to the touch. He wore a button-down shirt, not ironed but not made of material that creased much anyway, unbuttoned one button past corporate casual. Khakis and hiking boots. And a leather jacket.

"Hi," Anne said with a probing smile, which said without words, "You're glad we are here, even though we are late. Right?"

He was. "Hey there," he offered enthusiastically to her. "I figured that hot tub might have sucked you ladies in for a while, so I told the others to meet us at half past."

The restaurant was a five-minute walk down the main street, whose sidewalk was only wide enough for two. Flint and Anne took the lead. Anne asked Flint for the brief bios of the awaiting party, and how he knew them. Flint explained the social structure of the ski town, the hospitable but unequal relationship between the locals and the imports, the clique of extremely attractive Australians that rotate through the rest of the instructor pool, the early nights and earlier mornings, and the busy weekends that make Monday the new Friday.

Flint, the girls, and Flint's friends Joe and Sally sat down at a wood slated table and ordered some food and drinks. The planks on the table were well worn, and made a gentle thud when Flint placed a black drawstring bag of wooden blocks on it.

"Up for a game of Stacked?" Flint asked.

Joe leaned onto the table with both elbows and smacked his palms flat against its sticky surface. "Yes!" he said.

Flint opened the bag and dumped out twenty blocks of wood, all different shapes, including some blocks, some half-spheres, some triangle pyramids, some rods. There were no instructions.

"Who wants to go first?" Flint asked.

"How do you play?" Mary questioned. Anne smiled, relieved that Mary had the confidence to ask.

"You just build," Flint explained. "There are two rules: you can only build on top of what has already been built – only the first piece can touch the table itself. And whoever makes the tower fall loses. We'll start going around in turns clockwise."

"I'll go first," Julie chimed in, quickly realizing that gave her an advantage. She picked a big flat piece, one that would be easy for others to build on. Joe went next, also with one of the larger cubes, followed by Sally, who put a rod on one half of the cube, allowing the next person to still build comfortably on the other half.

Anne was up. She looked at the pieces left. While some were easy to build on top of, others were just nearly impossible: the half-sphere would be particularly tricky to balance another piece on. She grabbed it and placed it where it would be hardest for the next person. "Ha ha!" she said, throwing a (flirty?) icy gaze at Flint, who was next.

"Ah thanks," he grinned while taking a sip of his beer. He then grabbed a bridge-shaped piece, and balanced it carefully on top of the sphere, making it easier for the next person.

Mary took a small pyramid and balanced it on the rod. The tower started to wobble, but held, just. "Phew" Mary said. It was now Julie's turn again, and there were no easy places to put a piece.

"Might as well go down in a blaze of glory," Julie chirped, picking up one of the most awkward shapes left, and with great focus, tried to put it on Flint's bridge. As she started to release her grip, the tower started to wobble; surely this was the end. Slowly, carefully, she removed her finger; it held.

Back to Joe's turn now. Despite his practice with the game, there was simply nowhere left to go safely. He put one more piece on, and the tower crumbled. "Guess I lost that one" he shrugged off, still happy to be playing. "And I get to put the first piece down next!"

Anne's kept a poker face in the File, but when I checked back through her Memory, her mind was scanning, scheming for the hardest ones to start the game with. Surely, she thought, Joe will retaliate for us putting such hard pieces on his very easy base?

We watch Joe reach for biggest, widest, flattest base for everyone to build on. Now even in the File I can see the surprise on Anne's face.

"Usually we switch directions the second time," Joe explained. "Is that ok with everyone?" The group nodded. Anne did too, but you can see her take a bit of a gulp. Flint would now come before her and have his chance to make her lose.

Julie came after Joe, and again she picked a nice stable piece; Mary did the same. Flint grinned at Anne and licked his lips. "Hmmm," he said, "what should I pick…" He touched a conical pyramid that would be almost impossible to build on, and then settled for a simple block instead.

"You're up," he offered kindly.

Anne looked tormented. It's a game, she thought, where the point is to make someone lose. Why is everyone picking such easy pieces? Don't they get it?

She reached for the conical piece Flint had touched a moment before and placed it on the tower.

Sally, who was next, frowned, then found a narrow rod and placed it on another part of the base. Julie laughed ("here goes nothing"!) then also found a space on the existing base to put another cube, as did Mary ("phew"). Flint was out of good options, and when he tried to place the bridge piece back, the tower wobbled. The group inhaled all together and held their breath. When he removed his hand, the tower held.

It was now Anne's turn. Nervous both at the challenge ahead and the way that her earlier move had come back to haunt her, she picked up a pyramid with a slightly trembling hand. She realized her hand was trembling as it approached the tower, so much that it was visible to the others too, and that made it tremble more. She placed the pyramid on top of the bridge, but the unwanted movement in her hand makes the tower shudder. The group inhaled and again held their breath again. When Anne removed her hand, the tower collapsed.

"It's actually a good thing, Anne," Flint said, trying to comfort her. "Now you get to put the first piece."

In the File, she looked angry. When I interviewed her in my office, she told me that she was embarrassed. But oddly when I revisited her actual Memory, I learned that she was holding back tears. Tears for being a person that tries to win by making other people lose. Tears for making enemies when she wanted to be making friends. Tears for trying to win – not even win, just not lose – at all costs.

I wish I could say that Anne realized how her ambition was not serving her here. I wish I could say she had a great epiphany: that the whole point of playing this game was to build a big tower together with other people, not to make someone fail. I wish I could say that Anne then picked a big base, that would be easy for others to build on.

But while Anne will have gotten there by the end of this story, it's not in a moment of epiphany, and certainly not that day at this unnamed apres-ski bar.

"Good," she said, channeling sadness into bitchiness, as New York has long trained her to do. She reached for the conical pyramid, touching her finger briefly on it, before realizing that Flint will have to go after her, and she didn't want to give him something impossible – after all, she wanted him to like her. She settled for a long narrow rod, not as easy as the bases Julie and Joe put down, but not impossible.

Flint nodded, neither smiling not frowning, showing nothing on his face, "I can work with that."

The rounds passed, until almost everyone caused the tower to fall at some point. As the pain was shared, glasses were chinked, toasts were made, and food was ordered.

After the last round, Flint tidied up the pieces and pulled his drawstring bag closed. "Great playing guys. The next round is on me!" he offered, spurring Joe to pop up immediately. Flint stood up to take orders. "Alrighty, what'll it be? Beers and well-drinks only, tips accepted," he added. By the time he got the orders, Joe had already returned with another beer. As Flint headed for the bar, Anne joined him to help him carry drinks back.

Anne sat down on the stool next to where Flint was leaning on the bar, talking to the bartender. The bartender was beautiful, with an eyebrow stud calling out her jade eyes, and the naturally highlighted strands of hair that carelessly decorated her smooth forehead. Flint slathered on the charm, and asked if he could get a free drink for himself, "You know the tour guide privilege?" When she answered, her voice was almost prepubescent high but nevertheless extremely seductive, the way you'd imagine teenage Calvin Klein models talk. It was innocent and experienced at the same time. Anne guessed she could be from the East Coast, out here to snowboard and figure out her life for a while. In response to his request for a freebie, she offered him a free drink if he tipped her excessively, "commensurate with her degree in mixology." He laughed, agreed, and let her mix the drinks.

Then he half-sat on the stool and turned to face Anne.

Anne suddenly felt like a kid lost in a crowded museum

who sees her dad. Flint looked at her with such benevolence and compassion. How did he know her so well? His soft grey eyes seemed to open to a dense forest of wisdom. She noticed the stubble starting to grow out of his cheeks, the way his lips had fought the chapping dryness and sun, and then suddenly became aware of how dry her mouth was. She sucked on her upper lip with lower one, and then used the moist underside of her tongue to quickly lick her lower lip.

He rested his elbow on the bar and his cheek on his hand. Her jealousy of the bartender dissolved. He was looking at her silently with curious affection. She didn't understand how he could be so honest and so vulnerable. How could he see through the outer bitchiness and want to comfort the sadness that lay below the surface? While her mind whirred, trying to compute how she saw him seeing her seeing him, her face remained motionless, guarded.

"So," he gently offered to put her at ease, "did you enjoy Stacked?"

She thought about it. In truth, no, she didn't really enjoy the game. It was stressful. But it also made her hungry to play it again.

"It was alright," she replied. "I clearly need practice. How about you? Would you consider that to have been a good game of Stacked?"

"Oh, what happens in the game isn't really that important," he replied, rotating on his stool to face her completely. "It's who else you get to play with that matters."

Anne and Flint had their hands full with the drinks as they carefully wound their way back to the table. The six of them resumed chatting about the lowest common denominator – snowboarding – and it seemed the magic moment had passed.

Anne began to realize that she wouldn't have another chance alone with Flint to apologize for how mean she was in the game.

But just as this thought crosses her mind, five men in kilts with bagpipes entered the bar. I can't make this up. They were promoting some type of scotch Anne had never heard of and promised free samples to anyone who would try a Scottish jig. Flint put both hands on the table and shoved his chair back. "My free drink at last!" he exclaimed.

Flint made a complete fool of himself. He started out with a conservative attempt at a jig, before determining that his decade of experience with the Running Man move was his best move. Before being jeered off to collect his drink, he gave a last-ditch effort at the Robot. At the end, he smiled at Anne, and then he beckoned her onto the stage.

Anne took a deep breath out, tossed back the last sips of her drink, and walked to the dance floor. If this were my story, Anne would be a fantastic dancer, graceful to a tee, sexy as hell, and coordinated like the German army. But I have promised the truth, which is this: she tried.

After as short a time as possible, Anne walked off the dance floor and headed over to the table where the scotch was being poured. And where Flint was waiting.

"Hello," she said with a rusty attempt at what would later develop into a style of flirting. She couldn't remember a time when she really flirted before. All the previous men in her life were guys she had known a long time. Her relationships had started the old fashion way, before sparks and flints: with the patient use of a woodchip, bow and bark, gradually heating until smoke gave way to fire. She felt like she was wearing new shoes for the first time, a bit unstable and unsure how to take the next step.

Fortunately Flint slid down the bench so she could sit next him. They sat leg to leg, shoulder to shoulder. She leaned into him with a lowered voice, ostensibly so the Scottish promoters wouldn't hear, but also so he couldn't hear the nervousness in her voice. "Is it worth trying?"

He gave her his glass. "That's a Catch 22, isn't it? You can't find out until you try it."

She took a sip. A little too smoky, but a nice strong current of vanilla. The single large ice cube glimmered in the light, reflecting the green neon sign, the fairy lights across the bar, the disco ball above the dance floor. I found it beautiful to watch in the File, but Anne was looking straight through it, lost in thought.

"I'm sorry I was a bit of a jerk playing Stacked," she began, unable to make eye contact with him. "Where I'm from, there's no point in a game unless someone wins and someone else loses."

Flint nodded. "I know. You're not the first East Coaster I've taught to snowboard out West," he said. "Learning to play nicely with others just takes a little practice. If that's what you really want."

Was it? Did she want to play nicely with others? Anne always thought "nice" was what you said about people you had nothing else nice to say about. Where was the game, the challenge, the reward, in just passing the time pleasantly with strangers?

Slowly her eyes focus on the glass in front her, and a warmth spreads over her face, melting into a grin. She told me later that she realized then that this was truly a weekend away, a risk-free chance to try out a different persona. She wasn't in New York right now, and no matter what happened with Flint, she would be leaving the day after tomorrow anyway. Being nice for a day? It was worth a try.

"Maybe I could," she said, turning to Flint with what now most people would recognize as a flirtatious grin. "Maybe you can show me how sometime?"

By the time she was halfway through her drink, she had put aside the embarrassment and defensiveness. But she still couldn't believe he seemed interested in her and was still here talking with her. Could he really like her?

Maybe, she wondered at the time, he liked how she snowboarded or how quickly she learned. Maybe he had a thing for strong, determined women from New York. Or maybe there was some pheromone signal that resonated with his, and he just found her attractive enough to spend an evening or two with.

I never got to access Flint's own memories or talk with him, so I can't tell you what he was thinking. As usual, your guess is as good as mine. Of course, I did think about stalking Flint in the File, to find out what happened to him after Anne's ski trip, and maybe even before, but never felt that was appropriate or helpful for this story. You see, the reason Flint is important in Anne's story isn't Flint himself at all. It's how Anne was around him.

Just for that weekend, she lowered her typical defenses. She didn't feel the need to vet his friends, make sure he didn't have a girlfriend, conceal how she felt from Mary, Julie or the rest of the table. She let go of being embarrassed or worried. She just knew that she wanted another excuse to be alone with him for a while. She was like a kitten being picked up by the nape her neck around him; totally relaxed, and willing to be carried for a short while. Without realizing it, she was heeding his lessons back on the mountain: Relax.

Trust. Look at where you want to go.

She looked straight at him. Without putting down the glass, she slowly raised her other hand to touch the stubble on his cheek with her fingertips. It felt like sand more than sandpaper. She was sinking deep into his brown eyes, and to fall through them and wander around. She wanted to really understand him and let him change her; she felt sure that he would change her for the better. As she later put it, "I could tell he saw in me the person I could become. I just needed to find out who that person was."

Then slowly the sandy stubble on his cheek moved towards her, grazed against her fingertips, her fingers, and settled into her palm. He paused, awaiting permission from her hand which was gently pressed against his face. She drew her fingertips down his cheek to rest on his jaw. He leaned forward until his eyes were so close, she couldn't focus on them anymore. She could feel his breath against her lips and realized how she herself was holding her breath, as if waiting for another tower to fall. Her fingers started trembling against his jaw, and just when her lower lip started quivering too, he kissed her.

They stayed together until her trembling went away and her breath came back. Anne leaned back just a little. "Thank you," she said.

"See," Flint joked, now clearly flirting, "You already know how to play nicely with others."

They finished their promotional scotches, kissed a few more times, and headed back to the table to the same seats they started out in. The rest of the table had clearly seen what was going on the scotch-tasting table, but even Joe managed to avoid teasing them about it. It didn't seem appropriate, for some reason.

At 10:30 p.m., Sally's cellphone alarm went off. "This is when I turn into a pumpkin," she said. The ski instructors generally needed to start teaching classes at 8 a.m., sometimes earlier, so Sarah wanted to get a decent night's rest. Her heavy wooden chair screeched across the floor, and the rest of the group's followed. Flint was grabbing his coat off the back of his chair when Julie asked the girls what they wanted to do. Julie was in a pleasant and comfortable state and didn't seem inclined to head out just yet.

Anne was torn, between wanting to spend more time with Flint, and not wanting to be the kind of girl who goes home with the ski instructor from a bar. Under time pressure to respond, her cautious side won out. She would stay with the girls.

The rest of the ski instructors said their goodbyes and started for the door. Flint walked to Anne's chair and crouched down to be at eye level.

"Do I get to see you tomorrow?" he asked.

"Well," she laughed softly, "if we bought another set of lessons with you, that would somehow feel like pimping. But I might be free in the evening."

He leaned forward and pushed back the hair covering her ear with the back of his fingers. "Would your friends mind if you ditched them to have dinner with a hot ski instructor?" he whispered into her ear.

"I think they can manage without me," she replied softly. "It'll be tough though."

Not really caring that nothing is said, he kissed her again. Anne had read in *Life's Little Instruction Book* not to be the first person to break a hug. Over the years she had internalized this information and was famed for her back breaking perpetual embraces. But now, she didn't want this kiss to end anytime soon. It wasn't particularly sloppy or passionate. Just lingering. Pretty boring to watch, even for Julie and Mary.

When they finally separated, she stroked his soft gelled hair and asked him logistical questions and for tips on which trails to hit the next day.

And then he left. Anne parachuted back to the table, slowly descending, knowing that she would have to explain this thing to Julie and Mary as soon as she hit the ground. Which she did, relying heavily on the phrase, "I don't know what he sees in me, but I like it."

Julie too was a bit toasty and affectionate, and in a great mood about Joe. Anne was too caught up in her own thing to notice the sparks flying there. Apparently while she was at the scotch tasting table, the group had decided to get together tomorrow night, same place same time, at Joe's suggestion. Anne said, "Sorry kids, I can't join you," stretching her still-sore arms up and behind her head, "I've got a date!"

She clapped her hands like a seal, and suggested they head home.

* * *

The girls slept in. They were more tired from snowboarding than hung over. By the time they got up the mountain, it was already past noon. The first few runs were rough. They had lost confidence and were starting to fall back into old habits. Mary caught toe edges on almost every turn, and Anne was overcorrecting herself. Julie was still doing well and could now link together five or six turns together.

They had just gotten down the crowded part of the main slope, when Anne started to build up more speed than she could handle. To avoid crashing into a kiddie school, she plowed her entire body into the snow. She grated across the ice, narrowly avoiding the instructor himself.

She was lying on her now-sore back, winded and defeated, staring up through her orange tinted glasses at the clear blue sky above. She didn't mind lying there for a little bit. But then realized in a panic that others might befall the same fate and also crash into her.

As she propped herself up into a sitting position, she heard the slow approach of a snowboard behind her. It came to a stop.

"Hey," the instructor said, "next time be more careful about the little guys, Anne."

She whipped her head around to look at Flint.

"Of course," she said, thinking: Of course it's you.

He lowered his voice, humored by the situation. "So is this what you're like without me around?"

She gave him a playful "asshole" smile and an eye roll and accepted his hand to get up. Just then she felt a sharp knife pain from twisting her right ankle in the fall. Anne has handled pain before. She's injured her knees playing volleyball numerous times; thrown out her shoulder throwing baseballs from third base to first; kinked her neck leaning forward to see the screen as her eyesight worsened over time. And every time she did what she always did: hid the pain and carried on.

Flint couldn't see her wince behind her goggles and scarf, and she didn't want him to know she was hurt. Struggling to stand, she forced her voice to sound normal, and made a quick joke that she should join the kiddie school. Which reminded him that he was still teaching them responsibility. He said a quick "see you later" and shuffled off.

Anne lingered there, partially out of discomfort, partially to watch him work. What was it about him that captured her so much? He could be drinking with friends or leading a troop of ten-year olds down a mountain, and it didn't matter. He was so at ease.

She watched him snowboard, trying to learn how it did it so effortlessly. She heard him say from down the hill to his class, "Just do what I do." How lovely would it be to do what he does! To forget the details and the nuances, forget about balance or edges, just imitate him completely.

She started back down the hill, pain shooting through her ankle. She realized halfway down that she should make this her last run, a timid, painful, persistent slog down the hill. Alongside the pain itself, a dark cloud of sorrow now washed over her: she wasn't expecting her last run to be like this. By the bottom of the hill, the sorrow has turned to anger and then determination. She was determined to take another run.

And so again we see in the File as Anne grimaces. She winces back onto the ski lift and makes her way back down the mountain, injuring her ankle further, but proud that she has won her battle against the pain. She tries her best to be in flow, but it just hurts too much; she falls time and time again. Again, as she approaches the bottom of the mountain, the dark cloud returns; again she is determined for that to not be her last run. Up again she goes, gritting her teeth against the wind. The lifts would be closing soon; she only has time for one more run.

Down she goes, carving a fierce path through the slush and ice that has now formed on the sunny, frigid slope. The screech of board against mountain, as she fought her way down, fists clenched, ready for battle. With each fall she punches the mountain ("Take that!"). Each time she pushes herself up with her sore arms, she gets a surge of pride. Pain, challenge, pride. Pain, challenge, pride. She times this repeated cycle just right, so as she comes down the last time and unstraps her board, she has finished on pride.

"Yes," she thinks to herself. "I've won."

* * *

The three of them met up at the lodge as planned when the lifts closed and headed to get a drink. Different name, same kind of après-ski bar as the previous day. Anne never mentioned her ankle, her battle against pain. Julie was talking to Mary about the day, about the night, about this new fabric that keeps moisture away, weather forecasting and dynamite, avalanches and search dogs, seeing-eye dogs and disability rights and civil rights. Her arms fluttered in front of her, like a hummingbird, carrying her along by the passion of her soliloquy.

Mary at intervals nudged Julie on, whenever Julie's momentum in her wanderings seem to be waning. Anne has always admired Mary's talent for asking good questions. More than that, Mary always has been able to listen to the answers. She was leaning forward on her elbow, hand cupped around her chin; the narrow metal armrests must not have been comfortable for such a Thinker position. But Mary's eyes were bright, open fully, head pinned on a nod-nod axis, moving in sync with unheard classical music.

Anne had pushed her chair back so she could stretch her legs out fully and rest her ankle. Her body was draped across the metal chair, the ledge of her skull under her ponytail supported by its frigid back. This wasn't comfortable either. She reached behind her head and undid her ponytail. Her hair was so sticky that it mostly stayed just where it was, in pony-tail formation. But slowly over the next two drinks, you can watch the strands settle, coming to a peaceful landing spot against the back of the chair. The sweat on her neck beaded, then spread into a thin coat, then turned clammy. By the end of the first drink, it has evaporated.

Anne swam Mary and Julie's conversation like a breaststroker, sometimes coming up to pay attention to what was going on, sometimes coasting underwater in her own personal zone. She was thinking of the clouds meeting the mountains, the sound of Flint's snowboard the first time he sprayed her, the grating of his snowboard, the way he kept adding solid bases during Stacked for others to build on. Her ankle pain has dulled into memory. She reemerged into their conversation to find they are talking about feminism.

"You know," Julie says, "we're in a weird place. Before it made so much sense: find a husband quickly, have kids, and stick together. But now we are supposed to have careers and be successful mothers, be sexually innocent but experienced. And while the same time we are looking for love, while it's so important to have a boyfriend and someone to rely on, we are told to shun dependence. Freedom matters above all things."

Mary asked, "Would you give up your freedom for a guy? Just say you wanted to get a PhD for instance, and it required you to move to Bumble USA, and your boyfriend had some situation that prevented him from moving. Would you break up?"

Julie thought it over. "I don't know," she said seriously. And then she grinned, "Are the Bumble boys cute?"

Mary shook her head and rolled her eyes, then turned to Anne, sensing that she wanted to get involved in this discussion. "What about you, Anne?"

Her ponytail had finished settling. "I don't know," she answered. "I've worked too hard to gain the freedom that I have now. I don't think I would want to give up so easily."

Julie asked, "But what if you really loved each other?"

Anne considered. "Well in that case, I suppose he would understand why I had to go and support me in that. He would let me go."

So that was the Anne that eventually unpeeled herself from her chair, took a quick dip in the hot tub, and then spent a few minutes primping for her date. She spent a lot of time primping, actually, but half of it was to make herself look like she didn't. She put on makeup and then patted off half of it with a tissue. She brushed her wet hair carefully into straight lines, and then tossed her fingers through it to make it look less intentional. She wore matching underwear, just in case, but her outer garments weren't particularly seductive: a scoop-neck green cotton shirt that brings out her eyes, and her nice pair of jeans.

Julie gave her a few breath mints and a friendly pinch of the skin under her elbow. Weird, Anne thought, but sweet.

Anne set out.

* * *

In the File, you see her waiting under a streetlight. The pockets of her slim fit jeans aren't really meant to stick your hands in. Her hands have no idea where to go. When her weight shifts onto her left leg, her right hand goes to rest on the now slightly angled right leg. Left hand goes on left hip. Awkward. Left hand stretches out toward the left knee. Retreats. Descends. Ends up absently rubbing the outside of thigh, looking for a comfortable resting spot. Gives up and seeks her other hand out. The right hand comes over, and they meet in the middle, clasping. Too tight. They loosen their grip. Loosen more. Just hover near each other now not even touching. They sense her face is itching, and her right index finger finds her lip. I guess it's been bothering her because it's so dry and chapped. Rubs some dead skin off. Okay, back to the thigh. Back to clasping. Fixes a stray hair that has wandered over her cheek bone.

The hand is in the process of pushing hair back from her face when Flint arrives. He is carrying a rose. While her head is taking care of interacting with Flint, her hands gratefully reach out for the flower. Both hands want to hold it, partially so they don't have to figure what else to do. Anne is looking down at the rose and the hands that hold it. Her hands don't both need to be holding the single rose. One releases its grip, and drifts at her side. The other brings the flower to her nose.

It smells abnormally nice. She hides behind the rose like a singer behind a mike. And then speaks into it, hoping it can amplify a voice she can barely get out without cracking.

"Thanks," she says. "I really appreciate it." And then, "Where to?" Her hand drifts up and waves vaguely around, looking for the invisible current that will tell it which way they are about to go. Finding nothing, it flutters back down, drifting again by her side.

"Come with me," Flint answers, and he takes her hand.

* * *

They find themselves at a steak house. She orders the small filet mignon au poivre, and he goes for the porterhouse. This is the kind of place where spinach costs $8. So on one hand, she hopes he's paying. But on the other, she doesn't want to owe him anything. So when he asks her if she'd like something to drink, she says, "No, water's great." He says he was thinking about getting a scotch, maybe the brand they had last night.

What does he want her to order? she wonders, grating her upper lip with the lower teeth of her underbite. "That scotch was good," she states, allowing Flint to interpret as he would like. He orders two scotches.

Everything that had been effortless last night is a struggle for Anne. She's downright nervous. She feels like she's speaking into a microphone in a large auditorium, waiting for her words to echo off the walls. She waits to see how they play into his face, and in watching his reaction so closely, forgets sometimes to keep talking. Multitasking is hard. She wants nothing more than to listen to him, like one of his kiddie school students. For now anyway.

Flint obliges. He tells her about the first time he came to California to be a park ranger for a summer, ended up a historical museum site instead, went into tour guiding, traveled to Europe with over-privileged high school children, fell in love with a French woman ("He told you that?!" Julie would later exclaim), dropped out of college to live in France and study winemaking, fell out of love with the French woman, moved back to New Jersey to work in a liquor shop ("vintage wine shop" as he put it), and had just quit his job to work winters here. "I figure next summer,

I can head down to the coast and work on a sailboat for a while," he said.

"Do you think you'll ever finish college?" she asked him, concerned. Anne's mother had met her father before he had finished college, but Anne herself was trained to be snobby about education. She couldn't imagine having a real relationship with someone who had no ambition, not even to graduate from college. Later her definition of ambition would change, but not yet. And then, as she thought about it, she realized that she wasn't looking for a real relationship with Flint. She was leaving the next day. You can watch in the File as Anne's face processes these thoughts; a shadow sweeps over eyes. She regrets asking the question, trying to typecast him, to figure out who he wants to be. But it's the only thing she knows how to do.

Flint considers the question, as if for the first time. "I imagine so," he replied, "but I'm not in a hurry to settle down just yet. One day I'd like to have a job and a family and a mortgage, but not just yet. I love my job here on the mountain, love the people I meet, the air is amazingly clean, and I am in the best shape of my life. I have a little philosophy in life, which I picked up from a winemaker in France. He was explaining why his wines have been so successful for so many years. His company's strategy is merely this, he told me: 'When things are working, keep doing it. When they stop working, stop.' And this lifestyle, it's working."

* * *

The fluorescent lights in my office were buzzing overhead, casting a flickering light on the brown carpet.

Anne blew across the top of her mug of hot water. I waited.

She had told me about Flint and the snowboard trip several times before, in pieces, like a Picasso: fragmented, but vaguely suggestive of the whole. Her snippets of description had always been the vivid colors: the reds, the yellows, the bold greens, the bright whites. But as we were filling in the image of the snowboard trip during this interview in my office, the greys and browns and tarnished metal colors came through more and more.

There was nothing wrong with Flint embracing life, and living on a whim, she rationalized. It was alluring, after all. She fed on his excitement for adventure, and for exploration, and wanted to emulate that in her own life.

But when she describes the rest of their conversation over dinner during their date, her enthusiasm for him wanes.

She explained to me her theory on why: that as an American, she is taught to approach life as a shopping trip. Which experiences do you want to *have*, to own, to take home with you? Which people do you want to add to your collection of friends? It's an acquisition-based view, which involves holding on to something, and keeping it, indefinitely.

But the question of whether something is worth acquiring is a different one from whether something is worth experiencing. Acquisition makes judgments on the future: will this experience/product/person be useful to me in the future? Experience is much more rooted in the present.

Yet, while she knew from the onset that this snowboard trip would take place entirely in the present, there is something about going on a date that sets her mind in acquisition mode: is Flint worth acquiring?

As soon as she heard that he is the transitory type, the roamer, the experience seeker, he became uninteresting as an acquisition. As soon as she would hold on to him, he would vanish.

So roll to the video tape of the File. We see them now having their scotches and steaks and spinach. They smile pleasantly, now more familiar and less flirty, and talk about their respective childhoods. As they age in the conversation, they approach the present day, the season, the slopes, the mountains. The challenges of teaching, the challenges of learning. The waiter comes to clear the plates, and Anne grabs the sprig of parsley from the corner as he lifts the plate away. She munches it slowly, remembering the rainy day in her parents' garden many years ago when she first offered to pick parsley for dinner. The scotch is gone, the restaurant is emptying out, and there are three stains from water evaporating on the white tablecloth. Flint asks for the check, and Anne makes a half-hearted attempt to pay. They walk out to the front of the restaurant, where the headlights of the snow machines and groomers are visible on the dark slopes of the mountain.

"Thank you, for everything," Anne says, gratefully, conclusively. She takes both his hands, and moves into kiss him, lingering for a bit longer in his warmth, trying to hold on to this amazing person, this moment just a little bit longer.

The groomers go around a turn and the light fades. She steps back now and lets go of his hands. They fluttered empty now, rubbing against her jeans, her jacket, the icy night air. Still warm from his grasp, her right hand reaches up to touch his still stubbled cheek one last time, before she says goodbye.

PART 2 : UPHILL

The morning light coming through the window uncurled Anne and turned her toward the window. She smiled. From her window in Brooklyn Heights, she could see nothing but blue skies. She closed her eyes again and let her head sink back into her plush pillow, felt the thick foam mattress and the fluffy comforter around her.

She breathed like a pendulum. In physics class in high school, she watched a video of parabolic motion, the pendulum moving up, decelerating, pausing, accelerating down, decelerating, pausing, accelerating up. She felt herself collapse into a state with no potential energy anymore, the finality of expiration. Pause. Her unconscious diaphragm tugged gently, accelerating how quickly the blue sky filled her lungs and gently pushed her head back into the plush pillow. In her mind now, the teacher rotated the pendulum 90 degrees. And it became clear it wasn't a pendulum at all, but a circle, a wheel around which the once-pendulum rotated. From the side, the wheel had appeared to slow and pause and then head down; from the front, the wheel moved continuously, at a constant pace. And now she imagined her breathing like a circle, continuous. She fell back asleep, hypnotized.

Dishes clanged as her sister took them out of the dishwasher. A few minutes later the church bells across the street rang twelve times. Birds were chirping, and on the street below, trucks were gunning up their engines as the light turned green. It was time to get up.

Her sister had made her an instant coffee, 1% milk and Splenda, which she took. She knew that the reason she liked coffee-cart coffee better was that it was real coffee, whole milk, and real sugar. But she took what she was given and enjoyed it just as much.

Later she knew they would go to the bagel shop down by the Brooklyn Promenade, and get some bagel, egg and cheese (with tomato) sandwiches, and watch the summer sun light up the skyline of Manhattan. From the Promenade she could see the Windmill, where she worked. Since the chivalrous days of Don Quixote are behind us, this isn't the kind of windmill you tilt at. Large spinning windmills, the kind you see dotting Holland and mini-golf parks, work where winds are predictable. In New York, winds blow from different directions at different times, and sometimes many directions all at once.

Anne Kesheen had seen the Windmill there before there was a windmill. It was on September 12th, 2001, the day after 9/11. The white cloud over the World Trade Center site still lingered motionless. Silently. It reminded her of a young globular cluster, frothy and hot with the destruction of old exploded stars, and the birthplace of the next generation. The Twin Towers too had stood motionless and silent, immortal in the sky.

The difference here was the smell. You could smell it throughout the city, as it traveled up some avenues but not others, like a losing game of Plinko on the *Price is Right*. Apparently on 57th Street and 6th Avenue that day, you couldn't smell the cloud, but further north at 86th and Lexington, the unmatchable odor of plaster paper people pavement suddenly sucked the oxygen out of dazed pedestrians.

Anne stood on the Promenade, where only the smell made the white cloud real. She had watched the replays too often on television, and the line between reality and imagination had blurred for the last time. She came to truly believe that art and life were indivisible. (Later, when she was confined to bed with a torn knee, she would realize that the divide between body and mind was also bogus.) Some therapists might diagnose her inability to accept reality as Delusions. She called them Dreams.

So standing there, watching the silent, still city baking in the summer sun, she lost focus. Since I have access to her Memories, I can tell you where she went.

First: she was in upstate New York. On her back. In a canoe. On a temperate summer night. No lights anywhere. Just the Milky Way schmeared above her like cream cheese on a bagel, and a few shooting stars that reminded her of a screen saver. That last thought disturbed her, and she rolled, rocking the canoe, creating ripples of water and sound that eventually reached a loon, which crowed, and set off a round of howling from the local coyotes around the lake rim, which echoed against the mountains until eventually it faded out, as most things eventually do. The canoe eventually rocked her back to the present, and she watched instead the motionless Milky Way.

Back under the yellowing ceiling tiles and fluorescent lights of her high school, she had studied the night sky. How time travels at the speed of light, no faster, and so when you look out and away you also look back in history. The stripe of the Milky Way are hundreds of thousands of companion stars which we are washing around the universe with. Out there, behind the web of stars in our own galaxy, are other places, too far away to mention in this short daydream. But if you peek through NASA's eyes, you can see them: exploded stars, whose order-less mess of elements eventually find their way into bright-eyed and unjaded stars; steamy clusters where stars and planets and perhaps life is born, hugged together by gravity and sparked alive by the intensity of that hug; and constellations, the first way that we attempted to find meaning from the cosmos, before rationality dissuaded us from the merit of connecting the dots.

She could feel the infinite mass out there in the cosmos pulling her toward it, struggling against the wimpy pull of her own insignificant planet Earth. She panicked.

But Mother Earth held tight – mothers give the greatest hugs.

Two: She probably should have learned the metric system, but she was American, so she was taught distances in feet and yards. Her real sense of measurement though was the New Yorker one: distances are measured in blocks and height in stories. One mile is about twenty blocks, and one story is about ten feet tall.

So during a 40-block hike through Yosemite National Park, she saw trees gradually growing from the standard four story tall to ten, twenty, almost thirty stories. Thirty stories! Hoover Tower, the Stanford University landmark that Anne cycled around for four years, is only half as tall, and yet it dominates the campus. Imagine if that tree were imported and plunked down next to Hoover Tower!

She bit her lip and wondered if there was ever a time when people compared buildings to trees, and not the other way around.

Three: She is still at Yosemite. Walking up the stone-cut stairs next to a waterfall. There are three things that Anne can do all day: write computer code, watch people, and admire a waterfall. The computer coding is a mystery even to me, and I like to consider myself largely omniscient. People-watching is obvious, as I explain later. As for the waterfall, Anne once told me in my office over a cup of plain hot water why that was: "You can watch a waterfall all day. It's always changing. And never moves."

When I rebutted that it does change with the seasons, she rolled her eyes. As you will learn during this story, metaphors are like candles: extremely useful, and often beautiful, but they don't cast light on everything.

So she watched this waterfall next to her as she hiked up the mountain. The wet mist coated her face and the lens of her pre-digital camera. The roar of the waterfall remained constant, while the white cloud of mist grew denser, fresher, more alive. She was no longer watching the waterfall but breathing it. She looked up at her friend who turned from man to silhouette before disappearing entirely into the mist. Eventually so did she.

When she emerged on the other side, she could see the head of the waterfall leaping out of the sky, the foot of the waterfall kicking up tumultuous chaos, and between them the mist that still clung on her clothes. She looked down at her feet. Rainbows sprouted from her toes, forming full circles just in front of her hands. Through the mist, she could touch them.

She raised her camera and looked through the lens. And stopped. She wanted to remember this moment as it was. She did not want to remember her photograph of the waterfall.

She told me last week in my office that she still rarely takes photographs. She rested her cheek on her open palm, propped on the hard wooden arm of her chair. She looked distant, as if considering the endless cycle of the cosmos or how to make a cake when you've run out of eggs. She spoke confidently, but her face was streaked with discomfort. I offered her some plain hot water and reminded her that she could speak without fearing judgment. I'm not that kind of omniscient being.

She explained there are three reasons to take a photograph. First, to look more closely at something. Just the act of composing a photograph forces you to look more carefully – to see the color of the bird, the angle of the building's edge. But you learn the mechanics of framing a shot, how to appreciate light and shadow, color and hue, focus and depth, you see the world more vividly, and no longer need a camera in hand. She didn't need to take a photograph of the waterfall to see the beauty in it.

The second reason she gave for taking photographs was to remember something more accurately: how it looks, who was there, how the world once was in history. I suppose that's roughly how I use the File. She doesn't think photographs are accurate, no matter how high resolution they may be: history is interpretation, not fact. I agree. How often have you photographed a huge moon on the horizon only to see how small it really is? How often do you identify with pictures of yourself?

She brought in a stunning photograph of a New York City intersection at night after it had rained; in the blurred headlights of an oncoming car, you could see the motionless steam rising from manhole cover. Then she told me about the night she walked home, at night after it had rained, when the city turns black and grey and white. She said you could smell the comforting clean of wet pavement. You could hear cars sloshing by in the quiet of a New York night. And there was that same steam rising from a manhole cover, breathing into life through the bold headlights of the oncoming car. "It was like the photograph, but better," she explained, "for this had sound, smell, the energy of the amazing night out I had just had, the rush of blood in my legs after walking several blocks, the comfort of my plush bed waiting for me at home. How can you capture such a moment in a photograph, or in video, or even in words? How could I have possibly captured fully that moment in Yosemite?"

I nodded knowingly, and quietly captured her words for this book.

The third reason people take photographs is to share the moment with others, maybe people who were there, maybe people who weren't. "Maybe I'm selfish, but there is just too much beauty out there to waste time trying to capture it, package it, preserve it, throw a label on it. To do what? Share it with strangers?"

That's why she never took that photograph of Yosemite. She has it locked up in her mind and opens the drawer from time to time at her leisure to take a peek. Sometimes when she is on the phone with a counterparty, sometimes when she is riding the subway, in the shower, out on a run, or standing on the Promenade, watching the skyline.

The stench of the white cloud over the site of the World Trade Center jarred her back to present. She was still on the Promenade, but the white cloud was no longer across the river. She was in it. It roared around her and covered her clothes with white ash, and stardust, and mist.

Then it was gone.

Across the river she saw in its place a giant dandelion, as tall as the cloud, now the tallest thing on the skyline. It blew in the wind, but its seeds did not blow off. They tugged gently at the stem, first in one direction and then in the other. Then in all directions at once. For a moment, the Epcot-shaped flower head quivered. Then it was still. But just for a moment, before a new and unexpected wind caressed the top of it, and the seeds danced and jumped with excitement. She was looking at the Windmill.

She told me that since that moment, she never stopped seeing it. Intellectually she knew it didn't exist yet, of course; a giant dandelion doesn't just appear from the supernova dust of the World Trade Center overnight. But nevertheless she really did see the giant dandelion with her own eyes. (It's true: I've checked her Memory.)

So when she went out for a coffee and a bagel, egg, cheese (and tomato) sandwich with her sister that following weekend, Saturday September 15th, 2001, it took her a while to share her vision. Anne took a deep breath, then gave it a go. "When I look across the river, I see a giant dandelion growing out the rubble, like a windmill. Maybe it is a windmill, generating power out of motion. How beautiful would that be?"

Her big sister kept looking at the already surreal post-9/11 skyline. "That sounds nice," she said. "Why don't you build it?"

* * *

Everyone in New York knows the Windmill, but I never gave much thought about how it came about, and certainly didn't know when Anne first walked into my office that she was responsible for getting it started.

I checked in the File what Anne did later that Saturday morning. She and her sister threw their bagel wrappers, cups and lids into the appropriate bins on their way home from the Promenade. Then Anne immediately went online to see what she could learn about power generation, from traditional wind turbines, piezo generation, and tidal methods. By the Sunday, she had emails out to some of the academics and companies who developed these technologies, asking them if they had developed any designs that worked on low-speed and changeable winds and breezes. A few got back to her in the following week, one even with a link to patents that she had authored, asking who she worked for and if she was interested in licensing agreements. At the time, Anne had a normal management consulting job, advising companies on how to develop their businesses and identify market entry strategies. She had worked with a few clients in infrastructure, who bid for government tenders and contracts. But she had never run a project like this herself.

But as I said, Anne was driven and ambitious. So by the next weekend, she had created an Excel spreadsheet with high level calculations: if she could build this dandelion windmill cheaply enough, and it did indeed generate as much power as the academics had estimated, it could make a lot of money. It was worth a go. She spoke with her boss and asked for three months of unpaid leave to see if she could make it happen; her boss agreed, and off Anne went.

A month later, in mid-October 2001, Anne met with City Hall's urban planning division to understand who was working on plans for the 9/11 reconstruction and share her vision for the renewal. She wowed them with mock-ups of what it would look like in site. The Windmill's head is a perfect sphere. From the center of the head, affixed to the top of the stem, shoot 888 strands, each spaced equidistantly from each other, each painted the same hospital white, each identically pliable to capture the wind. At the tip of each strand is white polyester parachute. It is these parachutes that grab and sway the wind that rushes through, the wind that sometimes pushes and sometimes pulls, generating power by the kinetic exertion. For the Windmill, it doesn't really matter which way the wind blows. It gets energy just from change itself. City Hall's engineers confirmed it would work; the planners thought it looked great and verified it wouldn't disturb local residents; the finance department liked the lucrative returns from the power generated. Anne was checking all the boxes; everyone was on board.

By November, she was already shortlisting infrastructure development firms to run the project with her, and meeting with investors every other day. Her Excel models went from five lines to five tabs to five worksheets; she had to buy a faster computer to handle the huge design files; she negotiated license fees for the patents.

By the beginning of January 2002, it was clear she would not be returning from her three-month leave; the Windmill had become her new full-time job. As the project evolved and the funding got into place, she brought on board a well-known infrastructure development firm, whose team of experts obtained permits, procured materials and parts, finalized the engineering designs, and contracted workers to start building it. By March 2002, Anne was commuting to work at the future site of the Windmill itself.

Soon the Mayor himself was involved. He quickly took credit for this windmill concept and design. Like many New Yorkers, I remember his press release announcing that this would be a cornerstone in the plan for recovering from 9/11 – they would plant a flower, that produces energy, out of the rubble of terror.

I asked Anne the other day how she felt that the Mayor

had taken credit for the building of this iconic structure. "It's fine," she said honestly. "Having the Mayor himself promoting it definitely helped get it built."

The Windmill switched on the two-year anniversary of 9/11. Anne was at the opening ceremony, in the crowd around the Mayor, wearing a necklace made of dandelions. There was a gentle breeze that morning and the arms of the Windmill softly rustled across the sky high above them.

In her Memory, Anne closes her eyes to listen. When the breeze is slow it sounds to her like a tree in the woods with no one around; when the wind gusts, it sounds like a Yosemite waterfall.

She lets her shoulders relax under her shoulder-padded suit jacket. She realizes just then how tight they've been since 9/11, since that morning when a surreal television drama became real, since the morning of Wednesday September 12th, when she saw the Windmill in her imagination, since the first email back from the inventor saying, "Yes, it was possible." As her shoulders relax, she breathes out, a little breath, and when it finishes, she stops, holding her lungs empty for a moment, just as she's held her breath in for two years. In that pause, she hears the breeze pick up and shimmer across the top of the Windmill, down the side, along the bottom and, before it even arrives, hears it coming straight toward her. Its motion has now turned into electricity that races at the speed of light through the city, powering neon signs and hamburger grills and monitor displays. Just then, just as the breeze slows to stop in front of her face, spent from its journey through dreams and physics and history, Anne breathes it in.

* * *

Anne would continue to stand under the Windmill, to listen and breath over the next two years. It wasn't enough for her to build this dream-like, incredible thing; she wanted to make sure it worked and make more of them. So when the Windmill Company was formed, she created for herself a post leading the Business Development department. Some months she would negotiate offtake agreements for power or develop retail pricing strategies; other months, she would sell consulting and licensing projects to help other cities build their own Windmills.

Over these days and months, Anne would often go back down, to stand under the Windmill, in that same place she first got her breath back. You can watch these visits in the File (for instance, if you need a break from reviewing derivatives valuation spreadsheets). The shadow of the Windmill cascaded around her, constantly changing. As the sun swept across the sky, its stem traced across the flat rooftop like a sun dial. The light through the seed-like arms of the Windmill captivated her, and me too.

Stand under a tree on a breezy, sunny day, and you'll see this effect: the light pushes through the pinpoint gaps between the leaves, and spreads out in orbs on the ground below, diffuse, geometrical, in random motion. If it's raining, you can stand under the Windmill and dodge 78% of raindrops. This is statistical fact. I know this because I ran the study.

See, I had noticed one rainy day, standing coincidentally very near where Anne usually stands, that I was getting wet. The white dandelion structure above me is a perfectly symmetrical sphere, meticulously calculated, precision engineered. But the rain? It's total chaos. Some drops landed on me, some didn't; I was slowly getting soaked. The ground below me turned from light grey to dark grey. Like a shadow, you could see a perfect circle forming under the Windmill that was lighter than the rest of the ground. The edges were fuzzy, like shade at a distance. It seemed odd to me that the colors are so even, and yet the rain drops themselves were so random. How could that possibly be?

The Central Order is fascinated and frightened (and frustrated) by randomness and chance. Rainfall confounds us. Here we try to boil the complex randomness of the universe into a percentage, in the vane of economic studies. We in the Central Order are statistics junkies. We're exceptionally good at what we do; we rank in the top 1.3% of all statistical institutions.[1]

I've been working at the Central Order my whole career, and so my thinking has started to meld into its thinking as well. I joined the Central Order in order to understand the way the world works. I wasn't sure I agreed with it at the time but had (and still have) the firm conviction that the best way to understand something is to become part of it for a while.

So naturally I commissioned a study to quantify how much more rain there was under the Windmill than outside it. Our Statistics department took two approaches. First, they put out two pieces of tissue paper – one under the Windmill, the other outside it – and counted the wet spots on each page, comparing the results and repeating this a few times. To cross-check, they also put out two buckets, one under the Windmill, another outside it, for the same hour

[1] Results of a survey conducted by the Central Order, Statistics Department, June 2003. 10% response rate, accuracy +/-0.3%. "Top" defined as "most influential and most respected by peers."

of a rainstorm, and measured how much water was in each. They found there was 78% as much water in the buckets under the Windmill as outside it.[2]

What's fascinating about this phenomenon, not just to me but also to my friends in the Randomness Department, is that while I can tell you with great certainty that there will be 78% of rain that falls through the Windmill, I have no idea how to predict which drops will fall when and where.

I learned from the guys in the Physics department that that's how the fundamental particles of matter are designed too – you know with certainty how things will have worked out but have no idea how they will get there.

You see this concept across disciplines. In computer science, it bubbles up at recursion. Recursion is a concept Anne has patiently explained to me, but that is hard for a structured mind like mine to bend to. I'll try to explain anyway. Just say you want to count the people in a line. One way is for someone to walk down the line, counting each person. Another way is to stand at the end, and ask the person ahead of you, "hey how many people are ahead of you?" If that person says "100," you know that there are 101 people on the line – the hundred people in front of you, plus you. Well, you might ask, how does the person ahead of you know how many people are ahead of them?

They ask the person ahead of them. And so on, down the line. The person at the very front of the line knows they

---

[2] In the bucket study, there was between 76 and 80% as much water under the Windmill, depending mostly on how close to the center the bucket was. The tissue-paper method saw a larger reduction in drop count, to 72-75%; my colleagues explained that as water collects on the Windmill, it forms fewer but larger drops. I've included this (overly technical) footnote at the firm request of the Statistics Department.

are first person, so they can actually answer the person who asks them: "There's just one person on this line ahead of you – that's me." That person knows there's themselves, plus one person, so reports back "There are 2 people in front of you." The answer starts drifting back. And finally the person ahead of you has learned that they are person 100. Effortless.

When one writes a normal computer program, they have an order and a logic: first do this, then that, then the next thing. With recursion, they are writing questions, no answers, and just two of them:

(1) What is the question you want to answer? (In our example, that's "How many people are in front of me?")

(2) When does the recursion stop? ("When am I at the front of the line?")

Recursion is an incredibly powerful method in computer science programming. There are problems that can solved much faster with this method than with any others, I've been told, and some problems that can't be solved at all without it.

Anne says it takes a tremendous leap of faith and writing the programs can be frustrating. Because you don't know where they are going, and don't know if they work out until you run them. You must trust that things will work out in the end, even if you can't really understand deeply how they get there.

Fortunately, the English language has given us a tense to describe just this. It's the "will have" tense, which tells you how things will ultimately turn out, doesn't admit knowing how they get there, and acknowledges that the person observing in the future isn't the same as the person observing the event today. "I will have been glad to run," or "I will have regretted cheating," or "I will have finished my homework by class tomorrow." That's different from saying that I will be glad to run, or I will regret cheating, or I will finish my homework.

It's the tense the predicts how many raindrops will have fallen, how one will evolve over time, how plans will have come to fruition or not. It's a thoughtful tense too, one that judges the past with a more mature eye. It acknowledges that time is indeed relative, and that perhaps someday it will be pleasing to remember even these things.

In grammar books, they call this tense the Future Perfect.

* * *

Anne called them the Haystacks, her secret part of New York that only a few people knew were there, even though everyone saw them. She first discovered them the way you become fond of coffee: not the first or second time, but by association and through repetition.

If you stand on the top of the Great Lawn in Central Park, you too can see them. Look: south across the grand oval fields of lazy summer city slickers kicking hacky sacks or flying Frisbees. Beyond the anachronistic castle tower of Belvedere, see the buildings looming over Central Park South, guarding the entrance to the midtown skyline. The seam of the sky begins at their rooftops and stretches up and back until its directly over you. Planes rub their ribs as they depart for foreign shores, and they drag your eye across the immense and changing sky.

She had come from the Metropolitan Museum the first she saw them and had crowded with globs of American tourists in front of the celebrity paintings: Monet's haystacks, painted different hues.

So standing in front a pile of buildings on the edge of a field, she saw the way the soft sun glowed pink against the skyline's skin and realized she had never seen this skyline that way before. From that point on, they became her Haystacks, the static scene that constantly changed.

Derek noticed them too, and then eventually, noticed her. They shared a love of the Haystacks well before they would come to love each other. He lived on the Upper West Side and is the kind of guy who would have had a dog, had his apartment not been 400 square feet on the fourth floor of a brownstone that prohibited dogs anyway. You know the type, because you've seen them in movies and perhaps in your dreams: the sweet and gentle ambitious but not arrogant well-rounded athletic type, who knows how to cook two weeks' worth of dinners, dances well enough to hold up at weddings but not better than you, makes loves as sensitively and passionately as he dances, drinks scotch with the boys over poker on Thursday and drinks wine with his girlfriend over candles in the Village on Friday, misses dinner with his friend to finish fixing your mom's dishwasher, takes home the airplane's goody bags when his company sends him Business Class to Detroit, subscribes to *The Economist* and *FHM*, and sends text messages like "i miss u" five minutes after saying goodbye. He's the type of guy you're afraid to take home to meet your parents because your mom might wish she had found someone like him. He reminds you of your father.

* * *

Anne had started running in college after causing the

power in nearby Redwood City to go out. The night before the power outage, she went out to the campus gym at 10 p.m. to use the exercise bike. But when she got there, she realized she was bored of spinning around, going nowhere. She had hated running back in high school and was in terrible shape. But it was part of the Stanford culture, something everyone did. She was in a good mood. It was dark and she was by herself; she couldn't embarrass herself with no audience.

She started slowly. Halfway through the first lap, she was trying to determine what a reasonable goal was. Four laps? What's that, she pondered, a mile? A half a mile? She wasn't sure. (It's about a mile.) She did her thing, uneventfully, undecided on whether she would make jogging a regular part of her routine.

That second night she returned to the gym, but once again felt something in the air, some charge that made her stomach turn when thinking about another hour under fluorescent lights in a place that smelled of stale sweat. The evening was again cool, the wind was gently blowing, and she wanted to try running again.

She started to do her four laps, but then thought, "I did four laps last time. I wonder if I can do ten this time. Or twelve?" The thing with Anne that gets her into trouble is what I might call wonder-want-will transitivity. Some people wonder about something, and then think whether they want it; and of the things they want, they will choose a few that they will do. But for Anne, there's little breakdown in that process. She wonders if something is possible, inevitably wants it, and then almost always tries her best to will it into being.

So here we are back at that deserted track at Stanford,

one dark and imminently stormy night. Anne is just finishing lap nine, and feeling tired, but good tired. She determines that the last three laps she will run increasingly faster, or harder at least. So when lap ten comes around, we hear her chanting to herself, "C'mon, let's go" every few steps. Lap eleven she's more out of breath, merely puffing out "C'mon" to herself. And the last lap, lap twelve, it's more of a "c'm… c'm." She sees the finish line and has nothing left to give. For a moment, she debates just slowing down into the finish, but then decides that this moment is a time for celebration. So she, by herself with no stopwatch, no crowds and no race to run, crosses her own imaginary finish line and throws her arms up and head back in triumph.

Just as she looks up at the sky through the goal posts of her arms, it flashes a blinding light that fills the entire heaven. It starts to pour. The next day she heard that a bolt of lightning knocked out the power grid of Redwood City a few miles away. "Hers" was the only bolt of lightning the whole night.

From that point on, it was clear that Anne would continue to jog. She would explore the Stanford campus by what she came to call the "uphill" method: she ran forward randomly, just always uphill. When she got tired, it was time to turn around and run randomly downhill towards home. Not only did this give her confidence to explore anything – she knew the way back would be easier than the way going – but it also meant that almost every run was rewarded by a new and outstanding view. Clarity in a way.

Or as she put it: "I could see from the tops of the foothills that, even if I didn't know exactly how, I would eventually find my way back home."

* * *

It didn't surprise me that the morning she met Derek she was out for a run. On weekends she would often take the R train from her place in Brooklyn Heights to near Central Park South, and then jog a loop through the park. Two years earlier, she impressed herself by finishing the 1.5-mile lower loop, dodging oblivious tourists and piles of horse poop. With the help of U2's "Beautiful Day," one day she pounded up the hill on the east side near 72nd Street, and breathless and exuberant, and careened down toward the (also anachronistic) Cleopatra's Needle. The first time, she veered into the Great Lawn as way of shortening her trip. But once she noticed the Haystacks, she found herself pulled to the Great Lawn almost every jog. The Haystacks mark her half-way point, and she invariably felt the adrenaline of her aggressive charge up the hill and the secure comfort of knowing she had no farther to go than she had already gone.

So one postcard perfect Sunday afternoon, she reaches the bottom of the hill. Since Anne has no idea at this time that she will one day be in a book, she enjoys making her life resemble art, and the soundtrack is very important. When her MP3 player hits a sleeper song, stalling her, she shifts gears until she finds a faster one: the Black Eyed Peas' "Where is the Love."

In the moment that she took to look down and adjust the music, she sees the springing legs of some twenty-something jock pass her. He has calves on which are written the journal of his runs – he runs every day, she can see, sometimes through shrubs. His hair and tan end abruptly where his black jogging shorts end. While her own sweat-soaked shirt clings to her stomach and shoulder blades, his shirt is completely dry; even though his shirt hangs loose, she can see he has a well-sculpted back.

She doesn't want to see his back.

Her brow frowns down and in my imagination, she powers up like Sonic the Hedgehog getting ready to roll. Her legs are tired, but her arms are not, and she pumps them with the full force of her energy. She sprints up the hill just at his heel, always behind him but keeping pace. The finish line appears – really a white striped crosswalk just beyond the crest of the hill – and yet she is still behind him.

Anne Kesheen doesn't lose battles. With energy borrowed from the future, she erupts toward the line. Five feet to the line, they are nose to nose. And with the last of her strength, she leans forward into the invisible line and beats him.

He continues, unaware that they were ever racing. And she too continues. Her energy is no longer depleted, but fully recharged by the victory. Tight and relaxed, she turns toward her Haystacks. The sweatless man continues on his separate way, unaware that he too will one day be written about on this page.

Derek was there already, leaning on folded arms on the fence that lined the northern rim of the Lawn. To his left was a really crappy softball team – overthrows and hopeless pitchers and even worse batters – who were having a wonderful time. In front of him some foreign couple was working on turning their skin to leather, and to the side, a group of recently married couples were eating grapes and playing pickup sticks with conversation.

He noticed her when the fence sagged. Anne fully intended to run on by but couldn't help turning to admire the view. Someone else was doing so as well, and it seemed a true pity to pass by such a perfect postcard day to admire her Haystacks. She could continue running in a minute.

"The fence is okay to lean on," he said to her, "but I wouldn't trust something like this with all your weight."

She looked over with a squint, trying to figure out if he was insulting her or helping her. "There are few things that I do put all my weight on," she responded.

Derek smiled back anyway.

I've watched this scene several times trying to figure out what made it spark, what ingredients happened that could be repeated. I've distilled and measured and analyzed, and am sorry to say, I haven't been able to figure it out. Was it the fresh air and the scent of spring? The adrenaline of her run, and the confidence of her recent victory? Was it standing shoulder-to-shoulder, enjoying something beautiful? I had always assumed love starts with dialogue, the right words, said in the right order. The pickup lines and the responses, the witty jokes and the profound maxims. But watching Anne's File, seeing her Memories, I've learned it's almost never the words.

So I'll share what Derek says next, but it doesn't really matter. What does matter is how Derek felt that moment that Anne leaned on the fence. As Anne won't have known at the time – probably won't know until she reads this paragraph – Derek had spent that Sunday morning tidying his apartment, making a homemade chili, and donating his old clothes to the Salvation Army. He'd left his place to enjoy the beautiful day while his chili cooled, leaving his home, for the first time in a long time, in perfect order. Though he'd been in motion since 9:17 a.m., he stopped just then to look at the Haystacks – his first moment of stillness in the day.

So these two eventual lovebirds perched on the fence in silence for a while, and that was fine. They shared the beauty of the Haystacks, scorned the leather people now engaging in a Public Display of Affection. Anne felt the cool breeze move across her soaked shirt and heard it rustle the trees behind her.

"This is my favorite part of the city," Derek thought out loud, "and what makes living in my fourth-floor walkup worthwhile."

Anne told him about her Haystack theory and explained how she took the train from Brooklyn just to see them.

"Everybody's talking about Brooklyn these days," he said.

Anne explained how she and her sister had thought about getting a place on the Upper West Side, but then realized Brooklyn Heights was closer to downtown where they mostly spent their free time, was even more charming, accessible to every single subway line in the city without transferring, and a bit cheaper. Anne and Derek swapped rent prices and square footage, amenities and subway line proximity, all integral parts of the New York mating ritual.

He admitted that although he had been in New York for four years since college (she did the math: he was probably twenty-six, same as her), he had never been to Brooklyn Heights. To make him feel better, Anne confessed that even though she had been in New York for her whole life except four years of college, she had never been in Brooklyn Heights until the day she saw the place she now lived in.

"I should check it out," he said in all seriousness. "Do you have any recommendations on restaurants to go to or places to walk around?"

"I was just finishing up my run and am going home now," she replied, which was only a lie if you believe that life is deterministic. "You're welcome to come wander with me on the other side of the Bridge."

He looked at his watch in order to slow down time so he could think. This was the critical point, and I suspect he knew it. Since I didn't meet Anne until well after they had broken up, I never got to talk to him, so I don't know for sure what he was thinking in those few seconds. But if I had to guess, he was deciding in those moments to let the waves take him wherever they go, because they take all the good fish there too. Or, as I had learned in improvisation class, accept all offers unless there's a good reason not to. Watching the secondhand tick by, I suspect he wasn't thinking of why to go with her, but if there any reason not to. His chili was cooling on the stove, and he had been excited to eat it tonight. He planned on watching the Sopranos at 10 p.m. Brooklyn was a schlep from his apartment. She was a stranger. It was just random.

But the chili could wait, the Sopranos would replay, the A/C/E subway ran express to Brooklyn Heights (he had just learned), and there was no time like the present.

"Sure," he said. "Let's go."

* * *

We're in my office, air conditioner on at full tilt. My nose is dripping, and my coffee is already cold. I hate summer in the city.

Anne nurses her cup of hot water. She's in a good mood, being Friday and all. "And all" being that she is heading out this weekend with her fiancé to some place in Pennsylvania that advertises a bathtub shaped like a champagne glass. The actors in the commercial have Barbie and Ken hairdos that tack the ad firmly in the 1980s, which is the last time that Anne saw this ad on TV. But their brochures are still being printed, and she's been waiting a long time get in the champagne glass.

We had been discussing an article in *The New York Times* about the glass ceiling for women in the workplace, and Anne was expounding her theory that the glass ceiling is caused by what she calls "the concrete floor" – the fact that men don't often feel they can opt out of the workplace to raise a family or do more benevolent work (charities, lower income/status jobs, senior care). I don't entirely disagree, especially since the head of our group is killing himself so he can retire and go back to race cars, his true passion. His wife who stays at home with their two kids could go off anytime and join Nascar, no problem. Well, maybe it wouldn't be easy for her to break into something as historically-male as car racing. Actually that's a terrible example. But I digress.

Inevitably this conversation rolls around to the infamous New York City dating scene. People around the world know about it from the endless movies and TV series on the topic (*Friends* and *Sex in the City* come to mind). For Anne, dating in New York is unexceptional, and she explained that it's pretty much how you see it on the TV, all her friends do it, and the lanes of the road are marked with iridescent bumpers that make your car hop when you veer the wrong way.

According to Anne, you first need the right tools: two or three close and equally-animated friends; a refreshing shower; some black, conservative but attractive clothing;

subtle perfume; a couple of breath mints, to kill the taste of onion in your mouth, and maybe the taste of beer in his; a cellphone to change plans on a dime; 9 p.m. dinner reservations at some moderately priced but trendy restaurant downtown; $50 to $100 in cash with some small bills to facilitate splitting the bill at dinner; your contact case just in case you don't make it home; vitamin B (which her sister promised reduces hangovers); and lots of water (also to reduce hangovers).

Second, you need the right attitude. Guys aren't dumb, just lazy. If a girl walks into a bar and thinks she's hot stuff, he probably won't second guess her. (In the middle of the bell curve, it doesn't really matter much how she looks, just how she carries herself.) If a girl makes sustained eye contact, he won't be as intimidated to walk over to her and make some banal comment about the size of the party or the number of couples. Appearing happy is a good indicator of being happy, and isn't that what people are looking for anyway? Correct all this attitude with a dash of prudishness, and voila.

The challenge is finding the right fish without attracting the wrong ones. A glance, as mentioned above, is often seen as an invitation. So unless you are interested in a guy, don't look at him for more than maybe two seconds at a time. Here's what makes dating in New York challenging, and therefore interesting, Anne explains: you are perhaps intoxicated, in a dark loud room, with variable lighting, trying in a matter of a glance to determine not only someone's physical appearance, but their character, while trying to project an image (which granted may be accurate anyway) of being happy, confident and carefree, trying to dance and maybe trying to hold a conversation with the aforementioned two or three equally-animated friends. For six hours in a row after a 60-hour work week on a Friday night at two or three in the morning. In a condition that you wouldn't be allowed to drive a car in.

I asked Anne whether she thinks this method can ever work.

"Of course" she replied straight away. "It just takes some practice."

Practice in New York is easy. You can watch people all the time. You can practice walking down the street, on the bus, at work, on line for the bathroom, at dinner, at lunch, going for a jog in the park, picking up milk, doing laundry in the basement, getting dry cleaning from around the corner, waiting for a movie to start, sitting in an outdoor café, sitting in an indoor restaurant, with or without your iPod, on a rainy day or on a hot and humid one, from the distance of your 4th floor window or smashed up close on the subway. You can watch and judge and empathize and understand people all you want.

"That's the difference about New Yorkers," she continued. "We are great at watching people."

* * *

Derek and Anne board the C train at 81st and Central Park West, a station decorated with dancing elephants and floating planets, out of homage to the immovable Museum of Natural History and Planetarium above it. So Anne confesses a childhood obsession with astronomy and dinosaurs – both are probably products of this museum – and Derek confesses a post-childhood obsession with art – probably a product of the Metropolitan Museum of Art across the park. They start on a battle of the nerds, which Anne starts losing waiting to transfer to the A train at 59th Street, but then regains the lead by the time they find a seats together at 34th Street. Derek confesses his geeky study habits – meticulously recopying and organizing his notes after class. Her sweat is now just damp and heavy on her t-shirt. Derek pretends not to notice, but carefully makes sure he isn't touching her. He is leaning forward, elbows on knees.

By 14th Street, Anne starts on the chicken pox story, one in the classical Anne canon, which is about how she felt this need to study 100% well until she got the chicken pox right before final exams in 8th grade, and then realized she did not have enough time or energy to study everything perfectly. It went on the short list of Anne defeats, which included such glorifying moments as a foolish loss in volleyball to a worse team, canceling a street fair she had spent two months planning due to rain, dropping a class she was failing in college, getting outbid on what would have been her first apartment, and burning her second Thanksgiving turkey. Anne did not mention these other defeats, yet.

We're at W 4th Street when the person sitting next to Anne gets up and changes to an emptier seat. Derek tells Anne about a time he went to Australia and for various reasons was unable to wash his hair well for seven days before he had to board a plane for an 18-hour flight to California. "This middle-aged woman next to me on the plane actually moved to the only empty seat, in the last row, to avoid me," he said. "So I went to the bathroom, I'm in there you know trying to wash my hair with one hand while holding down faucet with the other. I've got water all over my shirt and down my sleeve, but it still looks terrible. So in a moment of sheer brilliantness," a phrase that is part of the Derek canon, "I think: 'Hey I know! I'll throw some hand soap in the mix!' So after a good fifteen minutes in the airplane bathroom, the flight attendants thinking lord-knows-what is going on in there, I walk out with a bucket of soap suds ALL over my hair and my shirt half soaked!

"My hair" he continued with the quick enthusiastic tempo of a story told often enough to get the timing and phrasing right, "was so thick with soap that it didn't even dry during the flight, and you know how dry plane air is. Man, when I got to the L.A. airport my girlfriend wouldn't even give me a hug until I showered properly."

Girlfriend. You can watch the word hit the corners of Anne's eyes, the one part of her poker face that she has no control over. Her mind was racing: Was this girlfriend still in the picture? Was he even single as she had supposed? They are way past W 4th Street, the train is picking up speed on the downhill, and her ears are popping. They are in the tunnel under the East River.

"When were you in California?" she asked in a failed attempt at an offhand manner.

"I grew up there, in Huntington Beach," he said. "But after college, I couldn't go back." The corners of her eyes relax; the L.A. girlfriend was probably also back in the past. The train plunges into the lights on the first stop in Brooklyn at High Street. "So here I am. I had always dreamed of moving to New York. Of becoming a part of this amazing city."

* * *

He waited in her living room while she showered. In the

File, you can see him looking at the pictures on the bookshelf; he picks up one of Anne and her sister, both desperately needing to wash their hair but smiling in front of a tent. Still holding it, he checks out the liquor cabinet, noticing in particular one almost-finished and several unopened gift boxes of Glenfiddich 12-year Scotch. He walks over to the window and sits on its ample ledge, looking across the street at the historic churches and townhouses of Brooklyn Heights. You can hear the birds chirping and the shower turn off. Derek is fidgeting now with the photo frame.

Back in the bathroom, Anne has thrown on a bathrobe, towel dries her hair and combs it down. She decides against the combed down look as usual and messes it up just enough. She flings opens the bathroom door, runs to pick out some clothes to wear – jeans and a black V-neck cotton shirt and a silver necklace with two Shanghai pearls. She sprays some delicate citrus-vanilla perfume into the air and walks into the cloud.

Derek is still on the windowsill when Anne walks in a little too sprightly. "Hey," she says with a forced casualness that makes her sound like a perky cheerleader.

"Is this your sister?" Derek asks, holding up the photo frame. Anne comes to the windowsill and squeezes in next to Derek. He leans forward with his elbows on his knees to preserve the bubble of space around him. Anne explains that that photo was taken almost a decade ago, but yeah, that's her.

"She's amazing," Anne adds earnestly. "I feel so incredibly lucky to have this time to spend with her, to live with her. It's an amazing thing to have a best friend built right into your life."

"She's pretty lucky to have you as her sister too, you know," Derek says, keeping his eyes locked on the photo. Over his right shoulder, Anne's face freezes. Does this mean he does like her? Derek senses her reacting, and quickly retraces his steps, "I mean, people you meet along the way come and go. Don't get me wrong, these strangers can change you forever, and may be the most important thing in your life. But there's something nice about having a relationship that can never be broken. It's one of the few things in the world that is certain."

Anne at this point probably could have asked the softball "Do you have siblings?" question, but instead goes for the jugular: "What's your relationship with your family like?"

He hesitates, then answers, "I wish we were closer. I sort of feel like in coming to New York, I was running away from taking care of them. My brother doesn't know what he wants out of his life, and my parents aren't helping him figure it out. But I'm twenty six, and I have my own life to live. It doesn't make me feel less guilty about the whole thing though."

Anne puts her hand amicably on his back between his shoulder blades, and tries to remember what she should say, which comes out as, "I'm sorry. It sounds like a hard situation." He breaks his eyes from the photo and sits up, which causes Anne to remove her hand. "Yeah, I know," he says looking straight at her, his eyes still vulnerable. The next moment, he takes a crisp deep breadth in and slaps his knees. "So," he forces out a grin, "you ready to go get some grub?"

* * *

The evening had gotten chillier, which is maybe why Anne was shivering in her black V-neck t-shirt. They had decided that the best choice was a BYOB Lebanese restaurant three blocks away and were on their way to buy a B of wine to BYO. Anne was unusually nervous. Their conversation was utterly uninteresting relative to the rest of the story I want to tell you, so I won't verbatim repeat it. But in it, we learn a little about Derek. We first learn that he is very allergic to garlic, which isn't a deal breaker for Anne, but close enough. Their subsequent dates will stick pretty much to Japanese cuisine, avoiding all Chinese and Italian food, unless they are at Anne or Derek's apartment and can control the garlic quotient.

The next thing we learned is that Derek had come very close to buying a dog the prior month. He hadn't because of the shoebox of an apartment that he lived in. He mentioned some aspiration to have a house big enough to have a dog someday, and Anne's face froze, which made Derek himself realize that he was talking about the Big Question: what does your future look like when you're *not* a 26-year-old kid living on a fourth floor walkup. The idea of a dog isn't that far from talking about kids, and the mention of a house means some plan to settle down in the suburban graveyard. Anne could never imagine herself shipping off to the lawn-buffered car-dependent smile-saturated soccer communities of Jersey or Long Island or Westchester, and somehow that emotion percolated up through her face. Derek hadn't dated a real New Yorker yet, not a born-and-bred one that barely had a driver's license like Anne, and suddenly realized that not everyone dreams of having a house someday. So to dilute this dog talk a tad, he added, "And, you know, a white picket fence and 2.1

kids." It seemed to work, and led Anne to ask the gimme question she has skipped back on the windowsill: "So do you have any siblings?"

Derek explained that he grew up in Huntington Beach with his parents and brother who was five years younger. Derek had cycled competitively and was a stellar student, popular in high school though never part of the popular clique (perhaps due to the cycling). After college he managed to land an incredibly competitive position at the Central Order in their Financing Division. His little brother however was quite the opposite – he rarely left the sofa, lived with his parents, and worked part time at a crab shack. He barely passed out of high school, never had a girlfriend, and his only talent was playing Tetris. He had grown up in Derek's shadow and resented his parents and his brother for it. Derek in turn felt bad about that but determined that he couldn't live his life for his brother.

Derek shared that he had a few goals in life. One is to make money. That's why he was working at the Central Order's Financing Division (just a few floors below me, though I never knew him at work). It wasn't as high a salary as some Wall Street jobs, but it was more than enough to live as a bachelor in the city. Plus it was good for his resume.

As all of us at Central Order know, the organization is in the middle of a multi-decade long project to reduce risk in the financial markets and economy at large, with the theory that certain risks create inefficiencies and stress. The Financing Division wasn't going to touch every aspect of life, but they were constantly bickering with the Random Department about what things to control and what to leave to chance.

Fortunately for Derek, he was working well below that

level of internal politics. He wasn't arguing for an end to business cycles, for instance, but just using the business cycle projections that the Statistics Department gave him to price contracts. Derek had come through the analyst training program, and so had made good friends across all departments of the Central Order. While he truly did enjoy his job and felt that finance was incredibly important to the healthy functioning of human society, he was jealous of some of his friends in the other bureaus. There was something sexy, for instance, about the division called the "Power Department" which was under the "Energy Division."

Once Derek found out that Anne was working at the Windmill – indeed that she had essentially created it – he couldn't help grilling her about how it worked, and how it didn't work. There were somethings on both sides of the conversation that had to remain confidential, of course. Derek couldn't tell Anne specifics about the weather hedging contracts that he was drafting. But he wanted to help her succeed at her job, and so offered some advice on the financial world of weather risk management. When he was halfway through his explanation, he realized he was effectively pitching her like a client, and suddenly stopped. "Oh crap," he said biting his lower lip with his upper teeth, "you know yeah, it's just awkward because the Windmill is a prospective client of ours, and I would like to see you again, and that's just awkward, yeah, you know. So I'll just shut up."

Anne was flattered and felt a small herd of butterflies do calisthenics in her stomach. She pulled out the calendar on her Palm Pilot and found a date they could both meet the following week. That concluded, she slipped her Palm Pilot back in her purse, and paused. "So, how can you control the weather?"

"Well, I'm not talking about controlling the weather, just buying insurance against it," Derek explained. "The idea started with farmers buying weather insurance against extremes of drought etc. and has moved to more sensitive hedging instruments. We are trying to market trade-wind hedges to shipping companies, and snowfall hedges to ski resorts, you know that kind of thing. As for you wind energy guys, we have contracts that pay out based on the average wind speed over a certain period. So if the winds slow down, and your energy production falters, your wind insurance contract pays you money." He had an earnestness in his eyes that hungered for a pen and paper napkin, but alas, this restaurant only had cloth. So he just looked earnestly at her.

Anne was considering this against the Windmill's method of operation. It was an interesting idea, and indeed one she hadn't thought about before. "Well for us, we don't generate energy based on how steady the wind is, like usual wind turbines." Derek's earnest eyes dulled slightly as he realized he didn't know that much about the Windmill after all. I suspect he had the feeling that the client knew than he did, and when he realized that he was thinking in those terms, it hit him that he was still thinking of Anne as a client, and if that was the case, then maybe it was good that his pitch had failed so he could move on with their personal relationship. "You see, the Windmill's power doesn't come from the direction or the strength of the wind, but just from how random it is." Derek looked puzzled.

Anne tried to put it another way. "Put another way," she said, "if there were no randomness in the universe, there would be no power."

Derek looked like someone just told him Elvis had auditioned for the Beatles but was rejected. Yeah, the kind of face you probably have now: you want to roll your eyes at the ridiculousness of the situation, but you kind of want to go online and check out the Windmill's Wikipedia page. So he poofed out a little air through the pressure valve of his nose and said, "Wow, that kind of contract would take a loooong time to model up, huh. I might even have to visit the Random Department," he added to himself.

"The what?" Anne inquired.

"Nothing," Derek half-lied, "just an inside joke." He glanced at his watch. "Oh wow, it's already nine forty," he said.

"Do you need to go?" she asked

"No, it's nothing," Derek half-lied, again. "Just hoping to see the Sopranos at ten, but I'll miss it tonight I guess."

"Oh why don't you come over and watch it back at my place," she offered amiably.

"Wow, not even the first date and I'm already being invited back to girl's apartment," he commented to some invisible wingman, jokingly.

"Even better: you get to meet the family," Anne grinned, "because my sister will probably be home by now too!"

* * *

When they step out of the restaurant onto Atlantic Avenue, Derek walks with his hands in his pockets to keep them warm. Anne almost unthinkingly wraps her fingers around his elbow and shelters herself against him to keep away the crisp night breeze. This time he doesn't pull away.

It's only three blocks to their house, and a short elevator

ride. Anne's sister hears Anne's keys jingle and comes to door to open it. Anne had called her just before they left the restaurant to give her the heads up that they had company; she didn't want her sister to be in pajamas, caught off-guard by this handsome stranger that Anne had picked up in Central Park. Her sister is charmingly cordial to Derek, shakes his hand and welcomes him to have some green tea. Anne asks for a mug too, and the three of them sit on their recently purchased sofa in front of the TV, Anne in the middle. *The Sopranos* has just started, and Anne tries to understand what all the fuss is. She will never get it. The show finishes and Derek says he has to get home as it's after 11 p.m. on a Sunday, and he has to be at work by 7 a.m. the next day. Anne grabs a jacket to walk Derek to the subway. In the elevator down and during the brief walk there, they confirm the time and neighborhood of their next date (South Street Seaport, 8 p.m., Tuesday – the day after tomorrow). They arrive at the top of the stairs leading down to the A/C/E train at Jay Street.

So now is the time to say goodbye, and it's always awkward, isn't it. I am just glad I have the File to watch, because I don't know what I would have Anne and her eventual boyfriend do on their first date if I had to make it up. Should they kiss? Should they hug? Should they just wave and depart, leaving them both unsatisfied and uncertain what the future might hold? A kiss here would take some of the risk out of their relationship. Put their relationship safely in the "couples" box rather than the "platonic friends" (or "prospective client") one. A kiss here would be what both people seem to want, and yet for some reason, it's not obvious that a kiss goes here.

I asked Anne for details about this night, the first time

she met Derek, before realizing I could just use the File. She never mentioned a kiss, but I always assumed there was one. Afterall, she had mentioned that she had walked with him arm-in-arm on the way home. But the more I thought about it, maybe there never was one. Maybe it was the sobering effect of the green tea after a shared bottle of wine, or the third-wheel presence of her sister back at the apartment, or the blood and gore of *The Sopranos*, or the homeless person eyeing them from the corner of the station. Maybe they just parted ways with a date in their calendars and exchanged phone numbers.

So just imagine as I do that they are standing there, facing each other, at top of the stairs and the edge of the Future Perfect. Each knowing that they *will* one day *have* kissed, and that their relationship *will have gone* well. If they did kiss, it was to remove a certain uncertainty in their relationship, right? To nail something down once and for all. And if they didn't, it would be because they felt they didn't need to nail it down – because they felt it was already certain. So whether they kissed that night, or the next Tuesday, or the Sunday after that when Derek invited her over to cook some garlic-free spaghetti sauce and watch the Sopranos again, these things don't change the story.

But because you're curious (I know, I was too) I watched the File, and it wasn't until after dinner on Tuesday. Anne offered Derek a breath mint and they stepped outside to the quiet boardwalk next to the South Street Seaport, and they finally documented their relationship with something that could slip into a File at the Central Order.

"Yes," Anne told me over a cup of hot water, with a grin. "That was a good date."

* * *

Anne walked into Derek's apartment and saw the walls covered by yellow Post-It Notes. Each had a symbol; one had a triangle, another a circle, another a lightning bolt – each different.

"Hello, my beautiful girlfriend!" he shouted walking in from the bedroom.

"Hello, my beautiful mind!" she replied.

Derek laughed and explained that the descent into madness was for his business class on Presentations. The Central Order sponsored many of their "high potential" employees to do evening Master's in Business Administration (MBA) courses at NYU Stern; Derek had applied and been selected a few months earlier. I had also taken many of the same courses as Derek during my stint at the program, unfortunately now a few years ago, and really enjoyed it. I especially recall the Presentations class, which is still nicknamed "Drawing for Dummies." We were never sure if the dummies were the people doing the drawing or the people being shown them.

Derek's class started when the professor drew an arrow on the whiteboard. He asked the class, stacked in semicircular rows sloping up the lecture theater, "What does this symbol mean?" Since class participation counted for 30% of the grade, and this seemed like a softball question, a dozen hands went up. The professor wrote their responses on the board, alongside the arrow:

Causality
Time
Importance

Workflow
Growth
Change
...

He then asked what it was about the arrow itself that made it mean so many things: a line with two little lines coming to a point at one end. How was this symbol so universally understood?

Fewer hands went up. You might think that was because the question was harder; I think it was because those people looking to score participation credit already had and were back clicking arrows on their iPads.

Eventually the Navy guy (there's always one) put his hand up to answer the question. "It's taught, sir. And since we are built to learn, we learn."

The professor gave them an assignment that night: to develop a new symbol, like the smiley face or Nike swoosh, that would convey meaning. It had to be drawn with a marker on pen in black and white, and simple enough to be visible and interpretable from a distance. It couldn't be a depiction, such as a sketch of a tree to symbolize a tree, and it had to be novel.

If you try it now at home, you'll find it's not that easy. You start thinking of ideas, and other symbols come into your mind: start thinking about symbols that might have a circle, and you'll conjure everything from the Olympic rings to the peace sign, to the Audi logo.

So Derek had taken a Post-It pad and started drawing symbols to warm himself up. A circle, a triangle, a lightning bolt. He thought if he could conjure up all the symbols he could think of, a new one would form in the cracks between then. So he spent hours on remembering symbols. Nothing new had yet emerged. But his apartment did now look like a Mayan temple.

He boiled some hot water for tea and sat down with Anne on the kitchen counter while he explained the project. When he was done, Anne asked, "What is the meaning you are trying to convey?"

"Oh," Derek clarified, "it doesn't really matter for the assignment. It's not about expressing a meaning but coming up with a new symbol."

Anne looked perplexed. "How can you convey meaning if you don't know what meaning you want to convey?"

He thought about it for a second and shrugged. "That's a good point. But what meaning do I want to convey? I can't really think of anything."

"It doesn't have to be world changing," Anne suggested. "Look around. Surely even in this apartment there's something you'd like people to know or feel."

Derek had some more of his tea and considered. His eyes searched around the apartment, looking for things to instruct people on. He suggested having a sign for "take off your shoes" or "dance here," but those seemed to involve combinations of existing symbols. He needed something more lasting and abstract, maybe more optimistic. After all, he was in a good mood – on a rockstar track at work, dating a strong, smart and beautiful woman, and pretending to be a student again. He told Anne so much (she blushed) and that he wanted a symbol to convey this joyful happiness to others.

Anne asked him to describe optimism. His eyes wandered to the smiley face, which was the fifth symbol he had drawn. He picked up the pen and started sketching it out for her. It was like a game of Pictionary when you have been given have an impossibly abstract word like "forever."

His first Post-It filled mostly with lines, and these turned into arrows, pointing up, swirling with motion.

He tore it off, and started a new one: of a circle, a circle greater than that, a set of ripples extending in perfect symmetry outwards.

Next Post-It: a sine curve.

Next: an infinity sign, drawn around and around and around, darkening each line until he poked a hole in the Post-It.

Next: an infinity sign with a string through it:

He smiled at the last one, and put it on the wall, content that he had at least completed the assignment for tomorrow. "What do you see?" he asked Anne.

"It reminds me of harmonic frequency – when a string vibrates at the right speed so that the waves fit exactly in it, reinforcing itself," she answered reflectively. "Also a Froggie closing its eyes," she added with a grin.

"Done," he said, in exaggerated triumph, and stuck it in the middle of the wall.

He and Anne caught up about their day over the tea, and from time to time, his eyes would wander back to the Post-It. "What are you thinking?" Anne asked.

"I'm just not sure people will get the meaning; it's not obvious at all."

"It doesn't have to be, Derek. That's the difference between a symbol and a picture. I mean, think of any great symbols: the cross, the peace sign, the heart, the exclamation point," she said, placing her hand comfortingly on his arm. "No one knows what they mean unless they are told. They just gesture at an already-shared meaning."

Derek put down his tea. He reached over to grab Anne's hand and brought it up to his lips. "Like this?" he said, smiling.

"Exactly."

* * *

Anne's workdays at the Windmill were getting busier. She was working with fourteen cities at once, licensing them the technology, and was on a plane most weeks. She tried to be back in New York for the weekends and was usually able to get at least one date a week in with Derek.

In this ordinary rhythm of work-weekend, there came an ordinary Friday, just like any other. She and Derek had been dating now a few months. She was going to dinner at his place, which was still a four-floor schlep up to the top of a brownstone on the Upper West Side. She had been dreaming about this all week.

Some women had fantasies about men taking them to palm-lined deserted beach islands; Anne had fantasies about men sautéing onions. She told me this once at my office and speculated on the reasons. Maybe it was the humility of them: the simple, underground, white vegetable, that serves as an enhancement for so many recipes in many cuisines but is rarely the central item. Maybe it was the conversion: the eye-watering and breath-accosting sharpness of a fresh onion caramelized into something delicate and sweet through the sautéing process. Or the place in the cooking schedule: right at the beginning, as the pan heats up, and the edges of the chopped onion froth in newly heated oil, announcing the transformation of the kitchen from a static place to a chemistry lab of creation. If the Bible were written as a recipe, on its first page would be written: And on the first day, God sautéed an onion…

As she walked up the fourth and final flight of carpeted stairs to his apartment, she slowed to wrap a shopping bag with a bottle of red wine around her wrist and reach for her keys. She didn't mind slowing down; no matter how much she ran, walking up Derek's stairs always took her breath away, and she wanted to seem in good shape when she walked in. She'd gotten a pair of his keys a few weeks ago; it wasn't technically necessary as he was always there when she was, but it somehow marked a milestone in their relationship.

Like all good New York apartments, there were three keys on the set: one for the downstairs door, and two for the locks on the front door. (He hadn't, of course, copied his mailbox key for her.) He had left them on the table for her and gestured at them – "there are some keys for you" – in a nonchalant manner. At brunch the next Sunday, her girlfriends interpreted and reinterpreted this gesture, marking it against their soothsayer maps of relationship forecasting, comparing it against the season, their first date, the day they first kissed, and his first use of the word "girlfriend" to determine whether this relationship "had potential." As you'll recall from the MBA Presentations class, the meanings of such symbols are taught, and we are keen to learn them.

Anne found the keys and inserted the first. As the mysterious gears of the lock grinded against the metal, she heard a familiar sizzling noise conjured from a dream on the other side of the door. She was transported back to her image of a dream man, the perfect man, standing with an apron over his work clothes, in front of the stovetop, sautéing onions. She lost focus for a moment, fumbling with the keys, the plastic bag with the wine bottle cutting into her wrist so she adjusted it, then put it down, then used her hand to move the keys along the key ring. It took a moment, and there was a click, a beam of light, and then the smell of onions sautéing.

"Hello, beautiful woman," Derek said, in an apron over his work clothes, holding open the door with his elbow.

She kissed him a "hi honey I'm home" kiss and they entered the kitchen area which was also the living room which was also the dining room and entry. (When they said "one bedroom" they weren't leaving out much of the description of the apartment.) On the table was a baguette from Zabar's and a small bowl with oil, balsamic vinegar, and Italian seasonings. She remembered the first time he made that for her: she was in awe of his Italian seasonings concoction. Even later, when she learned that it was store bought, and after they broke up and she continued to buy it herself, she would think back in awe of his cooking acumen. First impressions die hard.

Derek was making pasta with meat sauce and broccoli. While she loves sautéed onions most as the symbol of cooking, when it comes to ingredients, there's nothing Anne loves more than broccoli. She once explained to me her fascination with the stuff: its natural appearance like a bonsai tree, its calcium and nutrient density, the variety in textures from the solid trunk to the delicate, bite size branches, its sense of healthiness and restoration, of treating yourself right.

"Eating broccoli feels to me like dogs must feel when

their owner takes them out for a walk," she once told me. She loved that Derek loved broccoli, or at least tolerated it, and made it for her to show he cared.

While he cooked, she sat at the table – big enough for two for dinner or four for poker – and lit the candles. There was no music. His onions were sautéing on the stove, and for a long time, he was silent. Then he sniffled back some tears and grimaced dramatically.

"I hate cutting onions," he said, and turned to her.

He was perfect. Apron around his neck, innocuously moist onion eyes, half masked smirk. He was making spaghetti and meat sauce and broccoli, but thought he was hot stuff for having a domestic side. Anne could tell he loved having a girlfriend. He was tired of all the games, all the cockfighting and boys' nights out, the one-night stands, the all-nighters, the lonely nights. He still loved flirting, don't get me wrong. But no matter how much he liked the game, he liked the idea of someone waiting for him at home so much more. I never talked to him so I don't know for sure, but I suspect that was why he gave her a set of keys: in the hopes that one day, she might be there before him, making it feel like home.

Where was Anne in all this? According to her friends' relationship astrology, she was falling in love with him. But when they asked her, she blushed and dodged the question.

Anne grew up in a country, a city, a school and a family that prized independence above all. Even in lower school, she would walk ahead of her family when walking down the street, hopping up on the stones that surrounded the sidewalk trees. Once she took a bus nowhere to see if she could. One of her most prized moments was taking herself out to dinner one night in high school (the excellent portobello mushroom and red pepper appetizer didn't hurt either). She refused to join cliques at any point in her life, from the treacherous days of middle school through the dorm selection process in college.

They had been together for months now, but Anne is always careful about where she leans her weight. She had watched her friends obsess over men, fall in love, fall even harder out of love, sway through bouts of depression and alcoholism, adopt predatory dating behaviors to work out their issues, gain or lose too much weight, do poorly on exams, get physically ill, all because of relationships. It was not something one undertook lightly. It was dangerous, and could hurt severely, as she would of course eventually find out anyway. Love sacrificed independence. It weakened you. It exposed you.

Despite Anne's protests, though, I agree with her relationship-astrologer friends: that night in the apartment, with the onions sautéing and the broccoli steaming, she had fallen in love with him.

Before I go on, I should clarify. I have been getting lunch recently with some colleagues in the Relationship Department, who would be unhappy with my using the word "love" in such a vague way. In fact, one of them once shared the advice that couples not use the word "love" early in their relationship, if at all, as it can mean such radically different things to different people. My colleague threw out a few common meanings or components of love: admiration, respect, concern for, attraction to, comfort with, and empathy. Or as Helen Fisher grouped it: lust, attraction and attachment. A different colleague at the table defined it by the activities we use to demonstrate it: spending time together, giving complements and giving gifts.

I've since looked up the definition in the *Merriam-Webster Dictionary*. Apparently "love" (transitive verb) can mean:

> *(1) To hold dear: cherish.*
> *(2) (a) to feel a lover's passion, devotion or tenderness for*
> *(b) (1) caress (2) to fondle amorously (3) to copulate with*
> *(3) to like or desire actively: take pleasure in <loved to play the violin>*

Which comes a bit short. Wikipedia has a long article on the topic, or long by the metric of my attention span on the internet (45 seconds), but it adds a few insights to my lunch time talks. I like Robert Sternberg's definition of the three components of love: intimacy, commitment, and passion. But maybe most of all, I like the *Confessio philosophi* by Gottfriend Wilhelm von Liebniz in 1673, which defines love as "to be delighted by the happiness of another."

So where, in this lexical map, is Anne at this moment? Anne expects structure from me in this book, so I've drawn up a scoring system and added my estimates:

Definition/Component	**Anne's Feeling (10=most)**	**% of Maximum Possible**
Components		**78%**
Admiration	7	
Respect	8	
Concern for	6	
Attraction to	9	
Comfort with	9	
Empathy for	8	

Fisher's definition		**77%**
Lust	9	
Attraction	9	
Attachment	5	
Activities-based definition		**57%**
Spending time together	6	
Giving complements	8	
Giving gifts	3	
Merriam-Webster definition		**70%**
To hold dear: cherish	6	
To feel a lover's passion, devotion or tenderness for	7	
To like or desire actively: take pleasure in	8	
Robert Sternberg's definition		**73%**
Intimacy	6	
Commitment	8	
Passion	8	
Gottfriend Wilhelm von Liebniz		**60%**
to be delighted by the happiness of another	6	

So based on this analysis, I have learned – nothing.

Surely while you are reading this you are thinking: "Isn't it quite silly to be creating a set of definitions of something as abstract as love, setting a scoring system to it, and evaluating for someone else where they fit in this system?"

Yes, my dear reader, yes, it is.

And yet, if I didn't put this in here, you'd ask, I'm sure – was Anne really in love with Derek that night? Rather than answering that myself, how much better, don't you think, to just watch them, and see what happens next?

* * *

Derek turns back to his cooking. He wipes his onion-stained eyes with the back of his right hand and jiggles the frying pan. He turns to the ground beef, wrapped in plastic on Styrofoam and starts to untangle it. He checks the date, weight and price on the label before throwing the wrapper out. His left hand, still untainted by the raw meat, continues to jiggle the onions. With his other hand, he pinches a few pieces of the meat and throws them in the pot. The smoke becomes a crackling cloud. The rich, hearty, homey aroma fills the room. Derek's apartment doesn't have a proper kitchen or a proper smoke hood, so he took the batteries out of the smoke alarm a long time ago; you and the happy couple are spared its screech. Anne gets up and opens a window, which helps.

"Thanks," Derek says. "This stuff only takes a few minutes."

Anne sits on the windowsill looking back at candles casting faint shadows on the walls of the room and glimmering in the bowls of the two wine glasses. The fluorescent light in the kitchenette illuminates a still rising cloud of smoke.

Derek has finished with the meat, throws out the bloody Styrofoam, and goes to the sink. He uses his uncontaminated left forearm to turn on the faucet and washes his hands with antibacterial soap. He dries them on a blue- and white-checkered rag set just for that purpose, which hangs off the doorknob of the fridge.

He opens the fridge and stoops down to get the tomato sauce. The refrigerator light illuminates his face. He is in perfect profile, gentle eyebrows and strong jawline, which is how Anne first noticed him in the park that spring Sunday.

"Do you want to open the wine?" he suggests, then turns back to the preparation. He pours tomato sauce over the meat, which smothers the fire. She walks to the table, and standing, pokes the top of the wine bottle with the point of the corkscrew. She peels the wrapper off, and with her right hand pushes the tip of the corkscrew into the bottle. She twists it all the way and Derek stirs the meat sauce and swirls the spaghetti. Anne grabs the rabbit ears of the industrial corkscrew with both hands, Derek turns the broccoli burner off with one hand and picks up the top of the sauce pot with the other hand, which is still holding the stirring spoon. He deftly puts down the lid and spoon and Anne strains to release the cork and Derek strains the broccoli into the sink, which fills with steam. He pours out the pasta water; Anne pours the wine.

Derek places the broccoli on way edge of the plate, so the meat sauce won't touch it. He is looking for a fork for the spaghetti when he notices her chin on her shoulder and her arms winding across the apron around his stomach. She leans on him to balance, as she props up on her toes to look over his shoulder at the stovetop – the meat sauce still bubbling, the pasta still steaming. She squeezes briefly, a tug really.

"It looks great," she says, and then releases him fully so he can finish spooning the spaghetti and meat sauce.

"I know, doesn't it?" he brags, with cockiness masking humility masking confidence, and takes off his apron.

She takes her plate, he takes his, and with one hand each they pull out their chairs, scrapping in symphony over the warped wood floor.

They chink wine glasses, take healthy sip each, and dig in. They both looked pretty pleased: her with him, him with the food. She knew that by the end of the night, she would have told him that she loved him, and that was enough. She didn't know how she would do it, when she would or why or with what words. But she glowed on the inside and outside, because she knew it would happen. It had to have happened.

This wasn't the first time that Anne found quiet comfort in the Future Perfect. One afternoon when she was maybe ten years old, she glanced in the mirror briefly while washing her hands. Looking back at her was an adult version of herself, maybe twenty or thirty or forty, she couldn't tell ages when she was that young, smiling back at her. She never forgot the expression on the adult Anne's face; she was sublimely content, confidence and reassuring. Anne knew then that things would have worked out by the time she was in the mirror looking back.

A few years later, Anne entered the jungle kingdom of middle school. Things were rough. Friends were fickle and few. School pressure was rising. Biology and other catastrophes were taking place. She doubted that things would get better. But her wise older sister, whom I introduced to you on the Brooklyn Promenade, told her, "Anne, it gets better in high school."

With this foresight, she plowed through middle school unmarred, mostly. It's a powerful thing to know that everything works out well in the end.

So back in Derek's apartment, we see Anne completely comfortable with Derek and their shared silence. Had he looked up at this moment, he would've seen Anne suppressing a beaming smile, which muffled, looks like a sly smirk. But he doesn't and instead says, "This is great wine, where did you get it?" which launches them into a discussion about the New York State liquor shop that only sells New York State wine to her chagrin, which then launches them on a winding trail of conversation through New York State geography (where are these vineyards anyway?) and ends them up in upstate, where they both had gone to summer camp as children, which unearths the roots of their childhood and a few painfully embarrassing moments of growing up, though women always win in those competitions, which gives Derek the chance to talk about puberty and his precocious sex appeal and success with the ladies, and by that time dinner is over and she gets the welcome hint anyway.

She clears the table meaningfully, rinses off the plates and fills the saucepan with hot soapy water. The dishes can be done tomorrow morning.

Derek gets up and stands in front of Anne. Her fanned fingertips come to lightly rest on the well-defined muscles above his ribs. He pulls her toward him, and her palms press against him. Anne lowers her brow and angles her head down, hiding her eyes under her kissable eyebrows. In sheltering her eyes, she appears vulnerable; in lowering her head and brow, she looks like a bull about to charge.

"You know—" she starts.

She chokes on her words. Bizarre, she can't believe that she can't say it. I love you. She'd read trashy novels and pop articles about how difficult it was to say those three words, but she never thought it would actually be hard to say. Maybe it's not true? Maybe he means a great deal to her, but not quite that much?

She breaks eye contact and her gaze wanders absently and bewildered to an embroidered crocodile clinging on his shirt. She knows she can't look at him and say it, and maybe needs a few leading words to gather momentum before trying to take off.

"I, I was thinking today." She needs to get this out quickly or not at all. She looks at him with all of her eyes, no longer like a bull, just completely vulnerable. "I think I've fallen in love with you."

I've watched this scene many times on File in the hopes that it would explain what happened later. As he processes her declaration, he doesn't look surprised, not exactly. Initially overwhelmed, balancing both what to feel and what to express. But in the next moment, his expression is one of kindness, generosity, I would venture to say love. Anne now remembers that moment through the filter of what would come. Over time, she became dependent on him, exactly as she feared and knew would happen. She needed him to need her. Had he been coolly indifferent that night, he could have squeezed her heart back in a jar. But instead he gave Anne just what she needed: a hug.

Anne and I both assume that he loved her too. He would

eventually say the magic words "I love you" a few weeks later in bed, and then repeat it in emails and on rooftops and to friends innumerable times thereafter. But now he was still unsure or unwilling to forgo his independence quite yet. Or maybe he just wanted to be sure that when he said it, he meant it, and wasn't just echoing her.

He holds her tightly, and then kisses her lightly. Then sensitively. Then passionately.

This is where I stop watching the File, and Anne stops telling the story. The present had caught up with the Future Perfect.

* * *

The early 2000s were the era of character-limited text messages (msgs), and Derek was a messaging fiend. Poetry is constrained prose, one could say, and there are few constraints more unforgiving than a character count. If a poet breaks a sonnet's rhythm, what repercussions are there, really? But if a txt msg breaks the character count, that's another five cents.

Neither I nor Anne consider Derek a great text messager, but he said the right things at the right times, and that's what made Anne happy. After the Haystacks and Sopranos, the kiss on the South Street Seaport piers, the Sunday garlic-free dinner back at Derek's place that lasted into Monday, Anne started getting texts at random times. Most were stupid, but some, well, he does kind of grow on you, no?

"u free 4 din 2nite or tom? i cook!"

"mtg boring. wywh. actually wiwt!"

"slipped on banana today. ate banana smoothie in revenge."

"memory foam is forgetting u. can u come over fri?"

"gr8 performance review! i am rockstar! drinks 2nite on me!"

"still on 4 mtg my brother sat brunch?"

"thx 4 ur note. my day is just ok since havent seen u yet ;)"

"still on for amusement park tom? boss says its ok 2 miss work"

"sorry to throw L word at u last night. meant it tho. i do love u."

"losing at poker w boyz. must be black cat in street."

"won at poker. i am rockstar! love u"

* * *

Derek jotted down the price of the 38th bottle of water that day: $1.00, 20 oz, kiosk, 57th and 6th. It was a bright sunny day, so he didn't mind walking around town in his Teva sandals and Ray-Ban glasses with Anne. It was kind of fun.

The professor had asked the class to write a two-page report on the "value of a bottle of water" using primary research; there'd be prizes for whichever students were able to find the most expensive water per ounce, and the cheapest. His record high: a $8 for a 375 ml bottle of VOSS water at a midtown bar (63¢/oz). The low: $6.99 for a case of 24 16.9 oz Poland Spring bottle at Staples (1.7¢/oz).

Some of his classmates skipped the primary research and just made up the figures: they thought it was quite stupid to have to wander around New York in search of water bottles for this study. They already knew, after all, that the price of water varied depending on the circumstance. But Derek was quite keen to do the assignment as described; he knew that people remember those things they experience, and had a hunch there was something valuable to learn in this lesson.

The next Monday night, Derek slid behind his name plate in the semi-circular auditorium at NYU Stern for Valuation class. The professor started collecting highs and lows in prices from water bottles. Derek's wasn't either – there was a Michelin star restaurant that apparently charged $15 plus tax and tip for a 500 ml bottle of still water ($1.11/oz), and a local deli that sold gallon jugs of water for $1.99 (1.4¢/oz). With the range of prices up on the board, the professor asked the class, "So what do you think determines price?" As they threw out reasons, he started to group them on the board as if placing them in an invisible framework. When enough students had responded, he boxed their answers into six groups:

Who - who will be using this product? Selling it?

What - what is the product like, exactly?

Where - where is this product being sold?

When - when will this product be used?

Why - why does someone want it? Want to sell it?

How - how will this product be used?

He took a step back to let the class jot down these six questions. Most of the class looked tired: they had been at work all day, valuing companies or currencies on trading floors, selling value to customers, day-dreaming if their class books would have any value when they sold. This was too abstract, too basic for them. The guy next to Derek unwrapped a Snickers. Derek hadn't had time for dinner before this evening class, and his blood sugar was low. Derek whispered "$5 if you have another Snickers bar"; the classmate responded that he didn't, but now had a new business idea if the whole finance thing didn't work out –

feeding tired MBA students overpriced junk food.

"So Derek," the professor cold-called, "can you explain the $15 bottle of water?"

Derek broke his longing gaze at the Snickers bar and sat up straighter in his chair. Flickering his eyes between the professor and the board, he explained that the people at the Michelin star restaurant were affluent, they were buying a type of water that was perceived to be high quality, in a gorgeous environment, at a time when they were thirsty and the meal – which cost well over $15 – would be compromised if they skimped on water. They wanted it because they were thirsty, but also to show their guests that they didn't really care about the price. And they would use it to drink with their meal.

"Sounds good," the professor said, jotting some of Derek's words on the board. "So why $15? Why not $20 or $10 or $100?"

The Snickers bar student raised his hand. "That's the price where marginal cost is equal to marginal utility – the supply curve intersects the demand curve," he offered.

The professor grinned, delighted that someone had offered such a perfect opener to his talk. He invited the student to draw the supply and demand curves for water on the board. Like a textbook of Economics 101, Snickers Boy drew:

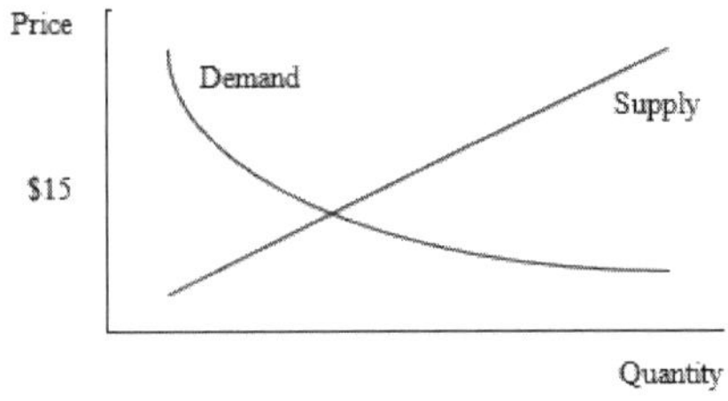

He let the student retreat to the security of the classroom benches before asking the class to explain the chart. What really does the Demand curve mean? What does the supply curve here mean? How would you draw it? He walked over to the six questions on the board. "Does the Quantity mean number of people, or number of bottles, or ounces? If they are buying it at a baseball stadium or subway kiosk, are they are on the same demand curve, or should we draw separate ones?

"What about the Supply curve? What 'marginal costs' should we include here? Surely the $15 bottle isn't the marginal cost for the bottle of water at that restaurant?"

He went on to explain that economists know these limitations; indeed, a great deal have gotten PhDs by defining and refining the curves Snickers Boy drew. But when economics is taught at undergrad levels or in business schools, the thing people remember is the easy thing: supply and demand curves intersect at a price, and that price represents something's value.

"What I hoped you saw by searching for water bottles all over New York," he said, "was that the price of something changes from instance to instance. The entire notion of value doesn't apply to a *product*, but to a *transaction*, at a certain place, in a certain moment of time, between specific people, for specific reasons, and for a specific purpose. If you change *any* of these variables, not just the 'what' but the who, where, when, why or the how, you change the value of the item.

"So in short," he concluded, "there is no true value to anything."

* * *

Derek is sitting properly on the cane seating at a round, white marble table. He cuts his ribeye steak and takes a bite. "This is great," he tells Anne's mom across the table, after he finished chewing, of course.

"So Anne tells us that you are doing nighttime business school courses at NYU," Anne's mom inquires.

Derek nods a few times, chewing another bite of the ribeye, and lifts his eyebrows to indicate he will speak as soon as he can. It's strange, isn't it, how long it takes to chew when you try. You watch him masticating the poor piece of beef, getting increasingly nervous that it's taking too long, that the eyes of Anne's parents whom he had just met are on him, and that maybe they will take his long chewing period to mean the beef was too tough or that he is lying about the classes. He gulps the piece down, a bit too soon, and clears his throat.

"Yes," he says, pronouncing the s with his professional voice, "I am really enjoying it."

They ask what he's been learning, and he describes the water bottle experiment and the who-what-where-when-why-how lesson in valuation. Anne's parents find this topic quite interesting, and within a few moments they are really engaged: what does the price of something mean, and how would you determine it. Anne is happy to sit on the sidelines and let her parents get to know Derek. He is doing well, with his pressed blue button-down shirt, looking like he's ready for an interview. Which I suppose this is.

Anne's dad brings up the topic of senior pricing at movies and on the public bus, and how Anne's parents get out much more because of the discount. Derek suggests that "early-bird" senior menus add on a "when" to the "who"; Anne's mom comments that those only exist in suburban areas with more capacity – an important "where." Together, block by block, they build together a story around senior discounts, with Derek and Anne's parents taking cordial turns.

Anne looks really content; she had been so nervous about Derek meeting her parents. I asked her why once when we were talking in my office. She didn't have a well-thought-out answer. Maybe it was that her parents represented something she didn't have a choice in, and therefore that she'd be judged on, and that her boyfriend represented something she did have a choice in, and therefore would be judged on. Or maybe it was that she was worried they would point out all the reasons he wasn't right for her, reasons that she knew herself, but didn't want to voice, or didn't know how to explain. And what if she introduced him to her parents, and then they broke up? How would she explain that failure – failure to form a relationship, or to identify a good one, or to hold on to a good man?

Or was it the other way – that Derek would see in her parents her past, her childhood awkwardness and reserve; or that he would glimpse into the future, what she would become when she was their age, and find something he didn't like?

If I look back at the chart defining love, I suspect that Anne wasn't ready for this level of intimacy. And judging from Derek's formal stature, I suppose he wasn't either.

Rise up above the white marble table for a moment and sketch out with me this moment in their relationship. How do we value it at this point in time?

Who: Anne and Derek. Two people, same age, same moment in life, same city, looking for a companion.

What: A boyfriend/girlfriend relationship. All the romantic perks, the norms of Western culture, without the commitment and burden of marriage and children.

When: At a stage in their lives when they want something to hold onto, as they change. Two years earlier, Derek wouldn't have wanted something so permanent, and Anne wouldn't have been looking for anyone to take up so much of her precious and intensely saturated calendar.

Where: In New York, a dynamic city. Meet Derek back in the suburban home that he will one day return to, and Anne would be uninterested. If Derek met Anne in Midland where she would eventually find herself, he may have felt distant, unsettled, intimidated.

Why: For Anne, at least, it was to fight off that seeping loneliness. For Derek, I don't know, but I guess it was the pride from dating an accomplished and attractive New Yorker.

How: Through spending time together, mostly on dates, and giving each other complements and gifts.

As they sat around talking about valuation, steak, Anne's embarrassing childhood memories, and the respective professions of Anne's parents, we see them laugh from time to time, their postures loosen in their chairs. Anne's smile, a bit forced, has flickers of genuineness, moments when she seems to be enjoying herself.

Anne's mom poured some Postum, a grain-based coffee substitute that Anne's family always drank; she'd only recently learned wasn't a common part of American culture. Derek tried it and smiled gratefully saying that it tasted good. But by the time the store-bought apple pie was finished, there was still two-thirds of the cup left clinging to the cold sides of the mug. It was nearing 11 p.m., and Anne suggested that they should go, so that everyone could get a good night sleep before work tomorrow.

They stood up, Derek perhaps too quickly, Anne perhaps too formally. They took their cups into the kitchen and put them in the dishwasher in silence. Anne's dad handed her her coat, and after she put it on, gave her a big hug. "It's great to see you, Anne." He let go and reached out to shake Derek's hand but had to wait for him to finish putting his arm through his own coat. "It was nice to meet you, Derek," he said.

"Nice to meet you too, Mr. Kesheen," he replied.

Anne hugged her mom, and they left, walking silently down the green and grey stripped carpet in the hallway. When they got into the elevator, Anne asked, "How are you holding up?"

"Yeah, good," Derek said. "Your parents are nice."

Later that week, Anne called up her sister to get some intel on their parents' impression of Derek. "Did they say anything?" she asked anxiously.

"Yeah," she replied, "not much. They said he didn't have a strong handshake. But that he seemed nice."

Anne exhaled, in a half-hearted laugh. "'Nice'" Anne told her sister "is what you say about someone when you don't have much nice to say about someone. Oh well," she added, defensively, "at least they aren't the ones dating him."

* * *

It's a lazy Friday in the city at the end of summer, those last days before the air becomes brisk and the leaves start to turn. Anne grabs a turkey sandwich on multigrain, no mustard no cheese, and heads to the roof of the Windmill.

The Map had just been finished and she took every lunch break she could to check it out. It was a people watchers dream come true.

The Map is a live 3D infrared satellite image of New York City. Cool things disappear, and warm things appear in various colors, from cool blue to fiery red. People are orange, the subway tunnels are indigo, hot water pipes are red. On hot days, some of the sidewalks start to blaze.

The effect is that the buildings disappear, and you can see people, with high resolution but no surface features, no clothes, no skin color, no hair wandering around the towered floors of Manhattan's skyscrapers. You can see people waiting in hot subway lines for their next train and watch the piston action as the subways push and suck air through the tunnels. Watch water boil on people's stoves. Watch body heat warm the bed under a comforter. Computers glow. Car engines burn.

The way the Map works, which is a mystery to anyone without a severe engineering degree, you can walk around in it without upsetting the projection. The first time Anne visited, she did what you'd expect: waved her arms to watch herself move in miniature. Looked at her apartment to see if she left the stove on, or the air conditioner. Looked at her desk, or rather where her desk would be if it were heat-emitting. Tried to locate Derek. Called him up to tell him to stick his arms out and turn in circles so she could find him. He did. She watched strangers near him watching him spin and she laughed into the cellphone. She bent down so she could see him more closely. She put her hand under him to support him, as the concrete of the tenth floor where he worked was invisible.

I can imagine what she felt at that moment, because I've

done similar things and watched other people watch the Map. You feel at once powerful, the feeling you get when finish a jigsaw puzzle or your first time behind the wheel. Before you is raw humanity, unable to hide in bathrooms or bedrooms. You see life at its core – the heat we generate, stripped of the images we wear or our appearance or even age. It's hard to tell how old an adult is in the Map. Watch Grand Central sometime at rush hour, which is a ballet to behold in real life, but on the Map is a colorful collision of merging and parting people, rushing to wherever. They look like atoms or bees. Or come at night, like Anne often does to check out the nightlife scene, to see densely packed clubs turn a sea of orange, undulating to the music. Even the subways are miraculous, strangers swaying the same turns on the tracks, strangers finding a common silent rhythm.

And yet you can't touch any of it. You can't really get inside these people, can't hold them, can't understand them. Here, at one of the great vistas of people watching, you can't really see people.

I've gone back to the File of this moment. Anne is kneeling. Her palm outstretched. A dizzy orange figure hovers, looking up towards some unseen heavens with his arms still spread wide, playful and loving. She smiles, warmly at him.

And then in a moment, the passion in her eyes gets sucked back down into her heart. The smile falls into emptiness, and her eyes lie vacant. She is now looking through him, at her hand. Which, she realizes in that moment, is empty.

I suspect that it was this moment, holding Derek's warm light in the palm of her hand, when Anne realized they were going to break up. Looking through him, she realizes that she will never really have him, never fully acquire him. That no matter how close they may be, they will always be two separate people, spinning through their own lives.

I watch as she grows sad. She no longer looks at her empty palm, she looks at nothing. She is completely inside herself. Alone.

These lonely spelunking adventures into her own soul would happen on subways and in rainy taxi rides home, lying next to him and tangled in him, during boring meetings at work, visiting the Map, and often under the 78% rain shield of the Windmill. They would happen when the credits rolled on romantic comedies or tragic comedies or tragedies or action movies, after four glasses of red wine, or as she turned at the midpoint of her run.

Was it shock or disappointment? She thought she knew herself so well, thought she was a solid rock or at least molten ire. Was there just really a great cavernous emptiness inside her?

* * *

We know now, and I think Anne and Derek knew too, that the dinner with her parents was around the apex of their relationship, when all the valuation metrics lined up, just before they didn't anymore. When the who-what-where-when-why-how made sense and worked. It wasn't amazing, or magical, or life-changing; just a comfortable relationship at a time when they needed a comfortable relationship.

But an apex is also a turning point, and as the next months unraveled, these value levers shifted, as things do. Derek changed into a man that Anne didn't relate to anymore, more obsessed with notching up ever higher on the corporate ladder at the Central Office and proving his value to his colleagues. Their relationship migrated into a commitment that neither really wanted just then, a bit too stable and predictable for their ambitions at this stage. Anne felt suffocated imagining herself staying in New York the rest of her life and saw that one day geography would get in the way of their relationship. And while she still longed for a boyfriend to fight what she called "the Great Loneliness," she realized in time that she had been okay being alone most of her life; she didn't need a man to make her feel complete.

The "how" of their relationship started to fall apart too: they stopped spending as much time together as Derek got more absorbed in his work and studies, and as Anne's work took her away on more business trips. And for some reason that Anne would illogically blame herself for even much later, they stopped giving each other complements and gifts. They assumed that they are already done enough, not realizing that maintenance of a relationship is like watering flowers: a little love is needed every day.

So that's it. That's how Derek and Anne's relationship eventually fell apart.

You may be realizing now that you have already read Derek's last line in this book – what was it anyway? And maybe a sense of regret or loss that you missed it, that you didn't realize it was the end at the time. Something feels seems incomplete, missing. You are perhaps annoyed with me for building their love story up and then not giving you enough time to prepare when it fell down. For not giving you closure. And maybe you are realizing that's how breakups feel, too.

Of course I considered sharing some of the details of the

decline – the teary conversations at Starbucks, the attempts to be friends again (and then friends with benefits, and then friends), the interrupted periods of "not talking," the sappy five-page long emails, and sappier if shorter sleepless text messages. But Anne avoids talking about it in our interviews and going into her Memories of this time is no fun. It's too real, even for me.

It's the sound of a tree falling in the woods, where you are the tree.

I read in my MBA a book called *Crucial Conversations*, where the authors talk about such crucial moments in relationships; when faced with situations of high emotion, people run either to "silence or violence." Anne, as you likely can tell, is a silence type. So when the fence she was leaning on collapsed under her weight, she didn't scream. She went back to holding her breath.

I've watched in the File and it's plain to see. She held her breath to silence tears and sobs, held her breath waiting for the time to pass, held her breath trying to figure out why she was so sad by ending a relationship she knew needed to end. As she holds her breath for minutes, then days, then months, you can see her body start to fall apart too. Her skin breaks out, her posture slumps, her joints hurt, her teeth feel cracked from grinding them at night, her lips constantly chapped from rubbing them anxiously, the skin under her eyes gets sucked out into dark hollows, her temples throb, light is often too bright.

She held it together at work, just about, shrugging off occasional comments from her colleagues ("you looked angry in that meeting," "we're in sales, Anne, we need to smile," "you're only feeling three out of ten today?"). So she avoided chat and small talk, focused on efficiently getting her contracts closed and the technicalities of her wind license deals lined up.

To cope with the stress, she still ran in Central Park, racing against whomever was close to her, happy to have someone to beat, somewhere she could win. She no longer paused mid-run at the Haystacks, which smeared like watercolors from her tears whenever she passed them. She never again ran past the fence that sagged that postcard perfect Sunday, so would never find out that it had since been removed, and the grass had grown full and green again. Instead, she ran further uphill, hard, until she ran out of breath, and then, with no fight left, limped downhill again back home.

In a term Anne would not understand until later in her story, the half-life of her recovery from breaking up with Derek would be months, not weeks. But be comforted, reader, that things will have worked out. You already know this. By the end of this book, Anne will have met her fiancé, whom she took last week to the hotel with champagne glass bathtubs. Be comforted too, that even back then, Anne too knew that, despite the loss and pain, things will have worked out.

Yesterday I shared some of these pages with Anne over a cup of hot water at my office. She sat quietly, sadly, but still comfortable with silence the way watercolors are comfortable with white spaces. "I think your analysis is right," she said. "I'd always thought that it was someone's fault – that Derek botched up the relationship, or that I did. But the way you put it makes it clear that the value of the relationship changed, not just because of us, but also when, why and where the relationship was taking place."

I nodded and let the silence fall around us, while Anne

stared through the square brown carpet tiles on my floor. Anne took another sip of her now lukewarm water and shook her head the way dogs shake off the rain.

"Oh well, at least I have some nice memories, some empathy for my friends going through breakups, and a vicarious MBA."

PART 3 : STILL

The wind stopped blowing at the end of the summer, when notebooks are on sale and the lines at the kid section of Harry's Shoe Store on the Upper West Side go out the door. In Asia, they celebrate the new year at the start of spring; in the West, the year starts a gloomy icy day in January. But I have always felt that the new year begins just then, with a new school year, with the cold fronts pushing away the damp moist air of a city summer. The last barbeques go up, and one day you wake up and find out that the pace of life is picking up again. That school starts, that there is only one fiscal quarter left in the calendar year to make your objectives at work, that vacations don't last forever. In a usual year at this time, hurricanes lurch across the Gulf of Mexico, and typhoons pound down on the skyscrapers of Hong Kong. Seasons change, and it's rarely pretty.

No one particularly noticed the first day the winds stopped, other than some sailors off the coast of Rhode Island who had been planning their trip for months. Maybe someone noticed that trash blew less frequently into the gutters, and the humid air hung slightly heavier. But no one can hear the wind over the din of traffic anyway, and the weather channel doesn't break headlines about non-weather.

Pick up any textbook now and of course you'll see the date clearly written there: September 1st, 2005, the start of the Still. But unlike 9/11, no one remembers where they were that day, not even Anne.

Thanks to the Central Order's immaculate File, we can see exactly what Anne was doing that day. She got up in the morning, after hitting the snooze button three times at 7-minute intervals, ran the tap for a little while, and then drank a glass of water to wake herself up. She filled the water kettle and plugged it in, dunked herself in a quick shower, and emerged to hear the click of the kettle turning off. She threw on some clothes, and made a cup of instant coffee, sitting in the living room window and looking at the Manhattan skyline through a slightly obstructed view.

It looked the same, or rather, no more different than Monet's haystacks would look in any given picture. She didn't realize that the Still would start her on a course that would pull her far away from anything she knew before.

Had she been paying attention she would've noticed how unusually quiet her walk to the subway was that morning. That the leaves on the trees were motionless. That the flags on the courthouse were limp.

Among the first people who did notice were the mechanics at the Windmill, who were busy determining the flows and angles of its 888 points, overseeing the plant's dashboards, and making judgments that artificial intelligence was not yet able to make. Anne worked on the business side, though, which took for granted that the wind on average always blows. Indeed, the Windmill's success was predicated on the law of averages, that over the course of a year, the pattern of the wind and the power output could be estimated based on what it had been the past year, analysis of ocean temperatures and other meteorological data, and complex but predictable computer simulations. For two years, these models hadn't been far off.

But over the next several days, what started as water-cooler conversation among the mechanics morphed into memos. The statisticians got involved, and when they noted something statistically significant was going on, they pinged management. Management at first seemed to think this was something temporary, for who would assume that the winds would stop blowing entirely? Who could have predicted or even imagined the Still?

It seems obvious now that weather could stop, that winds could stop blowing. With 20-20 hindsight, we can point to the clear signs that had been emerging: the completion of the Third Great Wall in Midland, the evolution of cloud seeding technology in Europe, the de-desertification processes in Arizona, the hurricane walls in the Gulf of Mexico, and the explosive adoption of multi-layered agriculture in Japan.

But imagine being back then, the week of September 1st: it would be as if the sun just didn't rise one day. Except that no one noticed.

* * *

On September 7th, Anne got the following memo:

> To: Anne Kesheen
> From: Lisa Cray, CEO
> URGENT
>
> As you may have heard or noticed, there has been no wind in New York for a week. The Windmill has therefore been completely unable to generate power.
>
> I don't need to remind you that wind power plants generate more than half the power for NYC. But we have recently learned that there is no wind anywhere in the continental U.S. and reports have come in that this "Still" has spread across the northern hemisphere. If this Still continues many days longer and the weather remains stifling and hot, energy demand will

exceed local supply.

We have already set up a meeting tomorrow with the Governor's office to discuss potential emergency deregulation of the market and strategic brownouts. Our financial team is meeting today to determine our solvency in the case of a prolonged period of stillness.

In short, the statistically impossible lack of wind last week has nevertheless happened. If it continues, our company will go bankrupt. The city either must dramatically cut back on power and/or pay significantly more for each kilowatt hour from other sources.

To try to avert this outcome, I am instructing you to immediately consult the Central Order's Weather Bureau to secure their assistance in restarting the wind.

Best regards,
Lisa

* * *

I held the door for Anne the first time she entered the Central Order. I have no recollection of this, of course, as I didn't know who Anne was at the time. But watching the File, there I am, on my way to another day at work.

When Anne first arrived at the Central Order, she thought it was a branch of the government, something which could help solve certain mass social problems, like transit strikes and epidemics. She figured that the Weather Bureau might have some chemical or fan somewhere that could restart the wind – a technological fix to a bizarre but inexplicable problem.

She arrives with her spiral notebook, a pen and a cellphone. The folks in the Weather Bureau watched the Six O'Clock News too often, and so have all adopted weather-related names: nothing as cheesy as "Storm Fields," but close. So the person that Anne has an appointment with is named, I am embarrassed to say, Gale Swarm.

Gale arrives a bit harrowed. She's annoyed that the local energy company would throw its muscle around to arrange a meeting at this of all times. Anne would find out later that the Still – and the politics leading up to it – had kept Gale at the office sixteen hours a day every day for the past six weeks straight. She wanted nothing more than to do her laundry herself, instead of dropping it off. There was something reassuring about washing your own clothes, Gale told Anne several months later. But with the recent weather crisis, both laundry and her social life had been neglected.

Gale's frustration with this unexpected meeting faded somewhat when she realized that Anne had no way of knowing how involved the Weather Bureau had been in the precipitation of the Still. So she gave Anne a pamphlet and told her to read it first.

I visited the Weather Bureau this morning to pick up that pamphlet, or at least the current version of it. It explains that the Weather Bureau has two Critical Mandates: to prevent the weather harming humans, and to prevent humans harming the weather.

The First Mandate, to prevent natural calamities from hurting people, doesn't mean "prevent natural calamities," just prevent them from actually causing harm. You may have assumed, as do a lot of my colleagues, that the Weather

Bureau fulfills the First Mandate by controlling the weather. That's one function, but certainly not the major one. Most people in the Weather Bureau actually focus on predicting weather. After the Indonesian tsunami at Christmastime in 2004 and Hurricane Katrina in the summer of 2006, along with myriad other natural calamities, the Central Order has been increasingly focused on giving governments more clarity around future weather patterns, both one week out and a decade out, so they can prepare defenses in time. Given the breadth of interested parties – from ski resorts to insurance companies to fishing boats – there has never been a lack of funding.

The Second Mandate of the Weather Bureau is to regulate the impact of humans on the climate. One tool they use is their authority to nix projects that will alter the planet's climate, unless sufficient Phase Three research has been done to assure that the benefits outweigh the costs. Since the impact of weather changes on the ecosystem is still not well understood, this requirement kills many of the large projects that apply.

But as you can imagine, the main human impact on the environment isn't from single-point projects. Most of the Bureau's time is spent figuring out how to regulate change that emerges over time from thousands and millions of smaller projects and billions of individual consumption decisions. One part of this, greenhouse gas emissions, are such a complex ordeal that they have their own department.

One interesting outcome of the Second Mandate to prevent human impact on the environment is the development of powerful weather controls themselves. The Bureau realized that some human activity had to go on, either due to a lack of political will, special interests, or in most cases, the fact that stopping these activities would bring harm to humans, thereby violating the First Mandate. So if you can't stop the activity or stop the damage, is there a way to reverse it post-facto? The Bureau has made tremendous strides and has now an arsenal of weather tools that could, if fully deployed, put all weather forecasters out of business – sunny and mild all the time, or so blisteringly cold that nothing could grow. The Central Order's Security Division has been trying to get the keys to this department for a long time, as some of the arsenal – hurricanes or unseasonable frosts – could be tremendously useful in the event of a war. I worry about that risk sometimes, and what would happen if terrorists gained control of this technology. I've read Vonnegut's *Cat's Cradle*; humanity may have survived a Cold War, but we could not survive an Ice War. So as you can imagine this department is situated well outside the Central Order headquarters, in an undisclosed but highly secure location. I think Santa's workshop would be easier to find.

So now Anne has just read this pamphlet talking about the Bureau's functions and Mandates, and is, like you, thinking two things: shock at the idea that there is someone out there who could turn the world to ice, and hope that these people might be able to stir the winds again. She puts down the pamphlet and looks up to see that Gale has left the office. So Anne folds her hands in her lap and waits.

A few seconds pass. Anne starts playing with her ring, a $5 silver thing with symbolic value I've never understood, which she wears on the middle finger of her left hand. She spins it a few times. Glances at her watch. Shifts her weight in the couch. Leans on the armrest. Starts to rest her chin on her hand on her arm on the armrest. Squirms. Her hands fall back into her lap, on the taut stretch of skirt across her thighs. She waits.

It's odd to watch Anne trying to be still for a while. You can watch her eyes darting to her bag (should she check her phone? she wonders) and to the clock (why are the seconds ticking so slowly?) and to the potted plant (real or not?) and to the strange little bruise on her knee (ah, probably from pulling in a chair at a table) back to the ring. She clearly isn't yet comfortable with being still. Her eyes dance and her fingers play with her ring for thirteen long minutes.

Gale finally returns, coffee in hand, still steaming. Too hot to drink just now. Anne waits for Gale to break the ice. And then as if being polite to a stranger in an elevator, she asks Anne "What do you think about this weather, eh?"

* * *

Anne's hands are now cupped around a hot mug of water. The mug is one of those Greenpeace ones that changes color when you add hot water to it, with a map of the world around it: "Stop Global Warming" it says, as the hot water turns the world map red.

Anne is now looking at Gale, and asks innocently, "Why did the wind stop blowing? And what can we do to get it going again?"

Gale shuffled through the papers on her desk until she found Anne's signature on the confidentiality agreement. She tried her coffee again. Still too hot.

"Well, there are many things that led up to this," Gale started to explain, "but the straw on the camel's back was the completion of the Third Great Wall in Midland. It seems to have created the condition for harmonic stillness.

Equilibrium that economists assumed existed but had yet to be seen in the real world has now happened with the weather.

"We weather people assumed that this equilibrium could never happen either – it's opposed to every assumption in our models. So we haven't yet been able to develop technology to start the wind again.

"Six weeks ago, we got wind, ha ha, of the potential for this Still to come. Our political team immediately flew to Midland and tried to persuade them to stall construction until a more complete study could be done. Midland refused, pointing out that only 2% of any large-scale projects that the Bureau has commissioned were conclusively determined to be safe, and suggesting that the Bureau's standards were too draconian. Without their consent, there's nothing we can do, as the Bureau has no jurisdiction over Midland." Gale tried her coffee again and took a satisfying sip. She closed her eyes and waited for the caffeine to hit her blood. The circles under her eyes were hidden under a thick layer of cover-up, but the stress she'd been under was apparent in her face. Anne suspected Gale had been on the team that went to Midland. (She had.)

Anne had come prepared to argue her case, to insist that the Weather Bureau restart the wind. But clearly, she would be preaching to the choir there. So what else could Anne herself do to help solve this problem? "What are our options?" she asked out loud.

Gale took another sip and put her cup down to use her fingers to count out the alternatives. First, develop technology to start the wind. But the Phase Three process takes two to five years for approval, never mind development, and she doubted there was the will to deploy a dramatic solution without careful due diligence.

Next, determine what else caused this Still. The Third Great Wall was the precipitating event, she and the Bureau believed, but not the only one. Scientists were already investigating whether removing the hurricane shields in the Gulf of Mexico would break the harmonic condition for the Still. But most of the causes were likely vague and irreversible: greenhouse gas emissions for instance, or deforestation in South America.

And third, persuade Midland to deconstruct the last and most critical piece of the Third Great Wall. This was a wall that had cost thousands of lives, billions of dollars, and at least ten years to build. And taking it down might not even solve the problem (Bureau researchers had estimated that there was an 84% chance that deconstructing this wall would restart the wind – or a 16% it would have no impact).

After watching this conversation on the File, I went online to see what other possibilities had been discussed. Many Op-Eds wanted to give the Weather Bureau special power to break its "do no harm" mandate in order to expedite deploying fans to restart the wind. Others suggested dumping chemicals into the Gulf Stream to alter its flow and hopefully create turbulence in the atmosphere, and others still suggested freezing then heating the earth rapidly using existing technology to create a convection effect that might stimulate winds. Some suggested that the Still would just unwind itself, and we should merely wait.

A few radical voices suggested that the Still was no big deal. These arguments were quickly rebuffed by a wealth of research that shows life cannot be sustained without changes in one's environment. But these radical thinkers pointed to other forces of motion: tidal motion permitting coastal water activity; diffusion permitting pollution to disperse, temperatures to change and chemicals in the oceans to move about; the earth's rotation causing night and day and changes in circadian temperature; the tilting of the earth's axis causing the change in seasons; variation in ocean temperature causing currents and weather patterns. "Who, except sailors and windmills need the wind anyway?" they argued.

Another set of articles started questioning the mysterious process by which the chief of the Weather Bureau was appointed. The Weather Bureau refused to comment on internal politics during the Still, but later – under different leadership – they increased transparency. In that process of opening up, we learned that the Weather Bureau Chief was chosen from the chairs of Bureau departments and was required to have a doctorate in meteorology. The Chief during the Still had been promoted out of the Desertification Department, where she had spent the bulk of her time working with the Chinese government on reducing desertification in northeastern China. But even after the new wave of transparency around the candidates' backgrounds, no information has yet been released on who makes the final decision about who gets to control the Weather Bureau. I suppose some things will always remain mysteries.

Back in her office, Gale's coffee had now cooled down to the perfect temperature. Anne explained to me that she did not have a clear reading on Gale at the end of this first speech. Was she the kind of person who welcomed suggestions, even from laypeople? Or would she become defensive if Anne offered advice? So she asked a softball question: "What do you think should be done?"

Gale pursed her lips to the left side of her mouth, pulling her skin taut across her well-defined right cheekbone. She held this contorted face and thought about how to answer the question diplomatically, or maybe how to answer it at all.

"Well," she began, letting her skin snap back into place, "I don't think we should start playing with fire. If we can take down the Gulf hurricane shields without creating devastating hurricanes, we should try that first. But I don't think the coastal communities are going to want to risk that for the more indirect benefit of restarting the wind." She took another sip of her coffee, then reached into her drawer to pull out a packet of sugar. Gale had a whole drawer dedicated to these sugar packets. Anne tried to read something into Gale's personality about them: maybe she was an environmentalist who hated throwing them away, or maybe she was an over-achiever who needed the sugar to power through 80 hour work weeks. Later when Anne and Gale become friends, Anne will learn that both are true – and that Gale didn't want to offend her regular deli-cart man, who gave the packs to her with a kind smile.

While Gale was dumping two packets into the coffee, Anne prodded further. "Why can't we just tear down the Third Great Wall?"

Gale laughed, one of those nervous laughs that might translated into southerner speak as "aw honey…." "If you want to figure that out, be my guest."

* * *

That night we find Anne standing under the awning of a shish kebob cart. It was almost midnight, she was starving, and it was raining. Between the rain, the Middle Eastern music and the sizzling of the chicken pita she had just ordered for dinner, her CEO could barely hear her on the phone. Anne couldn't be subtle about the situation, and so told her a little more abruptly than perhaps she should have that she needed a leave of absence from her job to go to Midland and investigate the Third Great Wall problem. She explained that she believed she could make a difference, given her expertise on wind power and negotiating skills. And that without wind, nothing else mattered for the plant.

Her CEO was one of those uniquely adaptable people who achieved tremendous success by processing new information and outputting rationale analysis in moments. She understood people intimately, and thanks to this empathy, never took things personally. She also knew which battles to wage and when and how. So she didn't ask her why or when she had made this decision, or even to reconsider, only: "So how long do you think you'll be gone?" The phone hummed with static while Anne considered. "However long it takes," she finally replied.

That was all there was too it. Between the time that Anne placed her order – chicken gyro with the works but no hot sauce and easy on the white sauce – and when the gyro man wrapped the sizzling dish in an aluminum wrapper, Anne had left her seat at the Windmill and was on her way to Midland.

* * *

It wasn't until Anne asked me to write this story that I started using the tools at the Central Order to really observe people. There are some folks in the IT department working on File search tools, with the hope that you can query something like "nuclear weapons in Iraq" and find all the nuclear weapons, with supporting visual evidence. The ultimate goal is a truly comprehensive search result, not limited by access, methods or politics; if my IT colleagues succeed, a lack of a result would be proof there were no nuclear weapons in Iraq, for instance. I've used the beta version of this search tool to help write this book. It can't prove non-existence yet, but still is both useful and fun (for instance, when you want to find moments of cats getting stuck in boxes).

I tried it out on a silly question the other day, to find out: where did Anne buy most of her coffee? The program gave me the result almost straight away – the coffee cart right next to the Windmill where she worked – and also gave me supporting visual evidence: a high-speed playback record of every coffee she bought between March 2002 when the site first opened and September 2005 when she moved to Midland.

It's amazing to watch, at least to me. The last time she bought coffee, at 6:58 a.m., you can see her speed walk out of the subway toward the cart. The coffee cart guy catches a glimpse of her out of the corner of his eye, and without interrupting his current customer, splashes together a coffee with milk and sugar into a bag with some napkins. Anne has $1.25 ready in her right hand which she hands to him in the same moment she grabs the coffee bag with her left, meeting his "Have a good day" with a "You too, Arun" over her shoulder as she dashes into the building. They are perfectly in sync, like an Olympic figure skating doubles team. How did they develop this incredible choreographed ritual?

I looked back at the first time she bought a coffee at this cart. It was at 6:25 a.m. on a chilly Tuesday morning. She asked the vendor whom she will later call Arun for a small coffee, non-fat milk and an Equal on the side.

"Here you go, ma'am," Arun said with a bright smile, even though the sky was still dark, putting the coffee in a bag on the window of the cart. "Fifty cents for you, my dear."

She smiles courteously and eventually fishes out two quarters with her gloved fingers. She struggles to open the lid with her gloves on, yanks a glove off with her teeth and shoves it her pocket, takes a sip, burns her lip, jerks the coffee away and causes it to spill all over her (thankfully still-gloved) hand. The split coffee is already dissolving the bag as she stumbles into the Windmill site office.

They don't meet again, until three weeks later, when she hurries out of the subway near the Windmill at 6:48 a.m. She checks the large display clock across the street and judges twelve minutes is just enough time to stop at the previous coffee cart before her first meeting at 7 a.m.

"Small coffee with non-fat milk and an Equal on the side?" Arun asks her before she even has a chance to speak.

"Wow. Yes, that's right," she confirms, astonished; she barely remembers what she ordered and certainly hadn't expected him to. "How do you keep track of everyone, especially when everyone's order is so similar?"

He flashes his white teeth, not stained by coffee at all, and answers, "It's the people that make my job interesting." He has already filled the small cup, and Anne confirms, "Still fifty cents?" He nods. She pays.

Later that week, she asked for his name, though simply forgot to tell him her own, and after that felt it was too late. But from that point on the routine is established. I watched most of these interactions in high-speed as they took place day after day, week after week. You see her getting to work always after 6:30 a.m. then always after 6:45 a.m. then always after 6:55 a.m. (sometimes unfortunately after 7:00 a.m.); her coffees go from small to medium to large; she switches from Equal to Equal with one sugar to two sugars; she goes from eating a high fiber cereal with fruit at home to a bagel with cream cheese at her desk; the price of coffee goes from fifty cents to $1.25.

Then suddenly, the day after she stood with a chicken gyro in the rain, this synchronized dance stopped. She was headed to Midland, and never returned to that coffee cart. I checked again to see if there was any warning in the days leading up to her last cup. But there's no farewell, no explanation given. I have half a mind to go down there and ask Arun if he ever wonders what happened to her. But then I remember that he never knew her name.

* * *

"Up," Gale answered. Anne had asked a string of questions about Midland – where it was exactly, how they were going to get there, and how long the trip would be. "Up" was all she was going to get for now.

Anne didn't know how long she was going for (maybe a couple of weeks?) so packed lightly. She brought a mid-weight coat, two pairs of slacks, four tops and a fleece, two weeks' worth of underwear, a month's supply of disposable contact lenses and her glasses, a notebook and pen, rainproof boots, some toiletries, a passport and a wallet. She had paused her (US-only) cellphone service; her lip balm, breath mints and purse she had left back in a closet in her apartment, along with all her going-out clothes, makeup, jewelry, shoes, and books. She wore to the airport a non-descript black suit, an even more non-descript scoop neck baby blue cotton shirt, and black walking shoes so non-descript I am uncomfortable including them in this description at all.

Their flight was delayed, and so Anne and Gale found themselves at a TCBY at the airport. Gale absently stroked her spoon down the side of the plain vanilla fro-yo. She occasionally lifted the spoon to her mouth and sucked on the plastic, passively. The fro-yo was melting faster than she was eating it, even though the airport was excessively air-conditioned. Anne had already finished hers in a few hasty bites and felt the chill. She wondered if she should've packed a heavier jacket. (She should have.)

I like watching the two of them that afternoon at the airport. Two strangers, off to a strange land. Neither one was interested in small talk, and yet there were too many questions about the big talk that had to go unanswered.

So Anne pulled out her notebook and started putting down bullet points. Next to each one was a little dash. She wrote in two columns on the unlined paper.

- *find the man upstairs – who is in charge of the Wall?*
- *determine if they knew about this consequence of the Third Great Wall*
- *find out why they built the Third Great Wall – who benefits?*
- *cost and benefits of tearing it down – political, economic, environmental*
- *will tearing it down restart the wind? (double star)*
- *find someone who can teach us how to negotiate with Midland government*

- *figure out what questions to ask (three stars)*
-

The last empty bullet is an old Anne habit. I recently asked her why she always had one more tick than things to do. "I never expect to leave it blank when I write it. But then I run out of ideas," she explained. I looked a bit confused, so she added, rolling her eyes, "I don't always have the answer, you know."

She looked at the list, looked up at Gale, and realized that while thinking her lower lip has slid under her upper teeth again, giving her the appearance of a grandma either frustrated with youth these days or pondering whether to change dentures. She relaxed her face and caught Gale's expression. She had that American pseudo-smile, just with the mouth, not with the eyes or heart, the little red mat at the door of one's face that says both "welcome!" and "no trespassing" at the same time. Gale continued to pet her fro-yo. Anne didn't know what to say, so as a last resort went to a get-to-know-you question she had been interested in anyway. "Did you have to say Goodbye to anyone?" Anne asked, with a clearly capitalized G.

Gale looked down and plunged her spoon deeply into the fro-yo. Well, halfway anyway. Deeply for her.

"Yeah," Gale said. "Sort of. I've known for a while I would need to go to Midland to pursue my career, I just never knew exactly when it would be until this week. So I guess I said goodbye a little while ago." She gulped down the spoonful. "What about you?" she added, more to discourage further inquiry than out of curiosity.

"Not really," Anne dodged. "Just a city I'm in love with."

* * *

Their plane arrived just before dawn. The last hours of flight were in the dark. The air was thick with something, and she couldn't see the runway until the plane smacked down on it.

The first thing that struck Anne about Midland was the luggage belt. There's that moment before it starts, when you have a chance to marvel at it. Where passengers posture for position, near enough to the beginning of it to protect their luggage, but not so close that you fight with the other vultures. Anne had all her stuff in a small carry on, but Gale had brought more baggage with her. Gale was anxiously anticipating the buzzer to go off and the belt to start winding its merry way around, quite usefully ending up where it began.

The buzzer went off. Anne at this point was staring at the infinite loop of the belt, as if she was looking straight through it into a wormhole of some future place. I haven't gotten around to checking the Memory of what she was thinking that evening, but the scene reminded me of something she said later about her breakup with Derek: "Things with Derek… at some point it just felt like it wasn't going anywhere. But once the break-up was set in motion, I was nostalgic for being motionless."

So maybe this is nostalgia that we see in Anne's face. Or maybe she was just tired. It was a long flight. Passengers with bags under their eyes grab bags under their arms. Anne was jostled out of her state when Gale's cumbersome black roller bag swung towards her. They went through gates: through customs, through immigration, and out into the smoggy air of the Midland City airport.

They were now truly in Midland.

Thank goodness the interpreter met them just outside the airport, because no one spoke English, and Gale and Anne certainly had no time to learn Midlandish. Midlandish is one of those odd languages that makes complete sense to the people who speak it, is far simpler than English, and has a poetic logic and millennia of continuous history; and yet since it shares absolutely no roots with English, is a complete headache for native English speakers to learn.

As we all know now, but Anne had yet to learn, Midlandish doesn't have the usual distinctions of most languages. Had she tried to look at the airport signs, for instance, Anne would have seen that the word for "entrance" is the same as for "exit." Both are roughly translated "the way." But those first days, Anne believed she could accomplish her mission without learning the language, simply by relying on an interpreter. She didn't have time to master a new language; she just wanted to understand the country, get a sense of their point of view on the issue, get them to change their point of view to be the same as hers, and return to the Windmill, her city, her life and her little going-out bag tucked in the corner of her apartment.

They hopped a cab to their Western hotel – with a clean Western-style bathroom Anne would come to appreciate later – and Gale headed straight to bed. Anne dropped down to the English-speaking, overpriced hotel bar to think things over. She was too jittery or excited to sleep soundly. The only other people still up at the bar were two American businessmen. They were a few beers back and talking loudly enough for Anne to eavesdrop effortlessly.

"Oh I think there's opportunity in the soft-drink sector. Everyone likes sugar, c'mon that's a no brainer," the older man was saying. "But the carbonated beverage market has just fallen short no matter what marketing we do: celebrities, free samples, ad saturation, product placement – it doesn't matter. They aren't biting. How can a country not like soda!"

"See, I think you can't think of traditional advertising here," Anne heard the younger man reply. "These guys go by word-of-mouth alone. If you want to get to these people, you have to speak their language."

Anne's gin and tonic arrived. It had lemons but wasn't carbonated. Anne drank it anyway. It's actually pretty good, she thought.

* * *

The next day, Anne and Gale headed out just after dawn to visit the Third Great Wall itself. It took a couple of hours in a newly built train to get there, and Anne used this opportunity to grill her interpreter about the language. She had learned "hello" and "excuse me" and "thank you" and "I want," and was now a fan of pointing at things out the window. They came over a bridge, and Anne asked how to say bridge in Midlandish.

"Chum," the interpreter replied.

"Isn't that the same word as 'wall' in 'The Third Great Wall'?" Anne asked, curiously.

"Yes," she explained. "Walls and bridges are the same in Midlandish. We don't have different words for 'separate' and 'divides,' so 'chum' is a word that means just 'a structure between two places that relates them to each other.' And I'm not sure that the English translation for the Third Great Chum is really accurate. You see, it's much more of a bridge than a wall, I've been told."

Anne looked at the interpreter genuinely perplexed. "A bridge to where?" she asked.

"To the end, of course," she replied.

* * *

You couldn't see the end of it. Anne and Gale are holding onto the icy railing of the viewing platform on top of the Ministry of Great Works. The wind dries the skin on their ungloved hands and whips the hair behind them. Anne deeply regrets not bringing a warmer coat. Gale has her red fleece ear-warmer tightly around her short hair. Her sharp nose and gaunt cheeks are bright red, and her blue eyes are tearing from the cold. With the wind howling over the top of the building, they can barely hear the Minister of Great Works. The Minister is bundled in a heavy coat and seems unfazed by the hurricane-force wind pushing him. This isn't the first time he's given the Wall talk.

The Wall, according to the Minister, was started ten years earlier, by the 12th Government of Midland, with the approval of the Ministry of Construction, Ministry of Great Works, Ministry of Transport, and Ministry of Culture. Its construction was inaugurated by the President and involved 17,245 workers, all proud to serve their nation in these harsh environments. It used the newest engineering technology available, developed at the Midland City University of Civil Engineering, with local materials wherever possible. He compared it to the Great Pyramids, the Great Wall, and the Eiffel Tower as a defining landmark in human history.

While his speech went into impeccable detail on irrelevant things, at no point did he explain why the structure was being built, or what it would accomplish when it was done. So Anne asked.

The Minister shouted back only, "It is required for modernization. It will have been a great work of history."

* * *

Anne went back down that night to the hotel bar. It was a lot to absorb, and she needed some alone time. A grey-haired American man was sitting downstairs at the bar, sipping whiskey and reading the paper. Anne sat down a seat away from him on a bar stool, ordered some mint cream tea, apparently a Midland specialty, and glanced over at the headlines on his paper. They were all in Midlandish.

"I wish I could do that," she said out loud, half to herself. The man looked up from his paper through the rims of his square glasses.

"It's not that bad once you get started," he said flatly. He looked back down at the paper. Anne swirled the plastic Midland Garden Hotel straw around her drink. A few minutes later, the man finished reading the paper, and put it down. "Here," he said, showing her a headline with his finger. "This says 'More couples find happiness.' Front page. Not in Kansas anymore are we." He gave a tired grin. His swampy grey eyes had no sheen to them. Anne guessed he was either exhausted or absolutely dull and gave him the benefit of the doubt.

"I'm Anne," she said, extending her hand, but not quite turning towards him in her stool. She wasn't sure if he was the sociable type just yet.

"Aesop," he replied, "yes, like the fable. First time to Midland?"

"First full day today. Saw the Third Great Wall. I think Great doesn't fully describe it."

"Wall doesn't really describe it either," Aesop added, his grin starting to warm up, a little anyway.

"What do you mean?" she asked, openly. Her sister had bought a book called *Conversationally Speaking* when they were kids, which in addition to having a clever title had a series of good advice. Asking "open ended" questions was one of them, and Anne used that ever since to get people to tell her much more than they normally would at a first meeting.

Aesop considered. "Well, it was built as a bridge, you know. And they projected that they would reach the halfway point this year, maybe in a few months. They still don't know where it leads."

"It's only halfway done?" Anne asked, genuinely surprised. "I thought it was just fully completed?"

Now Aesop was genuinely enjoying himself. His eyes started to glow like a cat sitting on a warm spot, aware only of his pleasant comfort, with no agenda and no real interest in the world outside the warm spot. Aesop had been in Midland for three years, he told Anne, trying to get a few joint ventures going. He had learned a good deal more than Midlandish in that time. And wasn't going to give his wisdom out for free to passing strangers drinking mint cream tea at a hotel bar.

But the warm spot does feel better when gloated over, so Aesop let one thing slip that night: "Anne, right? You have to understand that so much is lost in translation. The word 'complete' for instance. In America, you define set goals to achieve, and when the boxes are all checked, you consider them fully completed. Of course, then we just have to add more 'to do's – maintenance, repair, transformation, sometimes entirely new projects.

"But here in Midland, they think about all the lingering stuff upfront. So when designing projects, they don't give them 'completion' dates as we do, but something more akin to a 'half-life date.' It's the same concept of half-life scientists use to describe radioactive decay: since radiation decreases exponentially, never really getting to zero, it's more useful to identify when half of the material will be gone. Same here: a project is never really completed, but at some point, it's more than half finished. Now that Midland is opening up to the rest of the world, they needed some way to announce a completion date. So they've told everyone that it's done, but really, it's only half done, if that.

"Trust me," Aesop said, taking his glasses off and putting them in his shirt-pocket. "The Wall, if that's what you want to call it, is far from done. It will never be done. In some ways, it's just beginning."

* * *

It was the kind of cold you remember. Anne had been cold during most of the first two weeks in Midland, shivering in her meekly heated room, the damp air easily penetrating the ashy single-pane windows and grey concrete walls. She had bought a blanket to hang on the walls to keep the draft out and wore two pairs of socks to sleep. She hadn't been able to sleep through the night once since they left the expensive Western hotel after the first week. Her bed was so hard that she thought it might be better to sleep on the concrete floor – if it weren't so cold.

As time had passed, Anne's memories of those cold

nights became well-worn from retelling, and no longer had the sharp edges of actual experience. You often hear stories from Midland go through this decay, gradually wearing down into myths like statues on the shore. In time, Anne too would question whether she actually spent those years in Midland. "Sometimes I am not sure where the dream begins," she told me one day, "and if it's still going on."

But the day she first went on the Wall was definitely before the dream, if there ever was a dream, or ever a before. The wind roared over the side of the Wall and blasted Anne and Gale who were clutching at the handrail. Anne could see through squinted eyes as Gale screamed inaudibly, the wind whisking any sound waves violently over the side of the Wall and down into the mist below. The blood vessels fled her thinly covered nose into the depth of her stomach, abandoning the droplets of mucus in her nostrils to the outside world. She became aware of the gel in her eyeballs, cooling quickly, and squeezed the muscles around her eyes to protect them. Her fingernails dug into her palms under her mittens, as thick as boxing gloves but no match for this torrent. She could think of nothing but the cold. She couldn't even think of being warm, which was too complicated a question. Like a baby with a wet diaper, she didn't know what she wanted, only that she didn't want this.

Through her icy eyes she struggled to make out the Wall. There it was, so much closer than their earlier view from the Ministry roof.

Laid out before her like an ancient dragon turning forward into the distance, dipping in and of waves of clouds. Looking down its spine, she could see the peaks of the Wall curve up at regular intervals before plunging back down below the cloud line, invisible. It seemed in some places that the Wall might just disappear into the clouds, but sure enough further out on the horizon, there it was again, fading off into an unseeable horizon.

Through painfully squinting eyes, she noticed a black spot on the concrete-grey structure, a pinprick barely visible. She had noticed it because it was moving, she realized, moving slowly but moving towards her. But then it was gone, faded into the misty air a few miles away.

She stands there, motionless, perhaps waiting for the dot to reemerge on the other side of the clouds, perhaps because her body was paralyzed by the icy air. Her body no longer feels pain, just a sense of absence as if she is reading about this moment from a warm bed rather than experiencing it in person. The howling of the wind softens, and she can hear her own breath slow down through the pulsing blood inside of her head. Her eyelids are no longer struggling against the cold, and relax completely, falling into natural slits against the wind. She is now breathing out, ever more slowly, so that it seems she will never have to finish this breath.

She feels a tug on her arm. "Let's get out of here!" Gale shouts in her ear. Anne jolts back awake, panicked, the pressure of Gale's hand on her iced arm excruciating. Anne turns to climb back down the hatch into the Wall, but with her last glimpse, she catches the black spot emerging once again from the cloud. Anne follows Gale down the hatch, back into the company of the Wall's fur-wearing guards.

"How long were we up there?" Anne asks. Gale tells her that it wasn't even five minutes. "It felt like much longer than that. I guess when it gets that cold, time freezes solid too."

They had gone to the Wall to see if they could

understand it better just by being on it. By the end of the first week in Midland, Anne had not only tried every variety of coffee at the hotel bar but had also determined that Midland was a place that one learned only slowly. She decided to move out of the hotel in order to get a sense of how real Midlanders thought, and to get closer to the Wall itself. The people in the government were all there near her hotel in the business district, but they hadn't given her the answers she was looking for. There was something too fluently foreign about the way they spoke, as if they were writing a menu for a Mexican restaurant using only English words: "fried thin crispy corn cracker" instead of "taco." It wasn't working. So after one week of coffee and comforters, Anne rented a small apartment in the less developed outskirts of Midland City nearer the Wall.

Of course now many foreigners are starting to learn Midlandish in school and getting to know Midlandish philosophy (which has deeply influenced the language and vise versa) but when Anne arrived there, there weren't many foreigners willing to take the time. It takes a long time to learn a language as different as Midlandish. It's like learning mathematics, but with a different base of say, seven, instead of ten. It eventually will make sense, but only if you learn its own logic from the start – you can't just keep translating digit by digit, word for word from the language you already know.

Anne thawed out in the room under the Wall enough to unbind the scarf from around her head and yank her mittens off with her teeth. Rubbing her bright red fingers together, she realized that the soldiers were enjoying her predictable misery. Her still chilly eyeballs scanned the room and saw four young men on the verge of laughing at her. She headed them off by turning to Gale with an American mouth-only smile and said, "I don't care what the Wall keeps out, as long as it keeps us in."

Anne would later be involved in the Wall's military purpose, but it was not a direct one like you might imagine. This was no Great Wall of China, keeping out land troops. It wasn't clear to Anne from the politicians in Midland City what the Wall was keeping out at all. "It's for stability and security," they kept repeating. But what would make Midland instable or insecure? Who was the enemy?

When Gale and Anne had warmed up sufficiently and were about to head home, the hatch opened again. A small middle-aged man came down, wearing a full black bodysuit and goggles. Even his mouth was covered by a built-in mask. "I wonder if he sticks on antennae and goes as a bug for Halloween," Gale whispered.

The man pulled off his mask and smiled at Anne and Gale. "Nice day," he said in English, with a thick Midland accent.

"Were you on the Wall, going for a run, in this cold?" Anne asked aghast, miming the "up," "run," and "cold" as best she could.

The runner smiled and responded in broken English, "I strong." Then pinching his shirt added, "good clothing."

* * *

Anne called up her sister to run this decision by her first. She had trouble keeping track of the time differences, and ended up calling just as her sister was getting into bed

"Hey," she answered, groggy and comfortable under her warm sheets. "How are you? Long time no hear!" She had to wake up early the next morning but had been waiting for a call from Anne for two days.

"Good," Anne began innocuously. "Well, actually, I want to get your opinion on something, and I need to make a decision pretty soon." She paused, trying to figure out how to soften the blow. "You see, I'm thinking about staying here in Midland. For a while." She explained that by the end of their first week of cryptic and unhelpful meetings with Ministry officials, tours of the invisibly long Wall, pow-wows with Midland University meteorologists, and far too many coffees in English-speaking restaurants, Anne realized that she would have to make a longer commitment to Midland to get done what she needed to do. To understand how to handle the Third Great Wall issue, she would have to understand Midland; and to do that, she would have to learn the language.

"Learn Midlandish!" her sister interjected. "Doesn't that take years? How long do you plan to be gone?"

Anne sighed. "As long as it takes," she answered in what was becoming her most-used phrase. "I'll come back as soon as I can."

"Fine," her sister replied, clearly peeved. "I understand it, but I'm not happy you know. I miss you, Anne." She lay there with her eyes closed, drifting towards sleep. Then it occurred to her that maybe having her little sister on the other end of the world wouldn't be so bad after all. "Can you send over some Midlandish green tea?"

* * *

Twenty minutes before she has to be forty minutes away, Anne is standing in front of her mirror in her small Midland apartment trying to decide what to wear to the American Embassy Thanksgiving ball. In the last two months, she had managed to buy a few clothes, including a passable evening dress for this party. As for shoes, Anne has wonky feet and hates shoes: she hates shopping for them, hates talking about them, and probably hates that I'm writing about her hating them. So I wasn't surprised to see she didn't buy any last-minute party shoes to go with the dress.

So here she is, anxiously checking her clock, weighing her options: she can wear the dress she bought with the stocky boots and hope no one notices; she can wear her business suit with her nondescript black shoes and hope that she's not mistaken for catering staff; or go casual with long pants that hide the boots.

If I were not only omniscient but also revisionist (and benevolent), I could've told her one thing to help her out of her Cinderella quandary. Specifically, that her future boyfriend was at this very Embassy party, and that he liked women who were unafraid to stand out.

But I'm not, and that wasn't needed anyway. For Anne, there were always two ways to find an answer to important life decisions, like what to wear the evening you meet the love of your life: one is to find the answer that optimizes whatever you care about most (for instance, buying the cheapest toilet paper); the other is to find enough constraints that there's really only one solution left (like when you are stuck with ordering "the vegetarian option").

Anne decided against optimizing for comfort, or cohesion; she decided against optimizing at all. Instead, she put on her pearl necklace first, which really only worked with the dress. "I'd rather be limited by pearls I like than shoes I hate," she told herself. "I'll wear the dress that goes with the pearls, and hope no one notices the boots."

So now ten minutes before she needs to be (still) forty minutes away, Anne finishes up, throws on her too-thin coat, and stomps out in her boots and dress into the brisk night. She is flailing her arms at two dozen occupied cabs, regretting not wearing the warmer slacks instead of a dress. Just as she's about to turn back to change, a cab lets off a passenger magically in front of her. She puts her bare hand on the icy door to let the passenger out. The warm air from inside the cab envelops her and pulls her inside.

* * *

The American Embassy was under construction when she arrived. Literally. The construction was still going on that evening, despite the weather-worn red carpet being rolled out for this annual gala. In the frigid night, sparks from soldering irons illuminated workers, who were wearing faded green button-down work shirts, suspended from the rickety scaffolding, leaning back against the ropes tied around their waists. In the flashes of light, they reminded Anne of statues of "The Worker" cast in iron in the Moscow metro, undaunted by the challenges of the era, stuck forever in the canyons under the grey city's streets. Perhaps it was the strobe light effect, or the photographic way Anne's memory captured moments in static frames, but these men on the scaffolding playing with fire would remain recorded in her mind as motionless, eternal. Statues to the endless construction of Midland.

She arrived and reluctantly checked her coat. It was still icy inside, thanks to the heartless concrete that outlined the lives of Midlanders. But her coat was designed for function not fashion, so she ditched it and looked for the warmest spot to perch in. Gale had told her that she would likely be late, so Anne was currently alone. It didn't feel right to look for a seat in the dining room or loiter around the lobby, so she headed upstairs to the refuge of women everywhere: the ladies' room. After washing her hands under the thankfully warm water, she stepped outside, still alone. She checked her cellphone for non-existent text messages, and then noticed a plush couch covered with fuchsia velvet. It looked warm. She sat down.

She sits here for a full twenty minutes, watching various women coming and going, looking as stressed as she does. They walk out of the bathroom having just readjusted their hair, reapplied lipstick, now only needing to worry whether the small talk they carry around like their small black purses will last the whole night.

One woman with a bookbag size leather purse, far too large and practical to be sophisticated, emerges from the bathroom with her hair still a bit messed up. Anne notices she doesn't seem to mind and is relieved when she sits down on the side of Anne's fuchsia couch. She says without effort to Anne, "It's funny to watch all these people clutching their little bags like life rafts," echoing Anne's own thoughts. "Are you waiting for someone?"

Anne turns to the woman pleasantly and replies, "I'm just here with me. I'm Anne by the way," she added extending her hand. "Do you know anyone here?"

"I'm Grace," the woman answered cordially. "I work at the Embassy and helped organize this event. My husband couldn't make it tonight, so I'm here more or less by myself. I'd be happy to introduce you to people. Come with me," she said pushing herself out of the plush fuchsia couch decisively. "Let's go see who's here."

That night Grace introduced Anne to the political affairs officer of the Embassy – a person Anne would come to rely on in the future for many of the hurdles over the next years – and a bearded guy with two teenage kids who reminded Anne of an uncle she never had. The bearded man in turn introduced her to a young Midland woman who was responsible for external affairs, i.e. making sure that the American Embassy was allowed to work without interruption here. The Midlandish woman was here with a really handsome American guy, the kind that every Midland girl would swoon over, and who knew it. He was cocky though, and that's the one thing that completely turned Anne off. Plus he was with the woman. The cocky guy eventually dragged the sweet Midlandish girl over to meet another couple, leaving Anne alone. Again.

The party had started, and it was now appropriate to head to the bar to get a drink, which she did. She avoided the champagne, having heard that Midland champagne – sorry sparkling wine – was the worst in the world, and headed straight to scotch. It wasn't Glenfiddich, but it was a label she vaguely recognized, maybe it had a "Glen" in it somewhere. She waited.

If this were my story, I would have the hero arriving on Anne's right, no maybe left, asking the bartender to "make it two scotches, sir" and then debonairly introducing himself to the lovely lady to his right (or was it left). The Bond figure (it's an Embassy ball after all) would then talk mysteriously about his work in the "international arena" and Anne would comment on her efforts to "understand the weather, and maybe control it (laugh)" and Bond would lift his scotch glass and propose a toast to "controlling nature and all her bastard children" and they would chink glasses with a meaningful glance, and he would ask for, and of course have, the next dance with her.

But this is Anne's story, so she turns around now away from the bartender with her scotch on the rocks, unsure what to do next. She waits for innocent pray to wander by the bar, and debates even going back to the lady with the practical purse for further introductions. The bearded man is quite the gentleman, but somehow, she always ends up talking to the uncle characters and never gets to meet the razor-edged youths she had one day wanted to become (before realizing she really didn't want to become a razor-edged youth). But it would be fun to swim around in that school of fish for a while.

The cocky boy has his hand on the lower back of the beautiful Midland girl, nudging her into the spotlight of their conversation, perhaps showing her off to his similarly attractive friend.

This similarly attractive friend is tall, with a little stubble for fashion's sake, and a stylish button-up collar that Anne had seen once on a wealthy option trader who had flown into New York from London; the collar reminded her of a forgotten era of aristocracy. He was facing her but not looking at her, so she could take a close look without his noticing. He seemed unbearably comfortable in this awkward social environment, but not so unbearably comfortable as to be fully American. American men are taught to take up space, to express how relaxed and confident they are by wearing heavy-cut suits and crossing their legs with their ankle on their knee, creating a Bermuda triangle of demarcated territory. They speak loudly and gesture with their university-ring clad hands fanned out and lean forward into conversations when they speak.

But this friend of the cocky American, he had more of a more subdued sense of comfort. Composed, in Anne's imagination, like Darcy in *Pride and Prejudice.* The same soft eyes, Anne was starting to notice, but without quite the contempt. He was smiling at the Midlandlish girl, amiably touching her forearm while laughing at her joke. He swilled his red wine glass around a few times and then raised it to his smiling lips, which is what he was doing when he looked up to see Anne looking at him.

Anne's eyes dilated as if someone had shone a light in them. She felt her heart skip half a beat. But she didn't blink or avert her eyes, even though she wanted to. The two cubes of ice in her glass of scotch felt cold and clammy against her fingers, maybe because she was tightening her grip on the glass, just a little.

To explain relativity, my physics teacher used the metaphor of two headlights approaching each other in the middle of a completely dark road in Arizona. I wasn't sure why he specified Arizona at the time, but that's the image that held with me the first time I broke 100 m.p.h. driving there last year – you really can drive straight for hours without realizing there's a world that exists outside you. So imagine you too are driving on a moonless night in Arizona, in an automatic transmission car that drives as smoothly as a Cadillac, with your high beams on. There are no markings on the road for the sake of this example, and your windows are closed. You really don't know how fast you are going, you could confidently tell any cop that might catch you. When Frank Sinatra comes on the radio, you think you are going 55 m.p.h.; when it's Tom Petty, perhaps 85 m.p.h. You really have no idea.

Then on the horizon you see another pair of headlights, approaching you straight on. You can get a sense of how quickly they are approaching you – maybe you'll run into each other in one minute. But is that distance closing because they're driving 60 m.p.h. and you are as well? Or is one of you driving faster, one slower? Maybe they've stopped, and you are going 120 m.p.h. (which would explain the pair of flashing red lights in your rear-view mirror approaching you at a relativistic 5 m.p.h.).

The thing is, it doesn't matter as far as relativity is concerned. What relativity cares about is your relation to the other object, not to the space around you.

So returning from Arizona to the Midland City American Embassy ball. Due to the challenge of relatively, excuse me if I can't tell you whether Anne approached this Darcy character or vice versa. Blame it on Einstein, my teacher, or the mind-numbing fluorescent lighting in the office where I am writing this all down for you. All you need to know is that they approached each other. At about 4 m.p.h.

The Darcy figure, who's name will have turned out to be Chaucer, fires the opening shot. "Nice shoes," he says, incredibly dryly, in an accent that is unexpectedly mostly American. Anne will learn in time that Chaucer was born in Washington D.C. but spent half his childhood in London, before returning to the US for university and work. And in time, she will learn to love Chaucer's humor, with its obliquely dry sarcasm that occasional masks and more often than not illuminates deeper truths. But the ice cubes that were still chilling her fingertips had yet to melt, and neither had her nerves. So she takes this comment as any one of those ladies-with-insensible-bags emerging from the ladies' room might have: the wrong way.

"Er, thanks," she fumbles, embarrassed, "I just moved to Midland and thought four shirts and two pairs of socks would suffice, you know this 'developing country' misnomer and what not. Who knew there were balls in Midland?"

Chaucer leans back on the fold-out table that has been covered with a red tablecloth and doilies for the occasion. Gingerly, as it might collapse. (The country may not have been "developing," in Anne's judgment, but that catering company certainly was.)

"I have to say this is my first ball," he responds, smiling. "But I do like the shoes. You're the only one wearing anything sensible tonight, especially given how cold it is. You aren't cold?"

"Sure I'm cold. This scotch is helping, but I almost feel like getting my parka out of the coat check. I think they would officially kick me out of this champagne shindig if I wore that though."

Chaucer puts his wine glass down, gently, on the flimsy fold-out table and slides off his suit jacket. Without asking permission he uses both hands to place it around her shoulders. "Oh really you don't have you to" she says out of courtesy. "Thank you," she adds sincerely. "Mind if I ask your name? or should I just rifle through the pockets looking for a card?" Finally, and only then, does Anne's Cheshire cat smile return.

"Chaucer," he announces extending his hand to shake hers. Anne switches her scotch glass to her left hand and extends the icy fingertips of her right hand to meet his. His grip is solid, professional, and invitingly warm. She lets it linger there for a while to defrost, declares her name is Anne.

She still keeps her grip on his hand, until he lets go first.

"Why Chaucer?" she asks him. It's a strange question, no? One that over the next few months would have a range of meanings for her, but for now, is the only question she could think of. Back in New York, there are pedigree questions (where in the city do you live, what's your job, where did you go to school); at school there were the usual academic ones (what year are you? what are you studying?); and in Midland, it's been life philosophy questions (why are you here?). She was sick of the life philosophy questions, which often either blew up in her face ("I got fired from my job, and, uh, hear Midland was cool") or were canned ("I came to bridge Midland-US export channels").

But "Why Chaucer"? That was a new one.

Chaucer had a canned answer, of course, because that's the question everyone asked him when first meeting him. So he first gave Anne the canned reply, almost out of reflex: "Well, my parents were both English teachers. They liked Chaucer. My brother is Shakespeare." His stoic face paused for a practiced predetermined period, before cracking into a smile. "Just kidding, I don't have a brother." Anne snugged Chaucer's jacket around her, still chilly; the shoulders in the jacket were way too wide for her, belonging to a pair of shoulders she was starting to realize she would like to lean on one day. He continued, "You know though, I have this mental block against reading any Chaucer. Maybe it's that I'm afraid I won't understand it, or that people expect me to understand it intimately. Or maybe it's just that once I had to read the first few lines of *The Canterbury Tales* and never really got into it."

"So let me guess, you weren't an English major."

"Not at all, I got as far from English as I could without

learning Midlandish." Anne laughed, finally getting used to his sarcastic sense of humor. "I went into Computer Science, became a programming nerd. Worked for a while out in Silicon Valley when the going was good, and then, well, lost my job when the going was bad, and heard that Midland was worth checking out." Anne's face was held in place by social tacks, but that last line sunk him back on the level with the average lost Joe Schmoes she had met at every bar in Midland City – washed up, directionless, and worst of all, unambitious.

It was in a bar meeting a guy like that two weeks ago that Anne realized how important ambition was to her. She had questioned her ambition once in college, when her religious studies professor invited her into his office to discuss her plans after university. He had taught her an ancient Eastern philosophy that, in contrast to the virtue-sin dichotomy of Western religion, abandoned all ideas of assigning right and wrong to the world. It talked about following instinct more or less, about doing what seems appropriate at the time without overthinking the merits of it. In this course, she questioned for the first time whether she was really keen on being successful, on doing something "meaningful" with her life. Or was it enough to be content from one day to the next?

When she returned from Stanford that summer to talk about this new lease on life with her friends who had stayed on the East Coast to study, they teased her about this "laid back" approach to things. "C'mon Anne," Mary taunted her, "got a little too much California dreaming in there? I can't ever see you opening a surf shop and enjoying the sunshine for the rest of your life. You've got the same chip that I do, right – to do something with your life, whatever that may be."

But there was always something alluring about opting out of the rat race. Maybe its appeal was that she just didn't know too many people who did opt out of it; it was something to differentiate her. Or maybe she was afraid of the rat race and figured that by opting out she couldn't lose it, at least. Maybe there was something about letting go that was incredibly liberating. It's like that proverb about the monkey, which Anne reminded me of last week. The monkey sticks its hand into a jar of cookies and grabs all the cookies it can; it can't get its bulging hand out anymore, so ends up dying of starvation. "Letting go of ambition," Anne remarked, "is like letting go of the cookies."

As much as I'd like to restitch the fabric of time to show you a rational and linear progression of Anne's personality, from one who craves ambition, to one who lets go of everything, that's just not the way it happened. There were times, at Stanford or in Midland, when she did let go. Even in New York (though that's rarer), she was able to stand on a street corner, listening to her MP3 player, and let the world wash over her. But if you ask her what she was doing then, she'll tell you (with a frankness I appreciate) that she's actually being competitive about being laid-back. "Don't write this down," she told me in a tone I judged as insincere. "I always try my darndest; but isn't success so much sweeter when it seems to have fallen out of the sky, effortlessly?"

So I asked Anne, "Well why do you care? What is it all for?" As you may have gathered, she doesn't particularly believe in a religion or a set higher purpose. She doesn't have a calling in life. She was born into a life with enough freedom that she more or less could choose where to live, whom to spend her time with, whether to work or marry or fall off the planet into a spiral of drug addiction. So why does Anne make the choices that she does?

I know answering these questions is why she asked me to write her story in the first place. But I didn't see any harm in asking her.

"Do you mean why do I push myself so hard sometimes, instead of relaxing on a banana grove?" That's more or the less the question, so I nod. "Hm. That's a good question." She considers and gets up to the water cooler to pour herself some more hot water from the red knob. Her back is to me as she begins to reply, so her voice doesn't come across with its usual forcefulness and certainty. "I've always run uphill. This way if I ever get tired and want to head home, it should be easier going back than it was coming." She sits down and takes a small sip of the scalding hot water, then blows on it to keep it cool.

"Or maybe," she added with what I swear is a wink, "it's the chip that got planted in my head when I was born. I've always wondered what that was about."

Two weeks before meeting Chaucer at the Embassy ball wearing hiking boots, Anne was at an expat bar in Midland City, chatting with this boy who looked like a model, and seemed to look through Anne the way the magazine models look through the reader. Unlike Anne, who is driven even about relaxing, Magazine Boy genuinely didn't seem to have a care in the world. He was teaching English, had no plans to return back to the States, had a string of girlfriends, and lived by himself in an apartment big enough for him, some cereal, and his Xbox. Anne gave him the benefit of the doubt, partially because she has nothing better to do that night than watch Midland TV's news loop. When Anne asked him whether he was planning to return home for the holidays, it became clear that he hadn't spent Christmas with his family in several years; his parents split and got remarried, and their lives had rolled on without him.

"Wow," she asked, "so you are totally free to do whatever you want?"

"Yeah, pretty much," he answered. "It's a nice situation. I still get covered under their health insurance until I'm twenty-six too."

After she left him and the bar, Anne thought about how she admired this guy and his situation – to just go anywhere at any time, unattached. But that night when she got home, her fingers against her eyeballs about to pinch her contacts out, she looked at her fuzzy reflection in the mirror and realized that it wasn't him that was bothering her; it was herself. As she started taking out the second contact lens, she realized that she felt responsible, not only to her family and friends, but also to people at large, to make the most of the opportunity she was given. She felt responsible not to others, she thought, finally pinching the contact out with her thumb and middle finger, but to herself. She imagined a chip planted in her head that gave her a sense of virtue, whatever that meant, of right and wrong. She wasn't satisfied by this conclusion, she realized, frowning as she flicked the contact into the trash can, but it was time for bed.

So now, two weeks after Magazine Boy reminded her that she's supposed to do something meaningful with her life, we are back with Anne at the Embassy party. Here was yet another expat who came to Midland ostensibly for no reason, other than he heard it was the place to be.

"So is it?" she asked Chaucer quickly, catching him off guard. "Is Midland worth checking out I mean?"

"It's amazing," he replied without missing a beat. "Before I came here a few months ago, I thought Midland was just another pink blob on a map, a country like Germany or Brazil, someplace defined by borders and a country calling code and a government and a language. But now that I'm here, I realize this place isn't like any other place I've ever been." He reaches around her right hip to lift the red wine glass off the red tablecloth and takes a sip. "Something special is going on here, and I'm determined to find out what that is."

Determined? She thought. Maybe he wasn't the unambitious surfer she had taken him for?

"Well, have you been to the Wall?" Anne probed.

"Just once," he replied, "it was really cold, and I couldn't see much. Have they finished it yet?"

"It's half finished, which is as good as you get in Midland. Have you heard how they measure things in half-lives here?" she asked, both curious to see how much he knew, and to test how "determined" he really was.

"No, haven't heard about that. What do you mean?"

Anne sucked on her bottom lip, sizing him up. He could just be acting polite or trying to make small talk. But there was something in his tone, maybe the way his wine glass drifted aimlessly away from his mouth or that unforced glint of quizzical study in his eyes. Was he really a fellow nerd, Anne wondered, genuinely interested in learning about the quirks of Midland? Anne needed to examine him a bit longer to see where his character bottomed out. "Shall we sit down somewhere?" Anne suggested. He nodded, and she led him to a pair of catered folding chairs.

And so began a conversation that too would be measured in half-lives.

* * *

"So, Chaucer, why computer science?" Anne asked.

"Fair question," he replied. He figured that after grilling Anne for twenty minutes about the half-life method of project planning in Midland, the Wall, weather patterns, and project financing for such an interminable project, he deserved to be grilled in turn.

"The first course I took just to give it a try, see what it was about. I thought I would learn how to fix computers, or hack into government websites, or write websites. But the course taught us how to solve problems, how to break a question down, how to ask the right questions. I guess literature does the same thing," Chaucer started thinking aloud, "and a well-written program should be a nice read as well. You know, computer languages really are just that – languages. It's something that lets you express what's going on in here," he tapped on his head, "and investigate what's out there."

"So if that's what you're interested in, why not literature?" Anne pushed.

"If I studied English, there were no guarantees. My folks never had a lot of money, and that wasn't terrible. I mean we always had enough to buy clothes and celebrate Christmas and go to the movies and things like that. But not to travel. And I wanted to travel so much. Computer programming, especially in the late 90s, was very hot. If I could work for a tech company, I could hit the launchpad to success."

In her Memory, Anne spirals down into the conflicted part of her value system that she knows she has but hasn't debugged yet. He was mercenary, she decided, following the career choice that would make him the most money. She was as tired of dating guys who were only out to make a buck as she was dating guys who didn't care about money or any measure of success. She wanted to find someone who was passionate about what he did, and did it for that passion, not for what that passion would produce in terms of a paycheck.

But then again, he did seem passionate about computer science. And now he seems passionate about Midland. Maybe. So what's wrong, she mused, if he's finding a place where his interests intersect with profitability? Actually, isn't that the sweet spot in terms of a career after all? Those who are successful, effortlessly?

She asked him if he planned to go back to tech.

"I'd like to, maybe as a hobby. I've been really interested these days in trying to write code that incorporates chaotic phenomenon, like the weather, or chemical reactions. You know, if you just add one or two rules to a chaotic environment, like putting a catalyst in a beaker, all of a sudden something emerges out of nothing. Think of the lives saved by putting two simple yellow strips on the road.

"But since coming here," he continued rubbing his hands together, "I really wish I knew why it's so darn cold. I hear the Weather Bureau back in New York has some really good folks working on understanding the weather. I wish I could land a job there. Live in New York, understand the weather…"

Anne's jaw started to drop, slightly parting her mouth. To fill the gap, she took a sip of the scotch, which was now just melted ice cube water. She leaned forward and asked earnestly, "Are you serious?"

"Are you joking me?" he replied enthusiastically. "Think

how valuable you would be in elevator conversations around the world! What cooler job is there than actually being able to forecast the weather?"

The tip of Anne's tongue found the ice cube water on her top lip, tasted it while she waited to pause for dramatic effect. She smiled at the inside-joke that only she will get, and responded, "Well what about controlling it?"

* * *

Anne and Chaucer have now reached the lull in their conversation, that pleasant pause where you can just enjoy someone else's company for a while on this otherwise solitary path through life. Chaucer has found a glass of water on the table and a candle, and is staring at it, intently, silently.

"You still there?" Anne jokes.

He continues to stare at the glass, taking the question in and letting it settle like tea leaves in a glass of hot water before replying. "It's just so beautiful. I love candlelight. Just watching a little flame dance its merry way into and out of existence, this perfect little non-matter that doesn't go anywhere, tethered to its place by the wick that gives it life. How can you not be fascinated by it?"

Anne leans in to try to see what Chaucer sees. Through the glass, the corners of the ice cubes curve gently and let the light echo its crystal. The cubes look so soft and warm, even though she knows they are frigid and firm to the touch. They look weightless there in the water. The water looks thick, taking on form as the distorter of light. The flame dances and shifts with the invisible wind. Anne marvels, the way some people marvel at Monet's haystacks.

They are both silently staring at an ordinary tea light, when Anne feels a hand squeeze her shoulder through the thick padding of Chaucer's suit jacket. Gale has arrived, seemingly out of the blue. "Hey kiddo, have you been here the whole time?" They establish that Gale arrived about an hour earlier, having had a terrible time finding a taxi, and spent most of the time networking with her American Embassy connections. "Sorry I didn't get a chance to come by sooner. Word has it that they are actually trying to kick us out. Midnight has struck and everyone is going to turn into a pumpkin." She briefly introduces herself to Chaucer as "Gale who works with Anne." Chaucer takes out a business card from his pocket, just with his name, phone number and email on it – no company name or job title – and says to Anne, "I forgot to give you my card. Do you have one too?" Anne explains that they haven't had a chance to get them printed yet, sorry.

"You know, Anne, I never got to ask what you are actually doing here in Midland," he says trying to fill in the blanks.

"Yeah," Anne answers, stalling, "when I figure that out, I'll let you know." She smiles but realizes that he's still waiting for the real answer. "Gale and I are here doing research on the Wall. Had I realized how cold it would be up there, I would've volunteered for the Gulf of Mexico project," she adds glibly. "But let me give you my number," she says drawing a small notebook from her bag. "I'd be really interested to find out more about the programs you are writing. I miss writing code."

Chaucer replies surprised, "You can write code?"

"Of course," she says lightly, "can't everyone these days?"

"Indeed. Well let's see," he says looking at his watch,

"it's almost midnight. Gale, looks like you are right that they are getting us to leave. The bars around here all have to close as well. So looks like it's a night." Then looking up at Anne asks, "What's your schedule like later this week?"

Chaucer and Anne find a common date (Friday), confirm location and time, verify that they have each other phone numbers and queue up for the coat check. She hands her ticket in, and suddenly remembers she is still wearing Chaucer's suit jacket. She slips it off her shoulders, turning around to him, behind her. "I almost forgot to give this back. Thanks," she adds softly.

"You sure you don't want to keep it on until you get home? It's cold outside. You can give it back to me on Friday."

Anne considers. "Well it is good insurance that you won't stand me up…" she muses almost to her herself, "but yeah, I think I'll make it from curb to cab and cab to curb without turning into a block of ice." He shrugs his pre-warmed jacket on, and then reaches across the counter to grab the ladies' coats, helping each to put theirs on, before escorting them to the (very welcome) taxi rank. Anne and Gale say quick goodbyes to Chaucer on the frosty sidewalk before taking refuge in the heated cab. As soon as the door closes, Gale eggs on Anne to tell all, saying "So… Who was he? He's a cutie!"

"Yes, yes he is. And get this: his dream is to work for the Weather Bureau in the Controls department!"

"You told him about the Controls department!" Gale cuts in mortified.

"No, of course not. That's classified. I didn't even tell him that we are on assignment from the Central Order. All he knows is that I'm researching why they built the Wall and have a curiosity about its impact on the weather. But I'm really interested to see what his programs are all about. It would kill me if he is wasting his talent replicating work already done by the Weather Bureau. And maybe if his stuff is good enough, we can help him get a job on our project…"

"Whoa honey," Gale laughs, "slow down there. Go out to dinner on Friday. If there's no chemistry but he's got a sharp tack, then I'm fine having you interview him for a slot on our research team. Just make sure you know what kind of relationship you want with him. I don't want drama." Gale sank back in her seat. "Unless you also promise me some good gossip."

* * *

It was Friday. Anne leaned over Chaucer's shoulder to see the screen better. They had decided to meet at his place before dinner, so he could show her the programs he started working on. She hadn't indicated this was part of a job interview, because she wasn't sure it was.

His programs were beautiful. They were organized perfectly, completely easy to read and understand. You could see the questions laid out like railroad ties in front of you, his way of thinking direct and to the point, his answers organized and efficient. There were no errant or redundant lines of code. And it produced astounding results.

The first program predicted the weather in Midland City the next day. It took in live weather data feeds from around Midland, crunched them, and spit out an anticipated cloud pattern over the city as well as temperature charts for the following day's weather. He showed the output of the previous day's simulation and compared it against actual satellite images from Midland's space agency website of how the weather turned out. Not perfect, but so close she wondered whether he was making this up with faked screen shots. So she asked for a printout of tomorrow's forecast so she could check if the prediction worked. He was happy to oblige, completely confident that it would work again (it did), though he admitted he was still working on the bugs.

The second program was an attempt at longer-term forecasting over a larger area. It wasn't at a stage that produced any output yet. But he was taking her through the code, the parts that he had written and the parts he had only outlined, explaining his thought process. She was incredibly impressed. She hoped for a few moments that he wouldn't be as charming as he had been at the ball. She wanted him on her team, in both senses, but Gale had warned her to avoid drama. Could she possible date him if they worked together? Dating a colleague was unthinkable in New York; maybe rules were different here in Midland?

They were already an hour late for their dinner reservation, but while Anne went to use Chaucer's bathroom (did he clean it particularly for her or was he always that neat?), he had called ahead and made sure they still had a table for two. He yanked a bottle of imported white wine from his fridge; he chose this place in part because it was a BYOB, and Midland City restaurants didn't have the greatest wine lists. He met Anne at the door, just in time to help her with her coat. "You look great," he said opening the door for her.

"Thanks," she replied, smiling. "Shall we?"

They walked just a few blocks to Chaucer's go-to Italian restaurant, famed for its tragically bad pizzas and fantastic pastas. They ordered bruschetta and pasta and corked the wine. Chaucer poured and proposed a toast "to strangers in a strange land."

As he was still putting his white cloth napkin on his lap, Chaucer began asking Anne, "So, what are you doing here in Midland anyway?"

Anne knew this was coming, of course, but still didn't know how to answer. She didn't want to lead with business, but now he had forced her hand. She couldn't recruit him if he didn't know what the job was after all.

So she told him: that she was sent over by "some people in New York" to get the Midlanders to take down the Third Great Wall, or at least part of it, since it had stopped the wind all over the world. That she would need to understand their reason for building it in the first place and was not finding any straight answers. Something was being lost in translation, and it wasn't the fault of the interpreter. These people just thought differently. That Wall wasn't just a wall to them.

"I've hit a brick wall" she threw out, cringing just a little, until Chaucer laughed. She laughed too.

"I knew they were up to something," Chaucer interjected, waving a crust of bruschetta, "and I'm determined to find out what."

"What do you think it is?" Anne asked. "Where does that Wall go anyway?"

Chaucer finished swallowing the crust and cleared his mouth with a sip of the wine before trying to answer. "I'm not really sure. But you know when you left the US, how people joked, 'So you're going to end of the world now, aren't you!' And you laughed thinking, 'No it's not the end of the world, it's just another country, though maybe a bit colder.' Well, I'm beginning to think that this is the end of the world. And whatever that Wall is heading towards, maybe it's on the next one."

He could tell that Anne was skeptical, so he tried a different tact. "I mean, think about the greatest man-made objects in the world – the pyramids, temples, cathedrals, tombs, Stonehenge. They are all bridges to another world in some way, maybe to God or the afterlife. Some people suspect they are ways of communicating with extraterrestrials, people from other planets. Is it so strange to think that Midlanders are building something to bridge to another world as well?"

There was something about how Chaucer spoke, a lack of zealousness, a certain calm, which made everything he said sound convincing. There was something in his tone that convinced her that she could learn a lot from him. Man, she thought, I hope I can get this guy to join our team. Not only did he have all the technical skills – his programs were duly impressive and his way of explaining them distinguished him from the usual technobabble geeks she'd worked with in the past – but he seemed truly passionate about the Wall.

He seemed to have the beginnings of some answers too. Answers for questions that no one was willing to give her. She had been there, at the Wall, asking where it led, squinting through the frigid air to see if she could discern a destination, and was getting nowhere. But maybe he knew, or had a clue, or could at least point them in the right direction. What if they *were* building a bridge to someplace completely different, another society, another world?

"Do you think they'll get there, wherever they're going? Or that they already have?"

He answered, "Well, you yourself told me about their

half-life method of project planning. You know how it goes, if you have a certain distance to cross, and everyday cover half the distance that's left, you'll never get there. I think they are getting close, but they'll never get there. Not 100%."

"So why try? What are they hoping to accomplish?"

"Anne, aren't some things worth it even if they aren't perfect? Like, what's a good example," he searched the room with his eyes, "hmm, everything!" Chaucer now for the first time deployed what Anne will come to recognize as his go-to facial expression, the YouTube Cat Grin: he squeezes back his cheek muscles, fully revealing both rows of perfectly straight teeth, while raising his eyebrows in anticipation of a reaction. It's a smile that says, "I'm ridiculous but adorable, no?" which he has used since childhood when asking for forgiveness or a favor, or after a bad pun (which is often).

He held the cartoon grin until Anne eventually finally smiled too and said that he's right – there are a lot of things that worth pursuing even if it's clear it won't be perfect. "What would life be without its flaws?" she contributed. "Adds character, you know."

"Right," he nodded. "Like no one is ever in the perfect relationship. You'll never fully be able to connect with someone so that they understand everything you are thinking, or they love you as fully as you love yourself, seeing the world with your eyes. But even so, that doesn't mean we never try, right? My mom always told me, 'Chaucer, if you reach for the stars, you'll at least make the mountaintops.'"

Anne's eyes dropped to the candle dancing on their table, unable to mask the grin that is starting to seep out.

"What?" he egged her to divulge her thoughts. "Come

on, you don't agree?"

She watched the candle for a while longer, and suddenly looked straight into his, her face suddenly serious. "No, Chaucer, it's just that I'm in a pickle. See, my research team, i.e. me and Gale, we would be interested in having you work with us. To help pin down how the Wall is causing the winds to stop. We think you are insightful and your analytical mind would perfectly complement my delivery drive and Gale's political intuition. But—"

"Wait wait wait," Chaucer interrupted. "Gale hasn't even met me, except for a few seconds at the ball. And I still don't really know what you do, or who you work for."

"Okay, by 'we' I meant 'I'," Anne admitted, "but Gale trusts my judgment when it comes to people. As for what I do, I can't really talk about that until you are fully vetted and sign the appropriate confidentiality stuff. But trust me, once you find out who exactly in New York we report to, you would regret turning down this opportunity." Anne explained the job a little bit more: the requirements in terms of hours, compensation and benefits, what the background check process would be like – that his family and recent roommates would be contacted and so on – and emphasized that he would have to be extremely discrete about whom he worked on this project with. She told him that any software he wrote would become the property of the employer, so he couldn't reuse his own code later. But she was confident it would be a good line on his resume for future work if he wanted to go into something more lucrative. She told him that he, like Anne and Gale, would have an incredible amount of liberty in deciding how they would spend their days, and even when to go back to New York. That it would give him access to the people he needed to talk to about modeling the weather interruptions caused by the Wall. That it would give him the computational resources he didn't have on his own computer, and an unparalleled professional network to consult. That basically, it was an offer he couldn't refuse.

Anne was a professional salesperson, and Chaucer was sold. "Sign me up for the frisking!" he exclaimed.

Anne buried her head in her hands in exaggerated agony, "You had to put it that way, didn't you?"

"I thought you'd be happy that I will be working with you."

"Of course I'm happy about that," Anne answered looking at him. "It just means that now I can no longer try to seduce you."

Chaucer's face became stoically serious, an expression that Anne didn't yet know whether to read as sarcastic or not. "Well then, that plan blew up in my face." Anne asked what plan, to which he coyly replied, "To get the girl, of course."

Anne looked across the table at this man (who would one day successfully propose to her one predictably cloudless night). "You're joking, right."

Chaucer cracked the sarcastic façade and smiled as broadly as possible without going over. "Yes, of course I'm joking. That's not why I want the job. It sounds like a great job." Anne's icy glare had melted a little. Chaucer waited a few beats, and it melted a little more. Anne started forking the penne on her plate. He continued, "But now of course I'll need a new strategy to get you to come home with me. I'm open for suggestions."

Anne quietly sucked her lower lip, still thinking.

"Ok how about this," he proposed. "The two of us sign

a little confidentiality agreement, I take you home with me, and then Gale interviews me for the job later on."

Anne took a good look at him, her penne now motionless on the end of the fork that she was still holding in the air. His brown eyes were just soft enough to be sensitive, strong enough to bear all the hardships that life would throw his way. He had little dimples, no, she saw looking more closely, just one dimple on the right cheek. And the beginning of crow's feet around his eyes. He really was incredibly adorable.

She chewed the penne, still considering. She didn't like going home with guys after a first date, especially not expat men in Midland. She didn't trust them, and intimacy requires trust. Actually she once told me, "Intimacy *is* trust." And there was something about Chaucer, a certain pride that she hadn't yet labelled as cockiness or confidence. If cockiness, she had no interest in swelling his head any more than it already was, in being just another conquest.

But then again, she did want to spend more time with him. Immediately. She wanted to wake up to him the next morning. She would even save money on heating, she reasoned, now really reaching for excuses.

Not getting an answer, he carried on. "I think I have a copy of a confidential contract back at my place, if you want to come by after dinner," he teased, bringing her back to the present.

She stabbed another piece of penne holding back a smile, perhaps out of propriety, perhaps out of indecision. "Come now," she said still looking down at her plate, "I'm not that easy."

"No sex," he renegotiated, "I promise. Just hot cocoa and a movie. It doesn't even have to be a romantic comedy;

it can be an action movie. How about Jackie Chan?" Again the go-to YouTube Cat Grin. "My hot cocoa even has mini marshmallows. Mm?"

She was still looking at the plate, trying to spear a cherry tomato with a fork. The tomato kept dodging the fork tongs, and she ended up chasing it around the plate.

She finally stabbed it. "Okay, but I don't want to get your expectations up, Mr. Chaucer. I have high standards. I don't just jump into bed with a guy just because he is adorable and charming and brilliant, and it's crazy cold outside."

Chaucer happily twirled some pasta around his fork. "I can be patient. So does that mean that you'll come over and watch a movie with me?"

"Yes, it's a deal. I do love a good mini marshmallow."

Outside the restaurant, he raised one hand into the icy night air to hail a taxi, and with the other, took her hand.

There was something about holding hands that moved Anne more than anything. She told me once that when you are holding hands walking down the street, people don't see you as individuals, but as a couple, a joined entity. "It just seems like a very advanced thing to do in a relationship, much more real and sophisticated than anything that happens in private."

So when he took her hand, she jumped a bit but didn't pull away; it was cold outside, and it was so easy to be with him anyway. She was willing to let him lead the relationship for a while.

They got back to his apartment, where the heat had been thankfully left on. Chaucer excused himself to "the little boy's room" and then the kitchen, where he put a kettle on for the mini-marshmallow hot cocoa. Anne was instructed to rummage through the DVD collection in the meanwhile, but instead was drawn to the square window overlooking the apartment complex.

Midland architecture was built for function, not form. Midland apartment buildings tend to be rather tall, twenty to thirty stories. Parking lots are underground, though cars here are rare since the country is still "developing." Unlike New York, where each building is designed to be distinctive, here buildings are built in identical clusters. Chaucer's apartment complex had a dozen buildings that all looked exactly alike, though of different heights and with different interior arrangements. All were made of grey concrete with perfectly square windows, evenly spaced both horizontally and vertically, like a piece of graph paper.

Anne stood in front of one of Chaucer's three square windows (two in the living room, one in the bedroom), and looked across the street. The sun had set hours ago, and most people were home this Friday night. People in Midland don't have the sense of privacy that we have in New York, so most of the curtains were open. There was a red velvet one on the ground floor that was closed, but you could still see the light bleed through it. In the apartment next door, a pair of teenagers were sitting on the floor, examining a board game. In the window next to it, she saw the feet of two men and a woman under a dining room table. There was a bowl of bread next to it, the thick black stuff that they bake here and only here in Midland, which has the most amazingly moist density, perfect when toasted with a little butter. The windows didn't have bars, she realized. She wondered if they have burglaries.

She looked up at the penthouses, where she imagined the wealthiest folk live. Indeed, on the ceiling was a stunning crystal chandelier, brightly lit. On the intricate wallpaper directly above it were black soot marks, speaking of a time when this chandelier used real candles. When was that, she wondered, a century ago? Or did they not have electricity here until much more recently, maybe just a decade or two?

Directly across from her were a string of apartments with boldly painted walls, each of a solid color, so the windows looked like something from a Lego mansion: blue, red, yellow, purple. Nothing was hanging on the walls, since the walls themselves seemed to be the theme of the apartment. One room had a light on behind a frosted glass, and she guessed that the inhabitant was taking a shower. A moment later, the light went off, and then in the purple room she saw a woman about her age in a towel walk over to the dresser and rummage through the top drawer. She pulled out something Anne couldn't see and then walked to the closet. She was looking seriously for something to wear, pouting with dissatisfaction. She walked back to the dresser, ducking behind the bed to do so. Anne could only see the top of her head when a cup of hot cocoa appeared in front of her.

"Anything interesting?" Chaucer asked. Anne pointed out the sites and directed Chaucer's eyes to the woman in the towel in the purple window across the way.

"Ah yes, I've seen her before. In the past two weeks, she's had a string of different men come pick her up around dinner time. None have ever been in her apartment though. She mostly wears pretty trendy clothing, so I had thought she must be in fashion, but one morning I saw her getting on the subway in a normal business suit."

Anne looked up at him over her shoulder, teasing him for being a "stalker" and then they both stood there, watching the windows across the way. In her Memory, Anne wondered what they look like, this couple in the window holding mugs of hot mini-marshmallow cocoa, and what story someone might tell about them. From the street, she thought, you would see the lamp light cast a yellow hue against the ceiling on him, just a few inches taller than her, standing right behind her. She could feel the warmth coming from his body and smell his crisp aftershave. She wanted to lean back into him, dissolve against the warmth of his chest. She imagined herself with him as seen from the street, morphing into one unit. But she wasn't sure she was ready to be part of a couple just yet.

The stars were out now, somehow through the smog. They felt closer here. Chaucer pointed out Orion's Belt and the North Star, and a satellite wandering through the heavens. He followed it with his finger, his arm reaching up over her shoulder, following its arc through the sky until it went behind a building.

He used the satellite's disappearance as a cue to ask about the movie selection. He went to the rack and picked up *When Harry Met Sally*, throwing that on what he called the "danger" pile. "If we watch anything that romantic, you'll be all over me by the end of the movie, so choose that at your own risk," he joked.

They agreed on *The Simpsons Season 8*, and Chaucer brought a plush blanket over to the couch. As he put his left arm around her, keeping his hot cocoa in his right hand, he asked, "Is this okay?"

She snuggled into him a little and said reassuringly, "It's great. Best portable heater in Midland."

They watched an episode or two this way, and Chaucer seemed to be really enjoying it. He laughed at the jokes, and occasionally looked at Anne to check that she was enjoying it too. They watched another couple episodes; at the end of each one, he asked "Do you want to watch another one?"

"Sure, why not?"

Anne was stalling, trying to decide what to do with this man. As Bart was skateboarding off with some plutonium for the fourth time that night, Anne asked out of the blue, "Why are you here?"

Chaucer might have been taken off guard, but I don't think Anne does a very good job of disguising her "deep thought" face. I'm sure Chaucer could tell she wasn't really watching the Simpsons that closely. "Why are *you* here?" he asked back.

She thinks for a good time, letting *The Simpsons* theme song fill the void. After a while she found the words. "I came here to figure out why I came here." She lets that hang for a while, unsure what else to say, and then asked, "So what about you?"

"I'm just a moth. I always fly toward the light. And there's a big spotlight on Midland now."

"How long are you planning to stay?"

Chaucer hesitated a moment and then threw out, "Like you, I'll be ready to leave when I have figured out why I came." The theme song continued to chirp along. Bart wrote "I will not waste chalk" on the blackboard, and Anne and Chaucer laughed. "So when do you have to go back to New York for your job?"

"Same as you: when I'm done, however long that takes."

Chaucer took in a short breath, held it for a second, and said uncomfortably, "I know you have all kinds of confidentiality issues, but really, what do you do back in New York?"

Anne smiled, thankful at the way he phrased that question. "To be honest, I took a sabbatical from my usual job in New York for this assignment. I worked at a random energy generation plant called the Windmill, which looks like a dandelion – you may have seen it in pictures. When the wind stopped, they wanted me to come here to see what I could do about it. What about you? Where were you pre-Midland?"

Chaucer smiled, "Well I guess you'll find out soon enough anyway. I used to work for an artificial intelligence company working on social modeling. Basically trying to understand how masses of people think about things. We had a number of government contracts – so I'm used to this whole confidentiality thing – trying to assess the possible outcomes of various foreign policies. Mostly trade stuff, since that's a field that lends itself to numbers."

"So why'd you leave?"

"As I said, the tech boom busted, and people lost some hope in the all-knowing power of computer science. What seemed hot before – run an A.I. model of a policy – turned into sci-fi mumbo-jumbo, something from Asimov's *Foundation* series, not worth a real investment. We weren't cheap either. So some of my colleagues went to Wall Street, to work for hedge funds that were willing to pay big bucks for people who could use technology and brains to predict outcomes. I felt that I was still young enough to explore the world. Midland seemed to have a fascinating culture, which is certainly true. I always believed you cannot learn about a country if you can't speak with the locals, so here I am, learning as much Midlandish as I can, as fast as I can."

Anne turned to face him, pulling her feet on the couch under the blanket and her knees into his lap. She was sitting up now, no longer leaning against the arm that wound around her back. "So you modeled social behavior. Did it work?"

"Oh pretty well, given the appropriately sized question. I could tell you what a hundred people or a million people will do given enough assumptions, but I have a lot of trouble telling you what one or two people will do. I think the interaction between two people, which is what almost all of our relationships are at the end of the day, is one of the most complex and mysterious and beautiful things of all. It frustrated me that I couldn't model it, couldn't really understand it. But maybe that's my fault for leaving literature aside and pursuing computer science."

"Well I'm pretty impressed you can model societies. You have to admit that's pretty cool. Did it work?"

"That depends on whether you believe the world is deterministic. In some ways it is. Or at least humankind is becoming more so. I'll give you an example. There are a lot of people who trade stocks and other things with really transparent prices based on technical indicators. Technical indicators are supposed to be mathematical rules that explain human behavior; a trend will continue for so long and reverse when the stock has lost *x* percent of its price, or whatever. The funny thing is, the more popular the technical indicators become, the more people use them to trade, and so they become self-fulfilling prophecies.

"Or think about all the rules and customs we have, about when to shake hands or which side of the street to walk on, or even when to look at your watch. We have more and more rules that govern our behavior, taking some of the randomness out of play. I don't buy the 'free will versus determinism' debate. It's a spectrum, and now we are sliding

– although very slowly – down that path toward determinism. We'll never get there, just like the Midlanders will never finish building their Wall. But we're working on it."

"What if that's it?" she asked. "What if that *is* what they are doing? What if the Midlanders are trying to build a Wall, Bridge, whatever, to 'Order.' Trying to make everything more predictable."

Chaucer paused, considering carefully what she was saying, then replied, "That would explain why the winds stopped. Maybe the ending of the winds isn't some sort of strange side-effect. Maybe it's just the first test, the first stage. Maybe the Midland government wants to see if they can order the weather itself. It's not inconceivable that that Wall is like some Tower of Babel, to reach the next state of being, immune from floods and weather, when everything is predictable, and everything just works right. Some kind of perfect future."

Anne was silent for a moment thinking. "Shit," she said abruptly. "Sorry, for the language. It's just that my job may have gotten a whole lot harder."

* * *

They watched one more episode of *The Simpsons*, and Anne went to the restroom. She had too much on her mind, and somehow the mood was broken. Maybe it was *The Simpsons*, or the realization that she may well have to launch something akin to a religious war to get Midland to start the winds again. Maybe it was that it was already 2 a.m. and she was really tired. But it was cold outside, and she really didn't feel like going out again. Maybe she could sleep on the couch, under that incredibly warm blanket. That way she'd still get to wake up to Chaucer the next day, no commitment, no complications.

She came out of the bathroom, and Chaucer was back in the kitchen, washing up the mugs. She came over and leaned against the counter. "Would it be alright if I crashed on your couch tonight, Chaucer?" she asked.

"Of course, it's really comfortable. I've slept there myself when friends have come through Midland." He didn't seem disappointed, which surprised Anne. She realized that when he said "no sex just cocoa" he was being straight with her.

"Great. What time do you have to get up tomorrow?" she asked.

"Oh, I usually get up when the sun comes up. Habit. But tomorrow I can be all yours, so whatever time you want to get up is fine by me."

"Yea," she said clapping to herself, "I get to spend tomorrow with you too? That's great. Okay, I'm going to wash up and take my contacts out."

"Do you need solution or a case?" he asked.

"Oh no, I brought that with me," she said, heading to the living room to get her purse.

"You were planning to spend the night?" he asked, amused.

"Hey, guys carry condoms just in case. Women carry tampons just in case. And blind people, we carry contact cases."

Having finished washing the mugs, he dried his hands off on a towel and then started walking towards his bedroom. Anne had gone into the bathroom, leaving the door open, and started taking her contacts out. Chaucer handed her a set of men's flannel pajamas and a clean towel. "Thanks," she said in Midlandish.

Chaucer replied with the Midland form of "you're welcome" which translates literally as "some other time." When Anne was safely on the couch, under the blanket, she gave him a thumbs up and a cheery, "Goodnight!" Chaucer shut the light off and went to his room to go to bed.

* * *

That night Anne slept extremely well. The couch was indeed soft and comfortable, long enough to extend fully on, and as she would come to learn, wide enough for two people to fall asleep on. Just before she woke up that first Saturday morning at Chaucer's, she had a dream, which I've gotten to see through her Memory file.

In it, she sees the apartment from outside her window, the way that you or I might see it in the File. It zooms in on the square identical windows of his building as the sun's rays flow inside, past the chirping of birds which sounds recorded even in the dream, and through the substance-less glass of Chaucer's apartment. We hear now a toilet flush, and the running water of a sink coming from behind the door to Chaucer's room. Without interruption this sound of running water accompanies a sloshing pair of slippers across the hall and into the kitchen, where it is joined by the melodic clink of ceramic dishes. A snap snap snap of a gas stove with an electric spark going off and then the crack-sizzle of an egg on a hot frying pan. Suddenly the smell of bacon arrives, and Anne feels herself in this dream sinking deeper into a poofy white bed like that that she will one day share with Chaucer in their home. She hears a voice much deeper than Chaucer's, older maybe, or with some greater authority, like Charlton Heston in *The Ten Commandments*. For a moment, Chaucer (someone she knows to be Chaucer though it doesn't look like him) appears with creased lines on his weathered face behind a white, wind-torn beard at Anne's side, smiling gently at her. He strokes her still-sleeping head from her temples down to the ledge at the base of her skull, where her brain drops off into an abrupt end. He takes his time. Twice he runs his hand from her temples through her slightly greasy hair to the nape of her neck, while the sizzling eggs continue to solidify on the distant stove.

"It'll be alright," she murmurs absently to the Chaucer in her dreams. "We do find out where we are going in the end, right?"

He pets her one more time and then pushes himself up effortlessly and disappears out of the dream, which now backs out of the room and into the Midlands outside the window. Somehow though the sound of the eggs cooking persists as if the sound controller forgot to turn off the microphone, and we fly with Anne through the Technicolor background of a spring day that she imagines might be what Midland looks like in spring: saturated greens and blues, with cartoon birds singing from stylized trees. She is filled with a sense of peace and calm, and of completion. A wind comes and grabs her shoulder, rocking her gently and soothing any fears that the future would be less than perfect, assuring her that it may be even so perfect she wouldn't mind if things stopped changing. The wind rocks hard, now is pulling at her arm, and when she opens her eyes to look at it, discovers a hand.

Chaucer is crouched before her, his twenty-six-year-old

face beaming with more light than sunshine streaming through the window. "Hey Miss Anne, breakfast is ready."

* * *

The eggs continue to sizzle, and Anne assumes she is still in a dream. She doesn't have her contacts in, and the world is blurry, and the couch is extremely comfortable. She begins to realize that maybe the dream was a dream, and she clings on to pleasant ignorance for just a few moments. Chaucer is patient. His hand finds its way to her sleep-scrambled hair and pushes it back behind her ear, to the nape of neck. Twice. Anne decides that reality might be better than the dream, and stirs her vocal cords with a groggy, "Hey there."

She gets up and excuses herself to the bathroom. She washes her hands and as the water splashes over her palms, it catches the light in such a way that rainbows splatter down into the sink. She washes her hands way too long, watching the magic of the colors in this amazing sink. She unscrews her contact case and pulls her eye open to insert the first one, looking through her blurry eyes at the mirror. Over the ledge of the contacts, as she would tell me later with prophetic awe, she sees a younger version of herself looking back, questioning. Her face wakes up and cracks the kind of smile you see a mother give a daughter – proud, satisfied, encouraging. She finishes putting the contact in, certain she was on the other side of the mirror that she saw as a kid.

Her vision corrected, Anne steps out and looks around the apartment in daylight. It's a really nice bright place, and she understands why Chaucer normally wakes up with the sun. He's already laid out the eggs, bacon, coffee and some (fresh squeezed?) orange juice on the table. Anne exclaims surprise and appreciation, which Chaucer happily accepts. They decide that they'll wander around one of the parks today. They have some half-awake banal conversation about the neighborhood and location of various sites in Midland City, and then Anne follows Chaucer into the kitchen to wash up.

I think it's clear that Anne has a thing for men doing dishes. Or just dishes in general. I asked her about this one day, and she confessed: doing dishes is a very concrete and straightforward way of getting something done, of adding order to the world. It's cleanliness that you can see, completion and a simple task. Maybe the sound of water is soothing to her as well. There's something particularly wonderful about guys doing dishes. And making the bed. A few weeks earlier when Anne was complaining to Gale about being single, she said, "I just need a guy, you know, someone to make the bed, do the dishes."

"You don't need a boyfriend," Gale replied, "you need a cleaner."

Whatever the reason, Anne tends to have a mushy spot for guys in the kitchen doing dishes. Over the course of their relationship, Chaucer and Anne would often do the dishes together, no matter how few dishes there were or how small the sink was. They both enjoyed doing the dishes themselves and with each other. Maybe for the same reasons. Like some acknowledgment of their shared responsibility in the mess that the kitchen was in, and a shared sense of dedication to making the world a slightly better place.

So it may come as no surprise that this morning, after

Anne and Chaucer walk together into the kitchen, hands full of dirty plates and coffee mugs and orange juice glasses, after Chaucer takes the sponge and adds some soap and turns on the faucet, that just as he turns to see what Anne is doing, she leans forward and kisses him. It's one of those familiar pecks, her hands still full with dishes, that says thank you, or hello, or good morning. I also don't know why Anne thinks they skipped over a dramatic nervous first kiss into this one of familiarity.

Maybe you and I weren't surprised, but Chaucer was. Watching the File again I realized the whole date, he's been slightly tense; now as she puts the dishes in the sink, suddenly all the muscles in his shoulders and around the base of his neck just completely relax. He is standing there with soap dripping off both hands and the water running into the metal sink, grinning. "Cool," he says assessing the situation. "That works."

* * *

Over the next few months, Anne would end up spending most evenings with Chaucer, either out, or at his place, or (less frequently) at hers. One piece of laundry at a time, within three months she effectively had moved into his apartment. There was no defining-the-relationship talk; it just happened.

Sometimes they went out together with Gale or other friends they'd made. Some nights they worked their way through Chaucer's *Simpsons* collection. What surprised me was that, in time, Anne's guilt at "wasting time" watching TV dissolved. She had reframed it as spending time with him.

On Saturday mornings, they often took their coffees in mugs down to the park, just to sit and watch people. Or up to the hillside, to walk and watch birds fly from branch to branch. On weekday mornings, when the dawn light started creating a bright warm spot on their bed, she would just lie there, feeling the warmth, watching his stubble growing on his sleeping face. She could watch him breathe for hours.

I have poured through the File to give you some key dramatic moment in their relationship, something exciting to tell you. The fireworks, the brutal argument, the yelling or tears, the spark of passion, the tension. I have searched many of the records, but even with the help of the ever-improving File search techniques, have not found anything particularly notable. I've asked Anne for a clue, a date for that moment when she fell in love in with him, that moment when they became a couple. She shrugged and scratched her head. "Always?" she replied. Did she really not know?

Thanks to the File and some help from my friend in Data Analysis, I did find the first time she said the words "I love you" to Chaucer. She was on the phone with him one night after returning from a conference. "Ok, see you tomorrow, I love you," she said lightly, really in passing. "Love you too," he replied. So what do you think – does that count?

You know from my earlier analysis of her relationship with Derek back in New York that I don't think there's much point in trying to define when their relationship became 51% or 78% or 99% real. But for what it's worth, the clearest indication to me that this relationship was a keeper was on a call that Anne had with her sister, just a few weeks after the Embassy Ball. "It's just so easy to be with him," Anne told her. "I can just be myself without having to think too much." Easy. What a beautiful word.

So you won't be surprised to find them, for instance, one Sunday morning in a local park, watching an old man do Tai Chi, slowly. Painfully slowly. Chaucer had started learning Tai Chi when he first moved to Midland now nearly a year before, and Anne was starting it too. She'd continue to do Tai Chi it well beyond her time in Midland, both as she recovered from her eventual knee injury, and beyond; she even persuaded me to try it a few months ago.

I don't know if you've ever tried this ancient martial art, but it's much harder than it looks. You move so slowly and correctly that you are constantly straining your muscles all the time. Normally your body stays mostly in equilibrium, and you stand in a such a way that your muscles don't really have to strain. You don't spend much time in transition.

But in Tai Chi, you spend most of the time in transition. Equilibrium moments pass as just that – moments – indistinguishable from the moments of transition. I was talking to a colleague of mine at the Central Order's Economics division (one of the few friends of mine in that division actually) and he explained to me his great frustration with economic theory: it starts with equilibrium and works most of its models as modifications from that assumption. But life isn't mostly equilibrium points with moments of transition, like an hour-long movie made of a dozen frozen frames. It's mostly transition; equilibrium points are momentary blips. Economics in the real world is Tai Chi, not walking. Slow and continuous change.

Perhaps that's why Tai Chi is so popular here in Midland. Midland history is the same as history everywhere – a series of events created by people and strung together by retrospect – but it is told differently here. Exhibits are labeled by periods rather than dates, even though few people know when those periods happened, exactly. It's a concept of time passage as an evolution and a continuum. Partially the story has been told that way to polish over the crags and drop-offs in the history, the turbulent bits where the country wasn't a country anymore. But even then, when it was shattered shards on the floor, even when provinces were warring with each other and a shared sense of culture was demolished, even those are lumped into the sense of History that this country's present relies on. A sense of evolution, development, and patient change.

America got hooked on martial arts, the dramatic bits like smashing wood blocks and the knockout crane kick, taking on five enemies at once with flying swords and ninja blades. It would. American martial arts movies appeal to our young sensibility, our sense of immediate and possible change. That life moves fast, and always has. That change erupts. That companies disrupt. That progress happens right exactly now.

But watching the old man doing Tai Chi over in Midland through Anne's eyes, you see a different sensibility form. Chaucer has been living in Midland long enough to know to be patient. Anne is learning, and by the end of this story I hope will be mostly there; or at least half-way there, as the Midlanders would have it.

What amazes me is how long this new Anne can sit there, watching. Finding beauty in ordinary things.

The happy couple continues through the park, leaving the Tai-Chi man behind still going. They now are watching kids holding kites. Waiting for the wind to take them. There won't be a breeze today, or tomorrow, but the kids run around still, trailing their kites in tow, hoping that they can fly them without the wind.

Anne sees a vendor on the corner selling kites and ice cream, and grabbing Chaucer by the hand, drags him over to serve as translator. He asks the kite seller how business has been, and he replies that kids don't seem to be buying as many kites. They are buying more ice cream though. "Kids are resilient like that," he says, without irony.

Anne and Chaucer sit down on the hill, enjoying the hint of spring, and the sunlight and the silence of the Stills that are falling over Midland now too. The way the clouds hang there, motionless sometimes, or no, now that they have some time and can really watch them, just slowly moving across the blue face of the sky.

The untouchable sun continues its timeless march around the globe, drawn by the wheels of Apollo's chariot. That's something that won't change, Anne conjectures. Maybe, she realizes on that plot of grass, she should have gotten into solar energy instead.

* * *

The paper slip came in under her front door. It said, in English, "UNPAID TAX FINE" with a forebodingly large number of Midland dollars written in a box in red. Everything else was in Midlandish.

Anne showed it to Chaucer when he came over for dinner that evening. Chaucer's Midlandish was impressive – he was a natural at languages and had been studying with tutors for nearly a year. He looked up some of the more obscure and bureaucratic words in his dictionary and gave Anne as close a translation as he could: apparently, she hadn't submitted her tax returns, which here were due quarterly, and thus had been fined for tax avoidance.

Getting into trouble with the Midland government was the last thing she needed. Forget the consequences for her political outreach and role in representing the Central Order on a diplomatic dispute about the Wall, a more pragmatic concern was her visa: Midland had extremely tight and opaque visa policies. They could readily deny extending her rolling six-month visa if they didn't like her anymore. She needed to sort this out ASAP.

She called Gale who recommended she go to the Midland Assessment Courts in downtown Midland City. Gale had never been herself, but explained that in Midland, the court system and the administration system were much more closely interlinked than in the US.

Anne was used to the court buildings in downtown Manhattan: large, imposing stone buildings, raised up on stairs and lined with relief sculptures. The concept of "justice" echoed that: solid, fundamental, permanent. As Anne's taxi approached the Courts, she looked out the window expecting to see the same.

Instead they approached a large semicircular plaza, slanted toward a building at one end, the way that ancient Roman theatres were slanted to the stage. Anne estimated the plaza could hold a thousand people and wondered if they ever used them for mass assemblies, high profile cases, or class action suits. The building at the end was two-stories tall, and also shaped like a semi-circle. Together with the plaza, it formed a perfect circle. Unlike the stone facades of New York courts, the wall facing the plaza was made of clear glass and could be seen through easily. As Anne stepped out of the taxi and into the midst of the plaza, she saw that the interior walls of the Courts were lined with mirrors, reflecting the insides of the building and the plaza outside. It looked more like an airport than a hall of justice. There was no privacy anywhere.

She entered the glass-walled building and asked the (gratefully) English-speaking receptionist where she should go to dispute a tax fine. He provided her with a five-page form and a pencil and gestured for her to sit in one of the many tablet-arm desks that were scattered around the reception area. Thankfully the form was in English.

Anne thought it strange to fill in a form in pencil. All forms in the US required black or blue pen, to prevent modifications later. Perhaps, she said, this would only be used briefly?

The questions on the form were even stranger. While the first page was straightforward, asking her for her name, address, and tax ID number, the next four pages had room for longer essays. The first asked her to explain why she had not paid the fine, and then had an empty box. She wrote that she didn't know that she had to pay the tax, as she was a foreigner who had recently moved to Midland.

The next page asked her to list all parties affected by her violation. Here she was confused. What was this question looking for? She got up from her desk chair and went back to the receptionist. He explained that in Midland, all judgments would be made on behalf of those affected. One of the primary roles of the courts was to confirm that the set of stakeholders was fair and inclusive, and that their claims on their impact were reasonable. He recommended she spend some time thinking about all the people and organizations that would be impacted, positively and negatively, by her violation and the fine levied against her.

Anne returned to her desk chair and thought. She made a small dot for a bullet point, and then wrote next to it:

"Anne Kesheen." At least she knew she was affected. Then she added Gale and Chaucer, as they would be impacted if she were in violation of the law, especially if Midland invalidated her right to stay in the country. Then the Central Order, for whom she worked, and the Windmill, as her being in the country was essential to the work to restart the wind. And then she added, just to be complete, "The people of the City of New York," who got their power from the Windmill. She considered adding windmills everywhere, but that seemed excessive.

Page three asked her to describe what the impact on the affected parties might be if she was and wasn't fined. She was asked to limit this to parties where the impact would be "attributable and meaningful." She considered.

For herself, whether or not they fined her, she would right away consult a tax accountant and pay her due taxes. She added that she would inform others to consult tax attorneys as well; she wanted to give the authorities the impression that the deterrent effect on other "tax evaders" would be as strong whether she was fined or not. Secondly, if she were fined, she noted that she might lose her visa and therefore her job in Midland.

For Gale and Chaucer, she wrote that they would miss her personally as colleagues and friends. She flipped over the pencil to erase that, thinking it was too personal, but then left it; maybe the courts here weighed the value of relationships in their decisions? She added that they would have to recruit a replacement, which could take months, and that their diplomatic work would be stalled. This naturally brought her to write about the Central Order and the work that they were doing here, and why it was important: clean energy for the citizens of New York City through the power of the winds. This was becoming quite bold and poetic: an image of a soviet statue raising its arm to the heavens flashed into her mind.

At the bottom she added one more bullet: "Citizens of the world." They would be affected by increased political tension and pollution if wind power could no longer replace fossil fuels.

She handed the paper back to the reception desk, who gave her a table stand with a number on it, like cafes sometimes give their customers. The receptionist told her to wait with the number displayed on the table, and someone would be over to see her in a few minutes.

When she sat back in the moveable chair, she had a chance to look around at the place. It was strange being in such an open space to deal with such personal matters. Oddly, there were only a few police officers here. Perhaps they handled criminal cases in a different court?

"Ms. Kesheen?" said a Midland man in a perfect American accent. "May we discuss your case with you? This is Justice Wen and I am Hank, a translator here at the court." Both men were wearing lanyards with hologram photo ID badges on them. Anne was nervous but assumed they were legitimate.

Justice Wen and Hank looked around for an empty chair and pulled them over to form a small circle with Anne's chair. The Justice turned to the translator, and leafed through the application, explaining his comments to him in Midlandish.

Hank explained. "Ms. Kesheen, the Justice complements you on your consideration of the parties involved. He was impressed that a non-Midlander had developed such a thorough list. Most foreigners tend to have shorter lists, of just direct Affectees." He paused to show her the document. "However, you were perhaps a bit too expansive. It suggests here that you only list those parties that have an 'attributable and meaningful' impact as a result of the fine. While Justice Wen understands why you put 'Citizens of the World' and the 'Citizens of New York,' he doubts either would be able to attribute their impact to this fine."

Anne nodded, somewhat puzzled, but happy to have such patient teachers of the local law.

"You did make clear," Hank continued, "that you will pay the tax and encourage others to pay their taxes. That is very helpful to your case. After all, our justice system is a forward-looking one, that makes decisions based on what *will have been* the best punishment. We don't want to cause injury to you, your work or your colleagues, if we can achieve the same result without fining you. Therefore we will take you at your word. We will cancel the fine and strike this case off your record for visa purposes."

Anne gave a huge sigh of relief and smiled. "Thank you very much!" she exclaimed a bit too enthusiastically. "I really appreciate it."

Hank translated her response to Justice Wen. He nodded, still quite serious, and spoke again to Hank. Hank added sternly: "The Justice reminds you that this decision was based on your word in this application. If you breach your word, and do not pay the tax or do not tell others to pay theirs, then your word will no longer be trusted. Rather than just go through this administrative process, where the courts permit you to self-declare who you think is affected and how, next time you will have your word questioned by representatives and experts. It will be much more cumbersome and difficult, and the outcome potentially less agreeable."

Anne stopped smiling and nodded seriously both at Hank and Justice Wen. "Of course," she said, and then added in her limited Midlandish, "I understand."

Justice Wen smiled at her attempt to speak Midlandish, and then marked and signed the papers in pencil and handed them back to Anne. Hank instructed her to take them to the receptionist to make sure the verdict got into the system correctly, and to obtain a receipt she could use if she had any problems in the future with the immigration.

When Anne had finished the paperwork and was leaving the stadium, she finally relaxed. There's always something so frustrating and scary about administrative errors ruining your life. Imagine if she had been fined and kicked out of the country, all because she didn't know she had to pay her taxes! She was really pleased that the process had worked out so quickly and easily, but it had been traumatic nevertheless.

She met up with Chaucer later that day for dinner and recounted her experience. "You got off easy," he remarked, relieved. He shared a story about a fellow American, who had biked through a red light for the second time. The intersection cameras spotted him, and automatically mailed him a ticket. Rather than a fine, though punishment was a "weekend suspension": the government blocked the guy from making any payments between Friday at 8 p.m. and Sunday 8 p.m. The government regulates all the card providers who are required to enforce weekend suspensions. All online shops and services, transportation and nearly all physical shops in Midland only accept digital payments, so most of enforcement is automatic. If you get a weekend suspension, you literally cannot spend money for 48 hours:

no grocery shopping, no transportation, no nights out, no exemptions, not even for pharmacy purchases or heating and electricity. Since some shops still accept cash, the Midland police also publishes each Friday night a list of everyone with a weekend suspension. They say they publish the list so vendors can check it before accepting cash; Chaucer suspected it was also to add public shaming to the punishment.

Chaucer was uncomfortable with the principles of freedom and privacy that weekend suspensions violate, but appreciated that it was one of the most effective ways Midland prevented minor crime. For fun, Chaucer modelled the impact of this technique on behavior (yes, he has a strange definition of fun). He used epidemiolocal methods normally used for viruses (with obscure variables like "the R number") and was surprised to see how much impact weekend suspensions have. They are especially effective among younger people who normally go out on weekends with others – it's both embarrassing and public when someone's been suspended. For more serious crimes, like theft or assault, the government can issue up to six months of weekend suspensions in a row; beyond that, Chaucer explained, Midland researchers found that the negative mental health of social isolation actually increases criminal behavior; people suspended for months start to socialize on weekdays – often with others who are also suspended.

Anne told Chaucer his analysis resonated with the questionnaire: she had been asked to list everyone who would be impacted by both the crime and the punishment.

"Did you include me?" he asked.

Anne looked at him carefully, trying to guess what

answer he wanted. "Of course. I think you would be impacted if I had to leave Midland?" she stated, unable to keep the question mark out of her voice.

"Of course," he replied, "I definitely would. I'd have to leave then too."

* * *

Just before winter was over, Anne learned that there was a ski mountain (hill really) a day trip outside Midland City, and convinced Chaucer to go with her. The previous night, Chaucer had invited her over for dinner to use his new slow cooker. He didn't realize that a slow cooker was really slow, and the two of them ended up eating peanut butter at midnight, and then talking about nothing far after the lights were turned out.

Normally Anne has a ticking clock of productivity built into her conscience. When she is waiting for a friend for three minutes, she pulls out her flashcards to study Midlandish. It bothers her to be wasting any minute that could be spent learning, living, doing, moving. But once she turns the lights off at night, the world of productivity vanishes. With Chaucer, she squanders hours making stupid jokes or half-dreaming comments. Sometimes she says something random, like "I like pandas." Or shares her pre-sleep shutdown process, murmuring "did I charge my phone?" Sometimes it's a comment concerned for Chaucer's welfare, like "are you cold?" As she drifts further, it tends to get more esoteric, like "Why are airplane doors always on the left?" or "which is healthier, canola oil or sunflower oil?" And sometimes she'll crack inane jokes like, "I wish I would stop talking so I could fall asleep" which even Chaucer doesn't respond to – he has the good sense not to encourage her.

Chaucer for his part is a perpetual flirt and will take any motion from Anne in his direction as a come on. So he remains in stand-by mode, half awake, waiting for an invitation to make a move.

Anne and Chaucer's relationship has yet to evolve into a tired one, one that prioritizes sleep above these banal late-night interactions. So at 5:17 a.m. when their alarm went off to get ready for a day on the slopes (or more accurately, the slope), the happy couple was running on empty. But a plan is a plan, and Anne flipped on the lights full force. "Let's get going! It's going to be a beautiful day!" she said, more to herself than to him.

Chaucer shuffled out of bed, and bleary-eyed headed for the coffee maker. They threw on their ski clothes – not that much different from the usual number of layers they would wear in this frigid winter city – and headed to the bus station. They both pretended to sleep on the two-hour ride up to the hill, Anne's head on Chaucer's shoulder, sharing the headset of Anne's iPod.

It had been a while since Anne had snowboarded and the conditions were icy. The boots were relatively new and fit remarkably well though, perhaps because almost no one in Midland snowboarded. The bunny hill was littered with confused sprawling novices of all ages. Anne and Chaucer took one warm up trip down the hill, and then, fearing the crowds more than the conditions, headed up the sole chair lift to the intermediate terrain.

I wish I could pretend that this chairlift was a magical ride, like that one back the first time Anne was learning to snowboard with Flint. That it lofted the happy couple up through the clouds and above the pollution which hovered over grey-brown Midland. That it took them toward the light like a stroll in Dante's *Paradiso*. But no, the top was just as soggy, icy, and dreary as the bottom.

But Anne and Chaucer had woken up early to go, and Anne had great memories of snowboarding. She had assumed, I think, that it was the sport itself and not the mountain or teacher or friends or time in her life that made it so special. I think she figured that anywhere she went snowboarding, even on an icy hill in Midland, would be magical. Especially since she was with an amazing man, with whom she was in love.

Chaucer started to go down first but Anne was a bit more reckless, and quickly outpaced him. The first three runs down this slope were uninteresting. Anne was getting the feel back, listening to her iPod and moving to the music. For a few moments, when Coldplay's "Yellow" came on, she was brought back to California and Flint and the first time she danced into the clouds.

She got to the bottom and waited for Chaucer just ahead of the ski lift line. When he came down, she mocked him for being a slowpoke and then unbuckled her board to shuffle back to the chairlift. The chairlift was on a downward slope, and she found her momentum picking up and heading towards a barricade. She wasn't going much faster than a walking pace, but for some reason, suddenly tried to stop her momentum by putting down her unattached foot. She lost her balance and fell to a twisted stop. Chaucer laughed at her good naturedly. Anne was laughing too at her own sleep-deprived stupidity and tried to stand up.

You can't see her eyes clearly due to her goggles, but at

some point during the process, she has started crying. No, she's still laughing – after all she fell on her butt while waiting on a chairlift line – but she is starting to realize that there is something wrong. That she actually can't stand up. Chaucer shifts over in the line to let others pass and sits down next to Anne to unbuckle his board and help her up.

He has stopped laughing, and asks her directly, sincerely, "Are you okay?"

"Yeah," she lies, perhaps unwittingly, "let me just take my board off." She is sitting down and slides away from the line, her back now to Chaucer who is still behind her. She removes the board, carefully, and massages her knee.

"Did you twist your knee?" he asks again.

Anne is silent. Behind her she can hear the icy grating of others coming down the line. The chairlift engine grinds uninterrupted. She hears the click of Chaucer's braces coming off his board, and the awkward crunching of snow as he stands up.

He walks around to face her, putting his hand lightly on her shoulder as he crouches in front of her.

"Shit," she says, trying to pretend to be angry, or calm, or frustrated – anything to mask how distraught she is. Her knee is incredibly tender to the touch, and she fears she may have sprained it, or worse. She doesn't think she can stand.

Chaucer waits to see if she'll speak again, but when she remains silent, he asks in a tone so low and quiet you think he was trading state secrets: "Can you put weight on it?"

That question breaks her. She can't, she knows she can't, and now she is being asked to admit that she is broken. Her goggles fog up with tears and she removes them, leaving a deep red mark that crosses her brow and chisels a narrow indent across her cheeks. Tears pool in each of the fiery red marks, just above ice-burned plane of her cheeks. Chaucer takes a pack of tissues from his pocket, bites his gloves to pull them off his hand, and extracts a tissue from the pack. She is visibly shaking. Muttering to herself, cursing her own stupidity. He cannot make eye contact with her, and waits, the white tissue waving in the wind, for her to take the tissue to wipe her eyes.

When she turns to look at him, her eyes are now flushed with undirected hatred. "I just want to sleep," she stammers. Her eyes turn to the tissue in his naked hand, process its potential use and maybe even the compassion that lay behind the gesture, before dropping that line of thought completely. When she looks at Chaucer again, the fire in her eyes has been turned sharper. "Get me out of here," she insists, bitchy really. She is insistent, demanding. He stuffs the tissue back in his pocket, next to the credit-card sized mountain map and a stick of lip balm, puts his glove back on, and stands up. Leaving Anne, he walks to the chairlift man and asks him to call a stretcher to take her down to the lodge's infirmary.

Within minutes, we find Anne strapped into an orange stretcher strung out behind a snowmobile. During the process, her face goes mute; the anger is canned and preserved somewhere in the basement of her heart. As you'll see, it emerges from time to time over the coming months in particular, but in this moment, Anne is too occupied by the logistics of getting into a stretcher, the smells of motor fuel, the unsettling noise of the snowmobile's skis against the ice like nails on a chalkboard, the fear of getting her ski pass caught in something.

When they arrive at the infirmary, Chaucer is doing the translating, though he can't remember the word for sprain.

He indicates knee and is reminded that its Midland word is a combination of the word for "going forward" and "turning point." They recommend rubbing some Midlandish medicine on it, but Anne refuses any unknown medicine. Some Midlanders have gathered around and are arguing excitedly that this medicine is amazing. Chaucer laughs at one of their comments, and explains to Anne, who looks up at him puzzled, "This woman just said you should take the medicine. It isn't Midlandish. It's Soviet!"

The medics give her a knee brace to keep her knee locked until they can get back to Midland City, where there are Western doctors with whom she's more comfortable, and where Chaucer has some ibuprofen. When Chaucer recommends taking a cab – which costs as much as a month's rent – even Anne doesn't try to stop him.

So on this grey and unexceptional day near Midland City after a handful of runs down a mediocre hill with icy conditions, we find the couple painfully and carefully getting into the back an ancient black town car.

In the last scene of *The Graduate*, Dustin Hoffman and Katharine Ross are sitting on the back of a bus, having just run away from her wedding. Their faces are painted with relief from having escaped the worst part, excitement about the beautiful world that has opened up in front of them, and absolute fear and doubt as it dawns on them that have no plan and no idea what the future holds.

You see these same expressions on the tear-stained face of Anne and the solid compassionate face of her boyfriend as they sit on worn black leather seats heading back to Midland City, Anne's knee cradled on his lap. Neither of them likes to think the worst before it's been confirmed, and as far as Anne or Chaucer know, this could just be a bad sprain. But on their face is uncertainty, and a fear of the future which will turn out to be true.

* * *

The doctor at the Western clinic frowned. Anne had seriously torn up her knee. They could attempt surgery, but the outcome would be mixed, and the healing might take longer and be less complete than if they just let the knee rest.

Until the swelling and pain diminished, Anne would have to keep the knee elevated as much as possible and take pain killers. It was recommended that she not go out unless necessary, especially given the icy streets, as any twisting might risk reinjury of her knee or other joints that might compensate. The doctor suggested she take time off work while on the painkillers, and that she work from home after that. When Anne asked how long it would take to heal, the doctor said only, "As long as it takes." Anne forced a laugh and teased the Western doctor that she had clearly been in Midland too long.

Chaucer helped her out of the office on crutches. A wheelchair would have been better, but Midland wasn't built for wheelchairs – there were stairs everywhere, including up to Chaucer's and Anne's apartments. So she instead used crutches, carefully.

She later told me how much she appreciated Chaucer's patience with her, especially those first few days. She was broken, irritable, and sad, and incredibly slow in her movements, and yet Chaucer had unending patience. I watched the File of him helping her get up the stairs to his apartment, one step at a time. A third the way, she loses it

– frustrated, and cries, too exhausted to keep moving, and unable to sit down. He comes over and just gently hugs her. He doesn't say anything to try to encourage her, or praise her for the stairs she's already climbed, or try to make her laugh, or murmur words of empathy. None of that consolation would do. She needs in that moment to just hit the bottom of misery, so she can recover herself. So Chaucer lets her and waits. A few minutes later, she brushes the tears off and continues up the stairs.

* * *

She had no way to know it that day, but her knee would take seven months and twelve days to heal. Where do I get that number from? The start date of Anne's downfall is obvious: the chairlift line incident occurred on February 15th, 2006, according to the date stamp on the file. The end date was September 27th, a date set by Anne in a conversation held on March 25th with Gale, wherein Anne said, "I'll consider myself fully healed when I can jog a mile."

Of course when I asked Anne recently how long her knee was a problem, she replied, "It had a half-life of about a year." I found her answer vague and frustrating – Midland had gotten to her – but in the end, it's probably the most accurate answer. Something that Anne has taught me, or rather something I watched her learn, was that sometimes there is no exact answer to a question. And when that happens, we have a few choices: (a) don't answer the question at all, (b) make something up, or (c) find a way to define the question to make it answerable. Anne prefers the last of these, which she used to put a different way when mentoring her Business Development team: "When faced with a challenging question, challenge the question." So let's challenge my question.

I asked "How long did it take Anne to heal?" Which begs a new question, "What do you mean by 'heal'"? Anne will never be the same person who took that chairlift up the mountain with Chaucer. She breaks across every axis and dimension, and all the kings' horses and all the kings' men have to come put her back together again. She'll never be able to snowboard with abandon again (her doctors don't want her snowboarding at all, actually), and distance running will be discouraged too. She will jog a mile again on September 27th, yes, but in doing so, reaggravate her knee so badly she is stuck in a brace again for a month and has to go through another six months of physical therapy. So does that count as healed?

Or does she remain broken the many months she doesn't really recognize herself in the mirror, and feels like a different person? Is she only healed that day in May a year later, still doing physical therapy, when she feels once more at peace?

My friends in the Biology department told me that our skin changes every two weeks. Most cells in our body divide into their offspring, and their offspring carry on the business of being us. When we break, those offspring try to remember what we were like back before the break, the tear in the ligament or the cut, and restore us to it based on the code that's written there. They get pretty close, if you've ever seen a scar heal over, but not completely. History remains there, standing between us and where we came from. Even when where we came from is where we want to return.

* * *

I decided tonight that I don't want to be a video editor. I've stayed at the Central Order after work to look through the Files, so that I could recount a time in the seven months and twelve "official" days of Anne's injury that would give you a sense of the hell that she was going through. What tedious work. I am really not cut out for visual media. I respect anyone who can take hours of ordinary life and parse it into something interesting enough to compete with commercials. Reality TV show always seemed like cheating to me. No longer.

So I've given up, and instead of giving you the highlights or some awesomely poignant moment in Anne's seven months and twelve days of hell, I am going to cheat and pick a day at random. Maybe I'll challenge you to find beauty in ordinary things, and appreciate this vignette for its, well, ordinariness.

We are in Chaucer's apartment. Anne hadn't actually decided to move in with him full-time, just like she hadn't decided to let her hair grow long since moving to Midland. It just happened, and there was no reason to stop it. The day of the snowboard accident, she had sat in silence in the back of a black town car with her leg on Chaucer's lap, and they came back to his home, where she had spent the previous sleepless night. Maybe she had in mind to take a cab back to her own apartment, but after Chaucer made her some instant noodles, she didn't want to move. Or talk. So the couple watched the nightly news, then a reality TV show (I think the secret is the background music, come to think of it), then a 1980s movie about cars. I was fast-forwarding at this point in the File, so I didn't catch the title of the movie. And perhaps it wasn't even about cars, but it just had a lot of cars in it.

And then that was it. Anne is basically asleep, and Chaucer wakes her up only enough to carry her into their bed. He tucks her in, sheets all around, to keep her safe like the ski rescue crew had done on the stretcher before. She thanks him, mumbling. He has peeled off all his clothes except his boxers and a t-shirt, and climbs into the other side of the bed, sitting up against the pillows propped against the headboard. He sits there, watching Anne sleep. You can see his fingers kneading a fold of the blanket, the muscles in his left bicep tighten from time to time. He is frowning, and twice he releases the blanket to move his hand towards her head, as if to pet her hair. But then he retracts it, realizing perhaps he might wake her, and once again kneads the blanket between his thumb and index finger.

So now we go to the randomly selected ordinary day I've chosen. Let's start when the light comes in the window. 4:50 a.m., and the birds are chirping. The snow has melted off the mountains (or hills as they should be called). Flowers are in bloom, and the City of Midland has gotten used to the Stills that have finally settled over the city. It isn't clear yet what the impact of the Stills on pollution concentrations in the city will be. Without wind, toxins build up in the air around major urban centers, with no effective way to get them out again.

The Midland government, it will have been discovered, did consider potential pollution when they were building their Wall. They even hired external consultants to study the problem. The consultants' risk assessment showed the probability-weighted loss of human-life years was less than that caused by the invention of the car. So the Wall went on. You may want to ask a whole series of follow-on questions, about the incentives for these consultants (were their salaries paid for by the project managers who would get promoted if the project went through?), the metric of a life-year (is an additional year of life a valid proxy for a good society, and how do you estimate it anyway?), and the virtue of probability weighting itself (if on average I'm not going to have a car crash do I need to wear a seatbelt?). I hear at the Central Order that such problems are still being debated at the highest levels. I am sure in Midland, too, they question whether rationality and the consistency it requires truly lead to a good society. But for now, I'll judge their methods by their own measures. If you adhere to the Midland principles of rational and evidence-based decision making, the Wall was worth the pollution that would settle over Anne, Chaucer and the many citizens of Midland that day.

So it's through this rational fog at 4:50 a.m. that a garbage truck backs up outside their window, beeping, clattering bottles and boxes in a drumroll for the new day. Chaucer rolls over in bed, asleep, but Anne is clearly awake. It's a curse of not being able to work or do much of anything; Anne sleeps to avoid being awake, which makes it hard to sleep. So she lies there, not moving too much, listening to the garbage truck firing up its engine on its way to the next building. Maybe she hopes that if she lies there silently, sleep will just settle into her. She looks over at Chaucer, to see if he is on the verge of waking. Not yet. She shoves herself up on her hands and sits up against the wall. She takes a small book, something Chaucer had picked up at the airport when he first came to Midland and opens to the bookmarked page.

Two hours later, she finishes it. It's now just before 7 a.m., and Chaucer is sleeping more heavily than ever. Anne looks over at the clock, contemplating. She's finished reading and the alarm won't go off until 7:30 a.m. She doesn't want to get out of bed and disturb Chaucer's sleep, since it's a production to reach her crutches etc. And where would she go anyway?

She sits there. Staring at the wall. There is no indication of emotion on her face. Or of thought. Her eyes aren't darting around her mind, but instead are fixed, unfocused, on the off-white wall in front of her. My finger is on the fast-forward button at this time, but I hesitate to push it. She can't fast forward and it seems unfair for me to be able to. So I wait, and in real time, watch Anne watch the white wall.

She once wrote an email to Julie about this sense of emptiness she experienced often in that bed, her torn knee horizontal in front of her, her stomach acids fighting vigorously against the anti-inflammatory drugs she had to take, her eyes dry from wearing glasses all day instead of contacts, out of laziness or convenience or the challenge of standing on one foot and using two hands to insert the lenses.

She wrote, "Today I watched the wall, Julie. It was like watching a stop-action video of a flower blooming, but in real time. I saw the wall get brighter, and from time to time, would realize how bored I was, how much I felt like I am wasting my life, waiting. And sometimes I would stop, and try to squeeze value from the experience, for instance by appreciating the motionlessness that this moment gave me. Or by playing mind games, like 'how far is the horizon when you are sitting on a beach.' That would last for a few minutes, but then I would go back to staring at a wall. When it grew brighter during the morning, I would think, 'it's getting brighter.' And when it grew darker in the evening, I would think, 'it's getting darker.' Pretty deep analysis huh. :)"

At 7:30 a.m. the alarm went off, playing a scratchy version of the news in Midlandish, and Chaucer rolled over, first looking for Anne. He saw that she was already awake and had just reshuffled her face. She threw a hasty expression over the blankness in it. But, as she hadn't had time to figure out what expression to wear, she just seemed uncomfortable. Chaucer, who could see pretty well the moment he woke up, gave her space, and pretended to believe the smile she eventually produced. Good morning sunshine, one of them said and the other replied something equally nondescript back as well. Chaucer got out of bed and threw on a thick bathrobe. Winter was over and so central heating was turned off, but the mornings were still icy. He shuffled to the coffee maker which by now had been well trained to start brewing at 7:25 a.m. and came back into the room with two mugs of black Illy coffee, no sugar. He put them both down on the dresser next to Anne and went into the bathroom to shave while the coffee cooled. Anne listened to the news, trying to learn this challenging language.

It had been almost two months since the accident, and she was getting better, at least at listening to Midlandish. She didn't have much chance to speak. Chaucer had bought her some introductory books, but the language market was still undeveloped; very few foreigners even attempted to speak Midlandish, and there were almost no foreigners here in Midland City.

Chaucer dressed had started working unofficially for the Central Order just after his first date with Anne and passed security clearance to get his formal paychecks and benefits earlier that month. He now had a meeting every few days at 8 a.m. to discuss that day's finding and progress. When they made some major breakthroughs, meetings would happen in the middle of the night in Midland, as senior management in the Central Order expected overseas operations to report during New York working hours.

So he and Anne sit together and have coffee for a few minutes, before Chaucer goes to the corner of the living room that has become his "office." He puts on a soundproof helmet to make life harder for the spies who moved in across the street, and who sit at their windows with cigarettes and microphones. The Central Order was concerned about hiring him, for fear of espionage. They were uncomfortable with the development of new software in a country with as few intellectual property controls as Midland, by a handsome and unknown man who was sleeping with a member of the Central Order that he met at an Embassy party. It seemed too obviously Bond-esque even for them. But when they realized that the programs he was writing were predictive only, trying to estimate the impacts of the Wall on weather out two to two-thousand days, they let the project move forward. It just meant that the support they gave him was limited, and that he wouldn't be able to really advance unless he moved back to New York and underwent a more thorough background check.

Anne can't hear him talking, due to his helmet, and can't hear him typing due to the Midlandish radio station news. A half hour goes by, and the radio automatically shuts off. She struggles to the bathroom to take care of nature. She can't really go into the living room now, as that might disturb Chaucer's phone call; it's not like she could turn on an episode of *The Simpsons* while he is talking with his boss. So she goes back to the bedroom and picks up her phone. She sends a text message to Gale, "What's up for today?" and Gale calls her back.

Gale is thinking of interviewing some of the contractors who are constructing the Wall. She's been trying to hitch a ride on one of their trucks to the end of the Wall, to see where it goes, and to learn more about they decide how to direct where it turns. She wants to understand the decision-making process involved, how they decide which craggy path to take across the mountains, and who makes those decisions. Her Midlandish is still very basic, and while she has an interpreter, wishes she didn't have to go alone. Anne suggests Chaucer go with her, since he's part of their team now, and can work on his programming in the evenings. "It's not like I'm much fun anymore to go out with," Anne said to Gale. "He really doesn't seem to mind working evenings."

Gale assures Anne that's not the case, says a few vacuously encouraging words about Anne's knee getting better soon, and asks Anne to have Chaucer call her back when he's free. Anne tries to end on a chipper note, sarcastically joking that she'll "really be suffering here comfortable and warm while you are out trying to find the end of the earth." Gale laughs, as she's supposed to, even though they both know that Anne is telling the truth.

It's 8:57 a.m. now and Chaucer comes back in, helmet off, but his hair matted and damp. He doesn't seem particularly happy or full of energy, and Anne does nothing to boost his spirits. "Hey," she says flatly, "Gale called.

She's going to try to talk with some contractors this afternoon at the Wall and wants to know if you can join her." Chaucer looks at his watch so he has an excuse to break eye contact; he is excited to go but doesn't want to show it when Anne is stuck here. He pretends to do some calculations in his head, or maybe he does, and then asks Anne, "How long do think it'd take?"

Anne, always ready with answers for questions she couldn't possibly know, replies confidently, "Maybe the whole afternoon? Gale seemed to think you'd be done by the evening, if you needed to get work done then. And how late does anyone want to be on the Wall anyway?"

He pursues his lips and askes Anne more obsequiously than necessary, "Do you think it'll be worthwhile? Do you think we'll really learn anything?" Anne just shrugs, looking deflated, tired.

He goes into the living room to pick up his phone to call Gale. Anne hears his voice, instantly happier, on the line, "Hey Gale! Anne told me you wanted to make an expedition today into the wild white yonder... Are we to leave at three or are we supposed to get there by three? ... Sure, can you send me a text message with the address?... Great, talk to you soon, Gale." Chaucer comes back into the bedroom, having unmatted his hair a bit. His phone vibrates and he checks the text message before turning to Anne. "I have to leave at around one so let me pound out this module that New York wanted by end of day and then we'll grab some lunch downstairs. Sound good? My treat."

Chaucer goes back to the living room, working away, and Anne eventually lugs herself out of bed, dresses carefully, and walks with crutches into the living room. She stands balanced on one leg, and resting on her crutches, peels a banana. When she finishes eating – it's too hard to walk carrying things – she swivels and heads toward the plush couch in the living room, where her Midlandish books lay sprawled. She has set a chapter-a-day goal for herself, mostly to avoid depression and boredom. But even so, she finds studying these books a terrible drag. She wished so much she could go out more often, do her job, interact with real people. Staying in bed all day, or most days, is like being in jail.

She knows she should get out of the house, even if it's just buying bananas across the street. But she has little scraps of things to do – an impossible language to learn, a computer program to install, a shower head to fix, dust to sweep up. Her eyelids hang low, and she doesn't have any energy anymore.

Within her knee, blood is circulating. Little worker cells are doing their voodoo magic, building the pyramids of human health, surrounding the injury with scar tissue, dancing in and out of vessels and through membranes, carrying information and nutrients and waste like an ant colony. It seems an impossible task, and were the ants sentient, they might have given up a long ago. But they aren't and they don't question their existence and their goals, don't spend years of their lives deliberating their purpose and panicking at the vacant thought that maybe there is none. Instead they come and go and go and come, and eventually, a knee gets rebuilt.

Anne was in no position to learn from these worker cells, and so spent a significant part of her time ruminating and writing things in her head. From time to time, she'd jot them down, like this:

- *beauty in ordinary things/ order in random things*
- *the week should be 7 days, yes!*
- *why are you here? Because it's important. No because it's interesting*
- *I am trying to uncontrol the weather*
- *isn't that why God plunked us down on this planet? To name all his creatures, and find order in the chaos?*
- *beauty and the perception of motion*
- *rainbows follow her*
- *asking questions*
- *slow down, Tai Chi*
- *team sport*
- *Schrodinger's Cat*
- *turns invisible like Jane*
- *wind slows down > weather stops > Wind Bureau > foreign country building a large wall*
-

She's used this list in helping me to write her story, of course. Sometimes she'd show up in my office with these worn pages of all sizes – notepads yanked from hotels, the back of taxi receipts, torn out corners of full-page ads for beach destinations, spiral notebooks, Post-Its – and refer to them from time to time in helping me understand what to write next. I tried to keep the parts I understand, that help tell Anne's story. The bit about un-controlling the weather, being places that are interesting, those are themes I can work with. I have no idea what she meant about turning invisible like Jane, or rainbows following her, or why the excitement about the 7-day week.

But the notes people take are window onto their souls, and I selfishly loved watching her in the File sit on her exceptionally hard bed during her knee-problem era, deep in silence and thought, and from time to time, reach across her body pick up the notepad on her nightstand. There were days when she would write at length by hand, and others when she would jot down notes like those above, deferring explication to a later time, or maybe, presciently, to me.

Since she couldn't fit her life to her goals, she tried to fit her goals to her life. She tried to see the merits in patience and took time to write. And she started to read. Not just to read books that pertained to Midland politics and engineering, though of course she did that too, but books about any topic under the sun. She'd curl up with the Stanford alumni magazine on her impossibly hard bed, and flip through articles about archiving manuscripts, or grass breeding, or the mentality of walk-on athletes.

She often sits with her Midlandish book open, doodling. She is usually doodling the Wall, drawing each brick, the long way: she outlines each brick itself, so when put next to another brick, the line between them is drawn twice. The bricks' corners and spacing have a certain style to them that becomes distinctive in her Wall doodles. Over time, more than half the pages of her Midlandish notebook become lined with bricks, in the left margin of her vocabulary lists and along the top where she puts the date in *year-month-date* format.

You can interpret a lot about a person from their doodles, or so I'm told. But I have no idea how to do that, and it's not important for this story anyway, so I'll leave that to you. These doodled bricks aren't significant for what they tell us about Anne, but what they clue Anne into about the Wall.

It happened one day in the summer after the accident.

Anne now has a soft knee brace and hasn't yet jogged one mile. Her mood is somewhat better, but she bears the emotional scars and a heavy feeling in her body that comes from half a year of forced inactivity. She has continued to study Midlandish, driven in part by competition with Chaucer, whose Midlandish has never stopped impressing her. The more she learns, the deeper she realizes his knowledge is, and the more she adores him. She continues to doodle in her language books.

Chaucer had brought home a tiny blank-paged notebook from a conference in an upscale hotel, which Anne was using this morning for her mindless doodles. She filled the whole page with bricks, bricks, bricks, and then the next page, then flipping the page, the next and the next, flip, doodle, flip. As she was flipping the pages, you can watch her stop, right there at 10:53 a.m. that Wednesday morning, the page half-lifted above the notebook. She slowly raises and lowers it like a door, opening and closing. A gate in the Wall.

She dialed up Chaucer right away, and he picked up after two rings. They had started working that spring out of a small office a few blocks away, along with a few other people who had come over from the Central Order to work on other projects.

"Well hello," he answered flirtatiously, "and how may I help you this fine morning?"

"I think I know how to restart the winds," she told him. "We could ask the Midland government to build gates along the wall, through which the winds could pass. And I bet you can help them model where to put the gates and what the impact on the winds would be."

"Wait, Anne," he said calmly. "Let's not get ahead of

ourselves. Do you think it would really work, and that they would even agree to it?"

Anne paused. "I don't know, but I know who we need to ask."

* * *

Gale, Anne and Chaucer stood in the tower, waiting for him to come down from his morning run. It was the middle of the summer already, but still frosty up on the Wall. When the hatch opened and he came down, he was wearing a thin layer of microfleece, a cloud of mist forming every second as he panted out.

"Hello," said the bug-man said with unexpected warmth. Chaucer spoke to him in Midlandish, apparently explaining to him why they were there.

"He apologizes that he's not an engineer," Chaucer paraphrased after the man spoke, "and therefore does not know if the Wall created the Stills or not. I explained our theory, that the Wall was preventing the winds from blowing, and that gates would allow the winds to continue to blow through without obstructing the purpose of the wall. He seemed to think that made sense."

"So does he know the purpose of the Wall?" Gale piped in. Chaucer turned to the man to translate the question into Midlandish. The man removed his gloves and started talking for several minutes. Chaucer's face was blank.

When he was done, Chaucer summarized. "He's not a designer, and therefore apologizes again for not knowing the reasons. He said that every day on his run, he asks this question, where the Wall is going. If I understood him right, that's the reason he runs. He has been all the way to the end, he always runs all the way to the end, and so over the years, his run has gotten longer and longer. Now it takes him several days to run from here to the end." Chaucer quickly asked the man a question in Midlandish, and then clarified, "Actually, sorry, he doesn't always run all the way to the end, but every so often, he does, to see where it's been going, and if he can understand it more."

"What's it like out there, at the end?" Gale asked.

Chaucer translated the question and the reply, "It's apparently very misty and snowy, and you can't see anything. Kind of like it is here. It's not clear what's around the Wall out there. On one side, the wind is ferocious, and on the other side, totally calm, so he thinks that it makes sense that the Wall is stopping the wind pattern."

"So who decides what direction the construction goes then?" Gale asked.

Anne interjected, "We've tried asking that question to a few people, and we haven't yet found a central command that dictates where the Wall goes. I think it just is supposed to go 'forward' and that the engineers at the end of the Wall determine what the next step is. Has this guy ever talked to the engineers about it?"

Chaucer asked, and the man nodded slowly before replying quickly in Midlandish, "The engineers at the end decide."

Anne looked puzzled. "So the only central instruction they have is to keep building the Wall, and the individual construction workers determine where it goes? Is there a destination in mind that they are going to at least?"

Chaucer considered for a moment how to ask the question in Midlandish, to express the concept of 'destination' clearly. When the man replied, Chaucer translated. “He says that there is of course a destination. But no one knows where it is, so the central government has told the engineers to keep building the Wall forward, following the hills and valleys, whatever way is easiest to build.”

“How close are they to finishing?” Gale added. Chaucer smiled and asked the man, laughing at his own question so that he didn’t offend the man. The man and Chaucer chatted for a while, and then he turned to Gale and Anne.

“He said that they haven’t yet come to an obstacle that they can’t build over or around, so they have no reason to stop. And they’re not done yet. I tried to get him to explain how they would know when they are done, but he just laughed. I don’t think that there is a ‘done’.”

* * *

They finished their last soggy paper cups of hot water and went to the bathroom one last time. Before he went home, the running man confirmed that conditions were good today for a hike along the wall; but he advised they should turn back just after midday to ensure they made it back though before dusk, when the temperature drops even further.

They opened the hatch and the frigid air rushed down into the room, as they climbed the hard metal rungs to the top of the Wall. It was impossible to talk much during their hike. Their ears were bundled under thick fur hats, their mouths covered by scarves, and to the left over the precipice of the Wall’s edge, the winds thundered. They stopped every hour to take a sip of the water bottles which were kept from freezing inside their down jackets. Anne’s knee ached; they had to walk slowly.

To either side, for the first couple of hours, there were only grey, brown hills. On the right side, where all was Still, the patches of ice between the bushes were weighed down with bleak grey soot. On the windy left side, the bushes beat against the stones, whipping ice dust like sandpaper against the Wall, already smoothing the rocks that had been built just a few years before. There was no sign of life anywhere.

Around midday, when their shadows swapped from left to right, it was time to head back. The three of them, already worn down by the trek and frustrated that they learned nothing new, found a small alcove to sit in and eat the cold buns they had brought with them from that morning. It was in this alcove, sheltered from the wind, that Anne heard the bleats.

"Do you hear it too?" she asked Gale and Chaucer.

Gale cocked her head, then suddenly stood up to look over the edge of the Wall. There, making their way through the sooty grey landscape of the Stills, you could see two shepherds leading a small herd of goats. The goats looked up at the Wall; if you pause and zoom on their faces, their heavy eyes show a sense of loss.

"Hello there!" Chaucer shouted in Midlandish to the shepherds. They looked up and shrugged; they didn't speak Midlandish either. Of course, Anne thought. She had learned about this migrant minority group of shepherds in *Lonely Planet - Midland.* This group of people who were proudly not Midlandish and followed their herds across the wild frontiers of the country. The Midland government at times tried to celebrate their culture, with costumes and museums; but they also banned teaching their language in schools or television. Anne never expected to meet any in person.

We have to go down, Anne thought to herself, and started to scour the Wall for the nearest staircase. There was one not far away; she waved to the shepherd to indicate they would be coming down soon.

Chaucer looked at his watched, the sun, and then Anne. They should already be turning back to make it home safely, but this felt important. He nodded at Gale, and the three of them started their way down off the Wall.

As soon as they stepped down the first flight of stairs, silence fell. Without the winds, you could hear the crunch as their boots broke the grey soot surface of the refrozen snow, the snap of branches of icicled twigs in the bushes underfoot. The intermittent bleats of the goats.

The two parties approached each other, neither able to see each other's faces. Anne pulled down her scarf briefly, to show what she hoped was a friendly American-sized smile. The shepherds nodded.

"Where are you going?" Anne shrugged with her shoulders, pointing around, looking questioning.

The bigger shepherd waved all around, then pointed at the Wall, then punched his hand into his fist. Pulling down his face covering, he showed a pantomimed sad face. Then he pounded both fists into his chest and opened them up like a pair of doors swinging open. He walked his fingers like goats through the space he opened up and smiled a friendly American-sized smile back.

"Please," he said in Midlandish.

Anne recalled her doodles, the opening pages, the opening gates. She had the notebook in her jacket pocket and took it out, miming to the shepherd a gate opening, the goats going through. He nodded and bowed his head.

"Please," he repeated.

"I will try," Anne said in English, knowing the words would not be understood, but the meaning would.

Chaucer looked again at his watch, and at Anne, indicating it was time to go. The three of them bowed their heads in thanks and returned up the stairs.

As the howling of the wind picked up again, they found themselves on the top of the Wall. As they looked out, the sun had gone behind a cloud in such a way that they could see past the heavily polluted mists, beyond the shepherd and their twenty goats. Now they could see another herd, and then another, appear; hundreds of goats and tents appeared in the distance. The shepherd they spoke to pounded his chest once more: open the Wall, please.

* * *

A few weeks later, Gale, Chaucer and Anne are in a waiting room, drinking hot water out of paper cups that are slowly dissolving. There's a red rug on one wall, between the two double-paned windows, with a simple gold pattern on it. The floor is concrete and extremely cold. The hardwood chairs are far too deep and straight to sit in comfortably. The three of them stand, gloves still on.

After some time, the Minister's Secretary comes out, and shakes their hands. He too is wearing gloves, but thin leather ones so he can hold a pen comfortably. Anne notices the long underwear peeking out through his button-down shirt. He too looks cold. The Secretary walks over to an air conditioning unit on the wall and pushes some buttons. Vents open up and eventually warm water starts blowing into the room. But because of the concrete floor, the hard wood chairs and the windows, the heat doesn't last. They are offered to sit and hesitate, until they realize that this is it; there is no other place to go that is warm for them to meet.

He speaks enough English that it would be rude for Chaucer to translate, and so he doesn't. The Secretary welcomes them quite formally, and then asks them why they came and how he can help.

Gale starts off equally as formally, "Sir, thank you very much for your time today. We are all from the Central Order in New York, and really appreciate the great hospitality that your country has shown us over the past year."

He responds in kind, noting that the Minister has had the great pleasure of their visits on a number of occasions, and he is glad that after so much time he too finally gets to meet them.

Gale then proceeds to explain: "As your Minister is aware from our previous discussions, we are concerned about the Still, the lack of wind that has settled throughout the world. We are concerned that without that stimulus, certain natural processes in agriculture and aquaculture are not taking place. Weather patterns have changed, and as your government knows, pollution is settling over cities. Power plants that are run by wind, which has become an increasingly important form of energy especially in the US and also here in Midland, are unable to operate. While local teams are responding to short-term problems with apparently effective measures, we are concerned about the long-term implications of the Still."

The Secretary replied, "Yes, we know about the Still in other parts of the world and have heard these concerns in the past. We are also researching them, and hope to have a better sense of what some of the impacts may be."

Gale continued, "Your country and your engineers are respected worldwide, and we very much look forward to your findings. We also understand that the Wall may have been a part of the cause of the Still. We all understand the Wall's historical significance and are trying to understand the current purpose and plan for the Wall's expansion. We understand that there are good reasons to keep building the Wall. Therefore, we do not feel it is appropriate for us to come here, like some have in the past, and suggest that Midland stop building the Wall. While we do not fully understand the intention or use of the Wall, we trust your leadership's judgment in moving this project forward, despite the longer-term implications. We therefore want to suggest some innovative ideas that may help deflect some of the pressure that Midland is currently under from other governments, from the Central Order itself, and from some of your minority groups as well."

The Secretary listened to Gale speak with a poker face. "I appreciate the time that you and your colleagues have invested in studying the Wall, and your trust in our judgment that the Wall is critical for the long-term advancement of Midland, and of all people. It is not possible for us to stop building the Wall, but if you have suggestions, then we are happy to listen."

Anne handed Gale a manila folder with some architectural sketches in it. Gale took one out. "We think the reason for the Still is that the Wall obstructs the wind. We calculated that if you replaced short sections of the Wall with gates that could open and close, every few kilometers, the winds would resume, and you would still have a Wall.

We have started to analyze the exact spacing and width needed and could offer to provide this technical assistance to you. My colleague," Gale added indicating Chaucer, "is a very highly trained computer forecaster, and he can help you run models that determine that spacing, if you like." Gale walked the Secretary through the folder, showing him the materials needed, the cost projections, the method for construction, and rough simulations Chaucer had pulled together estimating wind flow-through. When she was done with enough of an explanation to allow the Secretary to report back to his Minister, she stopped.

It was Anne's turn. "We are here to help with technical advice around returning the winds and are not diplomatic representatives. As you consider this technical solution," she proceeded carefully, in pre-rehearsed words, "you may also consider that these gates would support the Midlandish Two Cultures Initiative to celebrate and support the goat herders whose traditional grazing routes were impaired by the Wall."

The Secretary remained silent, as they had expected, and revealed nothing. It is rude in Midland to start speaking before the other party had indicated that they are finished.

"Lastly, while the drawings here mostly focus on the use of the Gates in the open position, we have designed them in a way that they can close as well. Our modelling shows that when the gates are open, the winds will return to their previous patterns; but when closed, they will once again cause the Still. We can offer our support to develop models for other combinations, to better control the winds overall."

She paused, letting the Secretary try to draw his own conclusions. "Once the winds resume, we will go back to New York and continue over two dozen projects to build more wind-energy plants; indeed the International Energy Agency forecasts over half of the world's energy in thirty years will be wind-generated." Here Anne was treading on thin ice, touching very close to matters of national security. "I am sure it would be of interest to Midland to have a means of controlling the wind, and therefore global power production. But Midland can only have that control if there are winds in the first place."

The Secretary sat back and thought in silence. Anne, Gale and Chaucer gave him that silence, while their cups, now empty and completely soggy, turned cold under their gloved fingers. They were sitting on the edge of the wood chairs, the vents turned slowly from the heating unit against the wall.

After a minute of silence – a normal pause in Midland but very long for the three Americans – the Secretary shifted forward in his chair, and said, "Thank you. I will consider this and discuss with the Minister." And then he stood up, causing the three of them to stand as well. He quickly shook their gloved hands and went back through the door he had entered through.

"That's it?" Anne said under her breath. "We have no idea whether he thought it was a good idea or not?"

Gale and Chaucer waited until they were back outside to respond. "No, and you won't, not directly," Chaucer said. "If they liked the idea, they will take credit for it. And if they didn't like the idea, they won't cause you to lose face."

"The only way I guess we'll know if they liked it," Gale added, "is if they call us up to ask for Chaucer's model. Until then, we just have to wait."

* * *

The waiting ended when they were eating ice cream in a park. You could tell it was summer, as the trees looked tree-like, like they do when the sun spends more than half its time above ground. There were squirrels running around, looking for something – maybe nuts, maybe trees, maybe each other. When you take a step back, I suppose, that's what we look like too.

The Ministry called that day to ask for Chaucer's model. They were thrilled, and from that day on, Chaucer spent most of his time at the Ministry explaining and adjusting the model. Since this model analysis was rational and evidence-based, it fit snugly into their existing decision-making processes. The computer engineer helped write policy.

The next time Gale visited the Wall to speak to the running man, she heard that the construction was underway to replace the bricks with the gates that Anne had doodled one day in her lifeless apartment. Now Anne's time was mostly spent managing communications with the Central Order, estimating when the winds might return to forecast Windmill operations and sales, and managing communications with the global energy industry.

It was during this time that Anne started getting better. I can't pinpoint the precise moment of the trough of Anne's emotional state, her darkest day during her recovery from her snowboarding accident through its half-life. Have I failed Anne in writing her story, by not fabricating a pivot point filled with tension and transition? By not inventing some vivid moment at 4:13 p.m. on a Thursday when the light appeared at the end of her dark tunnel, where in reality there was never such a moment?

I promised you the truth, so here it is: an indefinite amount of time passed, and Anne's knee gradually got better – and so did she. The planet spun some more, heating and cooling as the plains of Midland faced and fled the sun, and Anne's knee got stronger, at least most days. By the time the trees were full and the squirrels mating, she could jog again. It was, like all things in Midland, an asymptotical approach at full recovery.

By the time this story ends, and it will end, in a way, she'll be able to run fully. But she will always have spasms of pain that drop her back to the darkest parts of her memory. Over time, she'll learn to accept those dark parts as part of her, invisible scars in her memory, that she observes and accepts, and then moves on from.

So Anne is out for a run now, on her ever-healing knee, through the dank smog that has come to define the city of Midland now that the Stills have settled in for this indefinite time. She has been advised not to jog outside, not to breath this toxic air, but the freedom of running is too great a draw. She jogs slowly, carefully, minding each step lest she reaggravate the knee. In moments, when the song on her MP3 picks up, she forgets this caution, and allows herself to fly downhill, briefly, paying close attention, responsibly reckless.

Her jog is over now, and she is walking back, the sweat damp on her back on this hot summer day, when the trees are tree-like and the plains of Midland lay flat and exposed to the sun's patient passage. What I did not want to say until Anne notices it herself, just now, is the cool breeze across the dampness, chilling her slightly. She pauses, here, to let the breeze surround her. She closes her eyes and turns forward into the wind.

I hate melodrama, but this moment was framed even without me, and I would be untrue to the experience if I didn't describe it the way it is, indelibly marked in time and memory. Anne stands in the middle of a plaza in a park, surrounded on both sides by flagpoles at the top of which drape limp red Midland banners. For the timeless time of the Stills, these flagpoles have looked like trees in winter – bare poles. Yet now, as the breeze begins to pick up, these banners start to yawn and flutter into life, like a butterfly coming out of a cocoon. There, in the middle of two flanks of flags coming to life for the first time, stands Anne, arms outstretched into the wind. The white smog that has accumulated over the timeless time collects and billows, softly caressed by a gentle breeze that is slowly gaining confidence and force. It pelts the flag poles. The unprepared red banners are lashed by the whiteness of the fog, fighting for their color to shine through the final struggle of the once-welcomed smog, now being forced to flee by an invisible ally of force that has rushed like so many centuries over walls, conquering all.

You see Anne, standing in the middle of the plaza, like Dorothy in Kansas, surrounded by this torrent of white. Look closely through her eyelids at the swirling mist, and you might see globular clusters of unborn stars, the rainbow mists of Yosemite, the acrid dust of the collapsed Twin Towers, clouds disappearing into the snowy slopes of Tahoe, the fading end of the Wall. You'll see in this cloud, shaped increasingly like the swirling white walkway of the Guggenheim Museum, a set of images: a Central Park fence bent by someone's weight, black bits of onion stuck on a frying pan in a kitchen sink, a swatch of Scottish plaid, three mini marshmallows floating on frothy cup of cocoa, a red flicker of flame twirling playfully through an ice cube, a dandelion on the shore.

And then it clears. The wind hushes into a breeze. The whiteness laps across the plaza, past the flags which are still waving peacefully attached to their poles. Anne stands there, arms still outstretched, and now opens her eyes. She watches the whiteness pour off behind her, leaving behind clearness.

Above her, the sky is blue. Not perfectly blue, of course, but blue enough that she looks up and breathes in its color deeply now, sensing the freedom of a new day.

When she lowers her head back to look at the horizon, you can see the smile fade, as slowly realization comes into place.

The winds had started again.

Her job in Midland was done. It was time to go.

* * *

They could see him clearly, wearing the same parka. A small spot out along the Wall, growing in size as the blue sky shone above them. Anne, Gale and Chaucer had decided to come back out here to the Wall, packing enough food for one day, which is how much the running man had suggested they bring.

The weather up here was still bitter and the wind biting as the sun rose that early morning, and the three of them were happy when the runner finally grew from pea size to life size, and extended a happy hand toward them. They went back down through the hatch, where he had left his own provisions, and warmed up for a few minutes before the journey. Taped up along the wall of the tower, like a middle school history timeline, were pictures of the Wall, taken as each segment was completed. It looped around the room now three and half times, an unbroken chain of bricks and now gates too, extending ever onwards.

The four of them set out. There was now an access road along the side of the Wall, and so the first few hours of the day, they drove. The running man sat next to the driver in silence, with Anne, Chaucer and Gale huddled in the back seat. When the road ended, the running man indicated with the Midlandish word for "here," which also means "there." The car stopped and the group got out.

They scrambled up some loose bricks that roughly formed a staircase along the side of the Wall. They climbed along the top of the Wall itself, up and down the hilly brick surface, listening to the wind whistle through the gates that Anne had seen first as doodles on a page some indefinite period of time ago. When the sun had moved up into the sky directly above the grey line of the Wall, they ate their peanut butter and jelly sandwiches. They sat on top of a turtle statue, a throwback to an era where time moved slowly and steadily, where safety was valued over advancement, and aged wisdom over youthful innovation.

Ahead of them, the Wall turned and stretched apparently on without end. They marched on. The sun was beginning to descend in the sky, at that moment in the day well before dusk, when the sky is still fully bright, but you first remember that all days come to an end. Anne wanted to ask the running man whether they should turn back, since it would no doubt take them as long to return as it had to get here. Chaucer too was looking at his watch as the sun wound down from its apex and she caught a look of puzzlement on his face. But there was nothing more than restrained silence from him too. The running man had run the Wall enough to know its features and route, and for reasons that they couldn't quite say, they trusted him to bring them home.

Around five o'clock, they came across a broken ceramic toolbox, long abandoned, holding just a crude hammer and a spatula speckled with white plaster. Twenty minutes later, they walked past a small cluster of wooden toolboxes, filled with rubber mallets and wire cutters, and almost illegible instruction manuals. They kept walking. Six o'clock, they came across four grey-haired workers wearing tweed coats re-surfacing the Wall, ensuring that its bricks were straight and clean. Gale waved hello, but the men were intent on their work, and did not look up.

It was getting colder now, and Anne was glad to have Chaucer's arm around her shoulders, blocking some of the wind. A few minutes later, they passed now a dozen workers actively hammering the bricks in, and several paces later, another dozen wrestling with steel wires. The Wall was narrowing now, and it was harder to walk on. The pockets of workers, originally just a dozen here or there, were now a continuous hive of activity. They must be passing a hundred workers a minute, two hundred, working in close unison to layer in bricks and structure wire into a solid Wall.

Now they press on through a wall of workers, ducking to stay out of the way, avoiding the wheelbarrows of bricks, the slung toolboxes and swinging mallets. White dust is kicked up all around them, making the ground hard to see amidst the chaos. The running man is leading them along through the work site, with Gale trailing behind. In between them, with no room to walk arm-in-arm anymore, Anne walks one step ahead of Chaucer, holding his hand tightly behind her. A mist has mingled in with the dust and it's hard to see the ground. Around them, the sound of mallets and falling bricks intensifies, carried on the back of a bellowing wind.

At times, there is no Wall at all. The mist grows thicker, and it becomes impossible to see the ground, and impossible to see each other. They pick their way ever forward, turning through the strewn bricks, the whiteness of the biting cold and the deafening rumble of the directionless wind.

Suddenly a shape solidifies out of the roaring mist, walking back towards Anne. "This is where the Wall ends, and so I have to turn back now," the running man tells her into the wind. "But there's more to see if you keep going on. Just ask whoever you come across for directions; they all know the way."

Anne looks at him closely across the inches that separate them and realizes that this is the last time she will have seen him. And so she replies in her now solid Midlandish, "Wait, before you go, can you tell me why all these people out here are building this Wall?"

He gives her a strained smile, and replies, "Well, if you lived out here, wouldn't you rather have a safe, level path to walk on? It's a lot more convenient and comfortable than walking over uneven ground."

"No," Anne adds urgently as he begins to turn into the mist, "that makes no sense. These people were brought out here to build the Wall; they're not building the Wall because they are here."

He faces squarely to her. "I don't know if building the Wall is the reason why they are here. I only know that building the Wall is the reason they will have been here."

He turns into the mist and is gone.

Still holding Chaucer's hand, Anne walks on. She can

now see nothing at all through the thick white mist that has collected here at the end of the Wall. Afraid of reinjuring her knee, she squeezes Chaucer's hand even tighter now. They walk along this way, figuring out what step to take next based on the step that has come before, always turning in the direction that they guess is forward.

They have come to the end of the Wall already but follow the sound of the workers who still surround them and lie ahead. From time to time, one solidifies out of the mist, and in answer to Anne's wind-muted questions, nods and points a mallet ever forward.

And so they walk on unseen ground, no road or structure underfoot, just other people to guide the way. As they move further past the end of the Wall, they are immersed in a sea of humanity. The din grows louder, filled not just with mallets and bricks and workers, but the sounds of children and dogs too. Anne hears a tea kettle whistling on a stove, bus horns, and bicycle bells, mobile phone ringtones and shampoo commercials, a washing machine finishing a spin cycle, oil frying in a pan, a receipt printing from a taxi cab meter, the rhythmic rumble of a train, the squealing howl of the 4 train turning into the 14th street platform in New York.

Anne won't realize until she reads this line that Gale has stopped walking on with them. All Anne has is the warmth of the hand she holds behind her, Chaucer finding his way with her through the fragments of unbuilt bricks and uncut wires, through the din of people's lives they never will have been in, and the relentless gale of endlessly changing winds. Anne wonders if any of this was real. The image that keeps coming to her mind, as the two of them pick their way beyond the end of the Wall, was one of a globular cluster of civilizations forming out of the mist. She imagines a Wall that will have been, formed by people who will have lived there.

Time stops mattering at end of the Wall, and so their peanut butter and jelly sandwiches, eaten on the timeless turtle sculptures some indefinite period of time ago, will have been enough for their journey. Anne would never be able to tell how long she was there, in the space after the Wall ends, as you couldn't tell how long you were in a dream.

As they walk in forced silence through the icy wind, ever forward, Anne's nose turns numb, and then her face, and then her hands. The warmth of Chaucer's hand in hers seems like a recollection now, and she stops to look back for him. Unable to see anything through the mist, she squeezes her now numb hand to feel if he is still there.

And in so doing, she realizes she is alone.

She stands still for a moment, while the wind howls around her beyond the end of the Wall, her hands hanging by her sides, empty. She raises them to her face to hide from the wind, and starts to cry.

She will stand with tears streaming down her face for a while. She'll want to go home but will be unable to conjure up a Kansas to return to or a pair of ruby slippers. She'll want some hot cocoa with mini marshmallows, and a warm bed, and a white tissue to sop up the tears and snot that are now freezing under her hands.

In time, she will get tired of crying. Crouching down in a ball, she'll feel a little warmer, and a little safer. In time, she will realize where she is and how far she has come, out here at the end of the Wall. The ground will seem inviting somehow, covered in a pillow-like mist. She will lay down onto the unkempt ground, and for a moment, close her eyes.

* * *

The morning light coming through the window uncurled Anne and turned her toward the window. She smiled and squeezed his hand.

He squeezed back, nonchalantly, more to tell her to let him sleep longer than anything else. And so she did, watching the sun rise up over his growing stubble, his shoulder, his back.

In time, he opened his eyes too, and smiled when he realized that Anne had been watching him all this time.

"How did you sleep?" he asked.

Anne considered carefully, and then answered, "Really well."

He noticed now that her cheeks were caked with salt from dried tears and reached out his thumb to gently rub one of the salt lines away. "Is something wrong, Anne?" he asked with the tenderness that she had come to love in him.

"I was just thinking…" she trailed off, as her mind wandered off to red flags and mist and uneven ground. "I guess I just wish someone could share my solitude, could know what I know and what I've been through so far, see through my eyes how beautiful things are. But no matter how close we are, we are always alone."

He looked at her closely. "Anne," he heard himself saying after a long pause, "you've always been a dreamer and who makes dreams come true. So why don't you dream up that someone? Maybe someone who is omniscient more or less, who could look back on any point in your life at will and empathize with you fully. It doesn't matter if it's true to fact, just as long as it's true to you."

Anne opened her eyes and looked clearly at him, and

with such blunt love. Her face relaxed, starting with her eyebrows, then the little muscles that crinkle the skin under her eyes, then as an afterthought her jaw, which widened into a yawn. "Okay then," she asked joyfully, "how do I go about doing that?"

"Oh, that part is easy," he replied. "You just create a narrator and office. Then one day you walk into that office and say: 'I want to be in your book.'"

If you liked this book…

I hope you enjoyed reading this book as much as I enjoyed writing it, and that you maybe learned a little along the way.

If you did, do tell a friend (or friends) and leave a review on Amazon.com or Goodreads.com.

This is my first novel (should there be more?), so your personal recommendations are invaluable in helping others discover this book.

If you'd like to read more of my writings, feel free to visit my blog, *Aabservations,* at www.lizaab.com.

I wish you the best as you make your own way forward,
Liz Aab

About the Author

Liz Aab is an international businesswoman and writer, born and raised in New York City, who has lived and worked in the US, China and UK. She structured derivatives on Wall Street, studied Mandarin and Tai Chi in Chengdu, advised multinational companies in Beijing, and commercialized new technologies at Shell in London. She studied International Relations and Computer Science as an undergraduate at Stanford University, and Business as a Masters student (MBA) at London Business School. She is the author of long-standing blog, *Aabservations* (www.lizaab.com). She lives with her husband and their two boys in London.

Printed in Great Britain
by Amazon

80552298R00148